DROP SHOT

VAI DENTON

Drop Shot

Copyright © 2025 by Vai Denton

Editing: Rachel Bunner (@rachels.top.edits)

Proofreading: Miah Onsha (@miahonsha.author) and Laura Hartley

Cover design: Vic Cavalieri (@weirdowithluv)

ISBN: 979-8-9904429-5-5 (paperback)

ASIN: B0FCSLRR3M (ebook)

First Edition: October 2025

10 9 8 7 6 5 4 3 2 1

content warnings

Drop Shot is the first book in the *Off Court* series. It can be read as a standalone and will have no cliffhangers.

If you are of the belief that content warnings are spoilers, please feel free to jump ahead now. For those who are interested, please be advised that this novel contains: brief mentions of postpartum depression (no descriptions and related to a character not shown on page), an alcoholic parent (not violent but verbally abusive), on-page caretaking of people when they're heavily intoxicated, mentions of dieting for athletic performance, neglectful parents, on-page sexual content.

This one is for the eldest daughters who spend their lives taking care of everyone else—I hope you find your Matteo <3

DROP SHOT / Noun

A soft and short shot often used when an opponent is expecting a powerful one deep in the court, catching them off guard.

one

othing says *I'm sorry for ending things* like a consolation burger from the players' restaurant.

To be fair, I think we both would've preferred The Copper Table, but neither of us finished our strategy sessions in time for that. Plus, Nicola, my roommate, best friend, and—soon-to-be former—doubles partner, is going to try to pay for my meal to make up for what she's about to tell me and, because I'm me, I won't let her. I'd much rather not allow her to pay for a burger from here than a risotto from our favorite but infrequently visited (because oh my god, is it expensive) restaurant.

Especially now that one of my main streams of income is about to disappear right as I was getting my financial footing.

Like she's read my mind, Nic looks at her food before her gaze meets mine, her dark steely-gray eyes cataloging my every facial twitch. "I'm sorry my session ran long. We can go into town tomorrow," she says, the subtlest of Greek accents curving her words. Sundays are our easy days. Morning stretching, yoga, more stretching, physio-therapy, and then actual free time, which is rare, even during the offseason.

It's odd hearing her apologize though. She so rarely does. The fact that this is now her second time in an hour confirms my suspicions.

Nicola is the kind of person who will glare you into submission if you so much as imply she could be wrong about something. The kind of person—and I can't say this with any great deal of certainty, but it's something I know in my bones—who could turn something as useless as a pillow into a weapon if you piss her off. The one our friend group sends into the fray when we want something badly enough—like a specific court at the facility or a table at a bar—that we're willing to look the other way while she works her unorthodox methods.

In short, I'm equal parts in love with and terrified of her.

Her dark, laminated brows furrow, and I realize I haven't responded. Twirling a strand of my damp blonde hair around a finger, I push my lips into a smile, radiating positivity. "It's totally fine. I went late too, and I'm in the mood for a burger anyway."

Say it, I plead. *Just say it already*.

Nic simply nods, taking a bite. Waiting on my own food, I look around the familiar restaurant. Low-hanging pendant lights cast a soft glow over the polished wooden tables, and a small bar made of dark reclaimed wood sits off to one side, its shelves stocked with liquor and glass-ware. My eyes fall to the only other table that's occupied this evening, where Austin is doing a poor job of pretending he's not eavesdropping.

His light brown hair is a mess from his shower and his blue eyes are narrowed, fixated on his table while he leans toward us so far, he may topple off his stool. I clear my throat, and his head snaps up. Nic follows my gaze, and when she rolls her eyes at him, he smiles, bringing his tray over and settling into the seat beside mine.

"I've been summoned." There's a tinge of worry in his tone, like he knows he needs to handle this situation with care. Handle *me* with care, though I've told him plenty of times I'm going to be fine. Our waitress drops off my Baja California burger and fries, and Austin nudges me with his elbow. "Did you manage to crack the ice queen?"

Nic glares at him, obviously not a fan of the nickname. "Not only did I not summon you, but nobody invited you to dinner, Austin."

"Actually, Delilah did," he answers, inclining his head in my direction.

I shake my head, smile widening. "Actually, *Delilah* did not. I told you I was meeting Nic for dinner at the players' restaurant, and you decided that meant you should come."

"Potato, potahto." He tosses a fry into his mouth. "I heard a 'sorry' and figured that was my cue to bring in the comedy."

A couple of whoops behind the bar pull our attention to one of the many large television screens lining two of the walls. Unsurprisingly, they're all turned to coverage of the Women's Tennis Association Finals, the last tournament of the year. Only the seven women with the highest number of points for the season are invited, plus the highest ranked of the four Grand Slam winners if she's not already in the top seven. One of those eight players? Anya Morozov.

There's a reason I made sure Nic was on the other side of the table, facing a wall blissfully devoid of TVs. She's been trying to break into the top ten for months, and seeing the person she loathes the most heading into the final round of the tournament has been grating on her. She's kept relatively quiet about it in practice and at home, but after spending nearly every day of the last year with her, I can read her like a book.

Even in November, when the season is all but over, the players' restaurant at the Morozov Tennis Academy insists on having tennis on every screen. Because if you're on the WTA or the men's ATP tours, you have to eat, breathe, and sleep tennis.

But watching reruns of Anya beating the number three in the world is in no way going to make Nic feel better. Her expression sours as she turns back to her food, swinging her wavy chestnut-brown hair over her shoulder and angrily biting into her burger.

Brightly, I say, "She's playing Emilia Kessler in the finals." The world's number one is on an insane win streak, and while I consider Anya a friend, I'm not sure I believe *anyone* stands a chance against Emilia with the way she's playing right now. "Anya's never beaten her, and she's unlikely to this time either. I doubt she'll end up winning the whole tournament."

Nic nods but continues chewing indignantly. Hoping to serve as a conduit for redirecting the conversation away from Anya, I continue, "This is the time, Nic. This is the season you dominate. Don't worry about the finals. I know you'll be there in no time."

Austin, ever the instigator, offers, "If it helps, at least she was gone a few more days than she would have otherwise been. You got an extra Anya-free week."

Nic's eyes narrow. She takes a second to finish chewing and swallowing, which is arguably scarier than if she'd simply snapped at him. "*How* is that supposed to help? I've been working my ass off for years and I'm barely twenty-sixth, and yet she cruises her way into the finals."

"Cruising" is a bit of a stretch. We all know that. Anya's parents own the facility we train at, and as world-famous tennis players themselves, there's plenty of pressure on the youngest Morozov. But I certainly won't be the one to correct Nic.

Austin holds up his hands. "If! I said *if* it helps."

I shoot him a look, which hopefully reads equal parts *What are you doing?* and also *Sorry, you know how she gets.* While I have about three jokes on the tip of my tongue, I recognize now's not the time.

A smile lighting up Austin's face tells me he knows exactly what he's doing. He's been in my life since elementary school, and while he might not be my brother by blood, he tries hard to annoy me and my closest friends like one.

He knocks a knuckle beside my tray and changes the subject. "Don't forget Matteo is going to start training here Tuesday."

"Oh yes. The scariest man on the men's tour is taking you away from me," I joke. The press have not-so-lovingly dubbed him "Matteo the Malignant Narcissist" for his behavior on and off the court, but I know better than anyone not to judge others without having the full picture. Matteo and Austin began playing doubles this year and have been doing well. Since mixed doubles is only played at a select few tournaments, as opposed to men's and women's doubles played at nearly all tour events, my and Austin's practices won't be as high priority as theirs.

Nic lets out a quiet, mirthless chuckle. "'The scariest man on the men's tour.'"

"He's not *that* bad." Austin says and then shrugs at her incredulous stare. "I've had fun playing with him."

She scoffs. "I'm sure it helps that he's ranked eleven and outmaneuvers half the other doubles teams."

Austin smirks. "It definitely helps."

They begin arguing the merits of riding coattails to championships while I finish my food. I'm just glad Nic is feeling good enough to bicker with Austin as they often do.

After irritating her to the point that she turns her body to face away from him, Nic finally gives me a subtle grimace—one I know means the consolation speech is coming. Too bad my burger is long gone.

She keeps it brief. Straight to the point. "My team and I have decided I need to take some time away from doubles." And then, "I'm sorry, Del."

With her trying to win a major and break into the highest level of tennis, focusing exclusively on singles is a logical choice. I was distraught when she mentioned the possibility of it late one night while we watched (well, I watched, she scorned) reality TV reruns on our couch, but

I've had a few days to come to terms with it. When she asked to get dinner out instead of eating at home like we typically do, I knew it was coming.

I do well enough. My sponsorships cover my tennis clothes and rackets. My winnings from playing singles are just enough to pay my siblings' insurance, books, food, rent, utilities, and whatever else they might need, along with my own apartment expenses, travel, coaching, academy fees, and the hundreds of other things I seem to have to pay nowadays.

Losing my doubles income isn't ideal, especially if I falter at all during the season. Shoulder injury flare-ups here and there have cost me hundreds of thousands of potential dollars in tournaments I've had to pull out of, but I'm on the mend. I worked hard to get into the top one hundred despite the injury. I might not be swimming in money, but I've been taking care of myself and my family for years. My whole life, really. This is no different.

It would be nice if, for once, I could be in a place where I didn't have to worry about my family's survival. If I could enjoy tennis, free from all the financial stressors of daily life. But if I take my eye off the ball for a second...

One day, if I keep my head down and continue working hard, if the twins get the scholarships they seem on their way to getting, maybe I'll be able to afford a week or two off, drink in hand, my butt nestled in a floatie, drifting around a pool in the Orlando winter. Or better yet, on a trip out of the country like Sahar and Harper and almost every other player on tour takes each year.

It's that image that brings a genuine smile to my face.

"It's really okay, Nic. You have to do this. You have plenty of majors in you; we all know it. It makes perfect sense."

Still, she looks worried. Or as worried as Nic can look. "Are you sure you'll be good?"

She means financially. After all, she's the one person since Maya—my previous doubles partner, who left the tour because of an injury—to actually see how stretched thin I sometimes feel trying to make sure I'm handling everything myself. Nic watched me battle tears when the rent for our tiny apartment across the street from the academy increased. Sat with me as I bit my lip so hard it bled so I wouldn't cry when Chase crashed the car he and my two other siblings share, leaving me to pay for the repairs. Offered to help pay, to the sounds of my vehement refusals, when Finn broke his arm during football practice.

"Of course I will. I'll miss playing with you, obviously," I say, emphasizing the last word with a meaningful look in her direction. "We had a great year. But it's not like we won't be training together all the time." And while we're rarely at the apartment at the same time outside of the offseason, we *are* still roommates.

She nods. "It'll be different though. Weird not being on court with you."

"If it helps, at least this means you only have to see Anya in singles," Austin chimes in.

"Stop saying 'if it helps.' And stop *trying* to help. Why are you here again?" Nic asks, shoving Austin's tray down the table.

He moves it back with ease, tossing another fry into his

mouth. "I bring the comedic relief you guys need after baring your souls to each other," he responds around it.

Ignoring him, I reach across the table, careful not to touch Nic but providing her with the option if she wants it. She takes my hand reluctantly, like it's more for my benefit than her own. Which, knowing her and her aversion to physical contact, it is. "Truly. I think this is great. It'll give me time to focus on my singles too. And if I keep doing as well as I have been, or *better* than I have been, I'll be set. It's been a fun ride, and it's not like we won't ever play doubles again. You have to do this." I squeeze her hand softly, then let go.

"Next season is your season. The season of Nicola," I say with a hand flourish above my head, as if the words will appear there in garish flashing letters. "I have no doubt about that. You're going to kick ass, and I'm going to cheer you on the whole time."

"Okay, I just…don't want you to be upset."

"Me? Upset? I don't even have the software for that."

Austin laughs and Nic smiles softly, knowing it's true. When we get ready to leave, Nic tries to pay for my food, as expected. I slap my card down with a smile, knowing this is the last time I'll eat out for a while.

And when we walk back to our apartment side by side, losing Austin somewhere between the CrossFit center and the indoor training pool, I grin and pretend I'm lying on the beach on the Amalfi Coast with Sahar and Harper, secure in the knowledge that no matter how much time I take off or how much money I spend enjoying myself, my family and I will be fine.

two

It isn't a Tuesday afternoon in the offseason if Nicola isn't smashing the ball so angrily across the court that I can hardly get to it. Granted, it's only our second offseason together. But still. I'd know the frustrated slap of her racket if I were blindfolded and three towns over.

Every ball I hit to her, she slams back with a ferocity that could maim. I'm surprised it hasn't yet. When Nic slaps a ball so hard down the backhand line that I can barely pivot from where I *just* hit a shot on my forehand side, Francesca steps forward, frowning. The weathered lines beside her eyes and mouth are more pronounced thanks to all the sun she's gotten in her years as a professional player and coach.

"Mannaggia, Nicola," my coach calls from near the net, a word I've come to learn means *damn it*—most frequently used when I'm frustrating her. "How is she meant to warm up if she can't get a ball back? It's warm-up. Stop hitting winners," she finishes, an Italian accent bending her vowels into something rich and melodic.

Nic mumbles an apology, one I don't need. With the finals still fresh, I understand why she's upset, even if Anya did end up coming second to Emilia like I thought she would. I know as well as any other player on the tour how therapeutic slapping the heck out of a tennis ball can be. I would rather she vent her frustrations now than beat me to within an inch of my life during our practice match in fifteen minutes.

"No worries!" I assure her.

After warming up our groundstrokes, Nic moves to the net to take volleys and overheads, and when she feels sufficiently warm, we swap.

Any other Tuesday afternoon, we'd finish this warm up and end on the same side of the net, doing doubles drills or playing a practice match. But now that Nic's done with doubles and Austin is practicing with Matteo more often, Francesca wants me to play a second singles practice match every week.

My eyes travel a few courts over, where Austin and Matteo are doing net drills together. I've been sneaking glances at Matteo all day, waiting for him to erupt like a volcano, spewing obscenities like lava and hot ash. For him to slam his racket against the concrete until it splinters into pieces. For him to storm off the court and tell his team he's done for the day.

I saw his volatility on a small scale this season the couple of times I sat in Austin's box during their doubles matches. Watched him struggle to leash his temper, angry tension between himself and the chair umpire clear from the hard set of his jaw and the rapid-fire Italian I later learned was all profanity, though it was directed at the fence instead of the umpire. It was never as bad as the media painted him to be though.

Other than a clenched fist here and there, I've seen nothing to indicate he's getting riled up today. No noise besides some amiable talking, a body slamming into the back fence when a ball had too much topspin, and Austin's boisterous laughter. It feels like vindication that I'm right about him. That there's more than meets the eye.

When I've put away enough overhead shots to know I'm good to go, especially since I rarely go to the net during matches, I head back to the baseline for serves and returns. A few minutes later, Nic's coach steps forward.

"Take a break before you begin," she calls, then turns back to Francesca, gossiping about some of the newer hires at the academy. They love to act like Nic and I distract each other when we practice together, and yet it's them who hate to be pulled away.

Thank goodness. The fact that our teams mesh so well, along with Sahar's and Harper's, means the tour is significantly less lonely for us than for most others. Even if, at the end of the day, we're all competitors.

I set my racket down and take a swig of water, glancing around the rest of the facility. A couple of women on the tour walk past, and I smile, giving them a quick wave.

The academy is always bustling this time of day, with more amenities than I know what to do with, though I certainly try my best to use them all. There are sixty tennis courts, indoor and outdoor, mainly hard court but some clay and grass for the players who fly back to train before those swings of the tour; a massive fitness center, a

CrossFit gym, and a separate players' gym; a training pool for those who enjoy that sort of torture; a full health and wellness center with medical offices and a spa; junior boarding houses for the prodigies hoping to make it big on tour once they hit eighteen, along with the school they attend to meet minimum education requirements; adult apartments for those who like the convenience of being right on campus; and, of course, all the built-in hitting partners I could ever need, including multiple top-ten players on the men's and women's tours.

It's every pro player's dream, and since I live off campus, I only pay fees the months I'm here. A no brainer.

My phone buzzes on the bench, and after a cursory glance at Francesca to be sure I won't incur her ire for looking at it during practice, I check my new messages. There are a few in the Sahar's Bad Berlin Bagels chat— aptly named for the time Sahar ate an entire stale, moldy bagel without realizing because of the cream cheese she slathered on it after losing at a tournament in Berlin, though also funny in a tennis context—and a couple of old ones in the bigger group chat with the guys that I swipe away.

SAHAR'S BAD BERLIN BAGELS

HARPER

8 images

We wish you were here!

Nic's phone is put away, probably in the locker room, so I show her the photos. Three of them are beautiful shots of the Amalfi Coast, three are of mouthwatering pastas and bread, and the final two are of Sahar and Harper in bikinis on a boat holding each other tightly, their dark hair waving in the breeze, cheeks pressed together, wide grins on their faces.

Nic's lips tilt up, and there's a flash of wistfulness across her features, though whether at the thought of vacation, being back home in Europe, or something else entirely, I can't be sure.

MAYA

I wish I were there too :(

Do I spy a Noah?

Now that I look more closely, my former roommate is right. I can see Sahar's childhood best friend turned coach in the reflection of one of the yacht's windows, the phone he's using to take photos covering half of his face.

SAHAR

I tried to tell him to stay home, but he insisted the offseason was for him too

Oh, definitely. We totally believe you

SAHAR DISLIKED "OH, DEFINITELY. WE TOTALLY BELIEVE YOU"

MAYA

Yes, totally. You guys definitely aren't doing anything nefarious.

HARPER

They're not!! Sahar and I are sharing a bed.

SAHAR

Yeah, there's no room for big oafs

I type the words *Nic and I wish we were there too* when the fence squeaks open, a couple of players walking onto the courts. Or rather, one player on the men's tour, Ryan Tremblay, and Anya's brother Aleksandr.

"You're kidding." Nic scoffs. "I thought they were going to Spain for a week."

Aleks waves the small orange cones in his hands at us, his lips quirking even more when he takes in the sour look on Nic's face. His dirty-blond hair is cropped close to his head, his blue eyes shining with mirth and his facility T-shirt slightly too small on his muscular frame.

"Nic, look. He's wearing your favorite," I tease, and she rolls her eyes, mumbling something about "stupid slutty little T-shirts." Still, I see the slight blush in her cheeks that wasn't there before despite our warm-up.

Francesca nods after the pair as they move to the empty court beside Matteo and Austin, responding to Nic, "Anya's in Spain. Aleksandr's doing strength and conditioning coaching for everyone at the facility during the offseason."

"Great," Nic mutters. She tosses her hair into a braided ponytail, then repositions her visor. "Exactly what I needed."

I smile. "I'm sure you'll never have to talk to him. You have your own performance coach anyway."

"And thank goodness for that." She stands, and I know our friendship is temporarily on hold. I've never met anyone more serious about practice matches than Nic. I tuck my phone into my bag and go to the other end of the court, doing a burst of high knees before getting set to return.

Each point is an absolute battle, but I lose the first set 6–3. There's a small momentum shift in my favor when Aleksandr laughs between a point and Nic glares his way. I win the first two games of the second set easily. Right as I toss the ball to serve into the third game, there's a loud pained "fuck!" from a few courts away.

I know that voice. Panic constricts my lungs, the ball I tossed coming down onto my shoulder. I don't care because three courts over, Austin is on the ground holding his ankle, Matteo standing above him with a grim expression.

I dart toward them, taking advantage of the fact that everyone else has halted their drills and matches to pay attention to the commotion. I'm by Austin's side in a flash.

"What happened?" I ask, voice wavering.

Matteo looks up, then back down to Austin, then does a double take. His brown eyes meet my blue ones, his thick dark eyebrows twitching upward. It's intense enough that I have to glance away, noting the pain on Austin's face.

Gruffly, Matteo says, "I fucked up. I shouldn—"

Austin huffs a pained laugh, his expression contorting as the small movement jostles his ankle, which already seems to be swelling—though that may be my imagination. "Shut up, man. I was being a dumbass. A ball fell out of my pocket. I said I was okay to keep hitting, knowing it was there. But then I jumped for an overhead and landed on it." He winces when he tries to lift himself off the ground.

Patty, Austin's coach, sets a hand on his shoulder and squats down, barely touching the ankle before Austin hisses in pain. "We need to get you to the health center. They'll want to do imaging and get it braced."

"I know. This blows," he grumbles dejectedly.

"I'm sure it's just a sprain!" I pipe up, then bite my lip nervously when Patty and Matteo help him up and it becomes clear the ankle can't bear weight. My eyes lock on Matteo's for a second, and I can tell he's thinking the same thing I am.

Ankle sprains are a product of the sport. All the quick starts and stops make them the most common injury. But I've seen Austin with plenty of sprained ankles, and never has he seemed to be in so much pain.

"I'm probably fine," he says, pulling his arm from Matteo's shoulder, but Matteo puts it right back.

Austin's trying to play it off—for whose benefit, I'm not sure. But I know that twist of his lips means he's holding back.

Softly, I agree, "It'll be okay, Austin. I'm sure you'll be back on court in no time."

Panic etches itself in the lines of his face as the trio moves toward the gate on the way to the health center, Austin's rigid shoulders belying the calm and collectedness of his previous words. I drift back to my court, an eye on them the whole time.

It's no surprise when Nic wins the next six games in a row and we call it for the evening.

Francesca meets me outside the women's locker room a little over an hour and a half later to go over game strategy and film, as we do almost every day. Only, my mind's not really in it. The entire time I did my bike cooldown, stretched, foam rolled, and showered, my mind was on Austin and his injury. He hasn't texted me back, which worries me more.

The expression Francesca is wearing does nothing to assuage my concern.

"What? Did you hear something?"

"I stopped by the health center after you finished." She blows out a breath. "It's a ligament tear. His foot is incredibly swollen. They want him in a brace and on crutches doing physio for a few months. He won't be able to do lateral movements for a while."

"How long is he going to be out?"

"Not sure yet, but at least three months."

I set my head back against the wall, closing my eyes. Austin may not be driven by money like me or glory like Nic, but like the rest of us who put our everything into this sport, he loves it. Any injury that takes you out, even in the offseason, is hard to bear.

"Did he seem okay emotionally? How was he acting?"

"Like he didn't want us to know he was upset."

My eyes open, taking in her frown. I should go into town to grab some things since he'll be home more often. I make a mental note I hope I won't forget in the three hours it takes to go through strategy and eat dinner. I'm sure Austin will get through physio in record time, but I still wish I could do more for him.

As I start toward the meeting rooms we use for film, Francesca says, "We should talk through your options."

"My options?" I ask dumbly, turning back to her. "What do you mean?"

"Austin's going to be out for the Australian Open. He *might* be fine in time for Indian Wells or Roland Garros, but you're losing mixed doubles income for the first major for sure. So either we follow Nicola's lead and focus on singles, or you try doubles with someone else."

Sahar and Harper will be playing together, and Anya plays with her older sister. I can't think of any other person I trust enough not to serve into the back of my head.

"I don't know that there's anyone left for me to train with. Everyone has their partners. Have you heard about someone trying to make a switch?"

"You could play with Matteo. Just for January. He's a great player, and if you train with him a couple of days a week for the next six weeks, you might make a significant amount of money from it. If Austin is still out after that and things are going well, you could see about continuing through the season."

"What?" I laugh at Francesca's attempt at a joke. It's not as simple as she's making it sound to up and start playing with someone I hardly know, even if we do have a couple of months to prepare for the tournament. Brooding Matteo, a top fifteen men's player who doesn't know me from Adam, seems a *bit* out of left field.

Earnestly, Francesca grabs both my hands. Her dark brows pinch together, and those wrinkles carved into her face become more severe. "Del, you know I believe in you one hundred percent. If you want to focus on singles, I think we can get you to more quarterfinals and semis. Hell, I know you can win these tournaments. And sure, we can find you someone else to play regular doubles with for the year. But if you want at least a shot at some big prize money early in the season, he's your best option."

"I don't…What?" I ask again, pulling my hands from hers and tucking them into my armpits. "Why on earth would that be the logical next step?"

"Because he has a similar style of play to Austin and you both need a doubles partner." I'm about to protest again, but she cuts me off. "And I guess when Austin mentioned he felt bad you would lose mixed in January, Matteo said he'd be happy to step in if he was okay with that."

"If—if *Austin* was okay with it?" I sputter. "What about whether *I'm* okay with it?"

She mutters something in Italian and then lets out a long-suffering sigh, like I'm a petulant child in a grocery store refusing to put a candy bar back. "Again, it's up to you. If you want to focus on singles and you think it will provide you with enough money to cover all the bills you pay for yourself and your family, we can do exclusively singles. You have sponsors for clothing and equipment. You're an amazing player with so much potential, so I would not be shocked if you showed up for the Australian swing, racket blazing, beating out every single other player. But I'm giving you this option at this *one* tournament to earn the money you could have won with Austin. If you lose first round, no big deal."

It is…an interesting choice. My primary endorsement

deal is set to end this month, and I have no idea whether they'll renew it. Even then, it's only for my clothes and shoes, so there's no actual money coming in from it, just a breath of relief that I don't have to worry about my many outfits on tour.

"Wouldn't we have to be lucky enough to get a wild card?"

"It's Matteo. You'll get it."

I back against the wall again, parsing all that she's told me. Doubles is a significantly smaller portion of my income. The payouts aren't anything to write home about in comparison to singles. But Francesca is right that it's low risk with the potential for a high reward. If we do well, and that's a big *if*, I wouldn't turn my nose up at the amount, no matter how small. Every cent I save is important.

I'd be going back to a three-day singles, two-day doubles training schedule though, and that would detract from my singles work. Plus, I like knowing that *my* work is what has freed me from the hell of financial insecurity. Jumping into a partnership with someone just because he's a great player and *might* help me make a little more money feels like admitting I need help.

I don't.

Before I can respond, Matteo steps out of the men's locker room, expression unreadable. His thick, water-soaked dark brown curls are held back by a hat turned backward, and it's been at least a few days since he's shaved, though there's nothing disheveled about him. Brown eyes lock on mine and hold, like they did earlier on the court. Once again, the intensity makes me squirm.

And then he's gone, sauntering down the hall and out the door without so much as a nod.

I square my shoulders, dropping my voice in case anyone else is around. "I'll look at my finances and think about it, but I'm leaning toward no. I think I'm making enough. I'll be fine without one tournament. We should focus on singles like Nic and try to get deeper in the draw so I have more to show for each tournament. I'll be fine." I have to be. I always am. Chase, the twins, even *Dad* rely upon that. Rely upon *me*.

There's no judgment in Francesca's face when she nods. "Alright." And then she grins evilly. "But don't complain to me when you have to do singles work five days a week."

"Diabolical."

three

My phone nearly drops from between my shoulder and ear as I wrangle my blonde ponytail into a braid three days later. "Sorry? Can you repeat that?"

Shay, my agent, laughs. "Stratosphere wants to increase your endorsement deal. You've been moving up the ranks, your social media is growing fast, and they're looking for more of your sunshine energy."

I abandon my braid, silent in my disbelief. Stratosphere has sponsored me for the last year. Renewal was the hope, but this? This would be money directly into my pocket. Exactly what I need to feel like I can exhale fully without doubles.

Scanning the walls of my bedroom, I think of all I can upgrade in this little space: a wooden bookshelf I found on the side of the street years ago, two of the shelves rotting enough that they're bending; a wicker dresser the person who lived here before me left behind; a bed frame I got at an estate sale that may (definitely) be haunted, ironically the same type of wood as the bookshelf, though not yet rotting; and fake plants galore since I'm not here enough to take care of real ones, and I'm not positive I'd be any good even if I were.

And finally, the many art pieces I've hung over the years, almost all from thrift stores and estate and garage sales: a blue-green fish with geometric patterns that could have been done either by a second grader or an adult with a deep love of marine geometry; a photograph of a cow, and beside it a photograph of cowboy boots, picked up on separate occasions, both of which have a sepia filter, though one more so than the other; a painting that could be Frida Kahlo or an unnamed, unknown woman with a unibrow. My personal favorite—a vintage pop art print of a blonde woman holding a dog with one hand and covering her eyes with the other, a bubble that reads "I forgot to have children!" above her, all of which made me giggle when I first saw it. Still does.

There are a slew of others and more in the living room behind our couch. None of them match. And yet the Frankenstein room I've built from other people's trash feels more like home than the ones I lived in for eighteen years.

Nic moving around in the living room, likely getting ready for the day, is what shakes my next question loose. "What are the specifics?"

"Six-month contract with the potential for an extension if you do well. They'll keep providing the clothes and shoes, and you'll wear them in social media posts here and there and on the court, of course. There's a clause that states you have to play in specific tournaments—Aussie, French, Wimbledon, US, obviously. And a few WTA1000 and 500 tournaments too. All the ones you already play in each season."

"Do I have to make it to a certain round for the contract to go into effect?"

"Nope! But if you get to the quarterfinals or higher, you get a bonus. The amount depends on the tournament. Here, I can give you the breakdown…" she continues explaining, but my mind is stuck on the last thing she said.

"The quarterfinal bonus. Is that only for singles or does it include doubles?"

I can almost hear her eyes scanning the document. For the millionth time, I'm sure. "Includes doubles. You get a smaller payout than if you get to quarters in singles, but they *are* separate."

"So if I were to make it to quarters in both singles and mixed at Aussie?" I need to hear the words again. It probably won't change my decision, especially now that I'll have more coming in without it, but it's good to know.

"You'd be making big money. I'll send it over for you to review and you can let me know if there's anything you don't like. I've read it more than a few times and added my notes where we can negotiate, but I think it's everything you've been hoping for."

For the sake of Shay's ear, I hold in a squeal and instead settle for a small happy dance. I'm a step closer to being financially stable, and it was all of my own merit.

"Del?"

"Yeah, sorry. This is…You don't know how amazing this news is, thank you. I'll send the contract back as soon as I can. Is there anything else I need to look at?"

Shay takes a second. Then, "No, that's it for now."

We say our goodbyes, and when Nic calls out from the kitchen to make sure I'm ready for practice, I allow myself that squeal.

It's easy to hate the monotony of on-court drills, but the predictability is precisely why I love them—running from the center of the baseline to the alley to hit the perfect cross-court backhand, then doing it another one hundred times until I can perfectly place it in the same spot every time. Once I get into a rhythm, all my troubles disintegrate.

When I'm playing a match, what I stand to lose is always on my mind. But when I'm doing drills? Nothing breaks through but moving my feet, using my core, and hitting the ball squarely in the center of my strings until my legs ache and my lungs beg for air.

Sadly, today is an exception. I've noticed Matteo practicing on the court next to mine approximately eighty-seven times. I can't help it. It's been three days of passing each other without speaking, and it's completely thrown me off after Francesca's claims that *he* asked to play with *me*.

Okay, not asked, but definitely offered.

Two days ago, during the first strength and conditioning session with Aleks, I went up a plate on the lat pulldown machine, so my set took longer. Matteo was standing a few feet from me, waiting, and when I finally finished and mumbled a quick "sorry," he just grunted. That evening, when I was heading to meet with Francesca for game strategy, Matteo swung open a door, nearly sending me flying into the opposite wall. All I got in response to my tentative smile was a brief stare. Then, yesterday, when Nic and I were doing our three-mile walk on our rest day, he jogged so close to us that he clipped Nic, who refuses to move out of the way for any man.

I thought she was going to kill him.

I've concluded, based on these very limited pieces of information, that he is preoccupied with something. Even on the court, he hasn't seemed all there. I have to wonder if it has anything to do with his offer of mixed doubles—if there's something more going on here.

Or maybe I'm being silly, as I often am. We've been at the same dinner table once, and I've sat in his box while watching him play doubles with Austin, but I don't know the first thing about Matteo Corsi. It's entirely possible (and with my luck, highly probable) that he has no idea who I am and simply spoke before he could think through his offer.

After about an hour of drills, a familiar voice calls my name. When I whip around, Austin is hobbling on his crutches to the fence behind the court.

"Taking five!" I yell to Nic and Francesca. I meet Austin at the fence, beaming. "See? I told you you'd be back in no time. Three days and you're already walking."

His head drops, nodding toward his booted foot. "Not so sure I'd call this walking, but it is good to be outside."

After strategy and dinner on Tuesday evening I thankfully remembered to swing by the store. I showed up to his apartment with a basket of all of his favorite foods, some of which he doesn't allow himself to eat during the season, and watched a few episodes of his favorite war show in the hopes of cheering him up. He was on the couch with his foot elevated, and just by the increased level of untidiness in his living room, it was clear he was putting on a brave face.

Now, at least, he seems to be feeling better.

"How was your first physical therapy appointment?"

He shrugs. "About as good as can be expected. She gave me the same timeline as the doctor but said I could be back on court practicing volleys and doing some basic racket work in a couple of months."

"That's great! For now, you can spend two months in the gym beefing up your arms," I joke.

Snorting, he says, "I'm absolutely doing that. Being at home all day is going to drive me crazy, especially with Dad swinging by three times a day to make sure I'm okay. Plus, I'm not allowed to swim yet, so it'll be the only thing getting me out of the house besides PT."

"And seeing me," I add, framing my face with my racket and free hand, smiling wider.

"And seeing you." After a glance at Matteo, he asks, "Did you hear?"

I feign ignorance. "About what?"

"I think Matteo is on the lookout for a new doubles partner for the beginning of the season," he answers suggestively.

"I'm sure he'll have no shortage of volunteers."

Austin tilts his head. "Del, I know Francesca well enough to know she heard his offer and took it straight to you."

I snort. "Okay, yes. I just haven't figured out what to

do with it yet." Though after today's call with Shay, I'm leaning toward saying no.

The *thump thump* of Matteo jogging over quiets us.

"Hey, man. You doing okay?" Matteo asks, voice deep and oddly quiet.

"I'm great. Like Del said, I'll be back in no time. I feel bad that you moved down here to train with me for the season just for me to get injured, though."

Matteo's eyes flick to me for a second before they're back on Austin. "I needed the change of scenery. Living and training in New York was getting old."

I turn my smile on him. "We're all glad you're here. It's nice to have new faces and hitting partners. Though"—I slant my head in Austin's direction—"hitting with him would've gotten old fast. Trust me, I would know."

"Hey! Is that any way to speak to your elders?"

I chuckle, rolling my eyes. "You're six months older than me." To Matteo, I say, "Anyway, I'm Delilah, Austin's friend. I'm on the women's tour." I hold out a hand for him to shake.

Matteo's thick, arched eyebrows sew together. He takes my hand in his warm calloused one and shakes it once. "I know who you are. We've met. Multiple times." He lets go, and when his fingers twitch at his side, he switches his racket to that hand.

I nod dumbly. I, of course, knew that. I just wasn't sure *he* did. After all, it was only a few times here and there at bigger tournaments this year. We trained on side-by-side courts at Indian Wells, where he asked me to toss one of their balls back to him after it rolled onto my court. Austin introduced us once at the Miami Open and then again at Roland Garros when we all got dinner, after which, Matteo told me, "It was nice to meet you, Delia," and I didn't have the heart to correct him. At Wimbledon, we nearly ran into each other in the players' tunnel, but he was so upset that his muttered "sorry" seemed more like an accusation than an apology—despite having beaten the number fifteen in straight sets. Most recently, at the US Open, I sat beside Austin's parents in their box during their fourth round and quarterfinal matches. At one point, when Matteo talked to his coach, his eyes slipped to me and stopped. Only for a beat or two, and then his focus was back on the court.

Nothing crazy. Certainly nothing memorable enough that it would stand out to the second highest-ranked Italian player on the tour—who couldn't remember my name after learning it twice and who hasn't so much as said hello to me this week.

"I remember, but you never know. With all the people you've met on tour, I'm sure it's not easy recalling names."

His eyes don't leave mine. "I remember. Delilah not Delia." It sounds like a joke, but he gives no indication that it is. Come to think of it, I've never seen him smile. Ever. Not after he slammed his racket, broke it in half, then proceeded to win in straight sets and held up the US Open trophy three years ago. Not after a five-set battle to win the Australian Open (after fighting with the chair umpire, of course) two years ago. Not even after he twisted his ankle horribly during the Roland Garros final the same year and still beat the number one player in the world in four sets.

Assuming he is joking, my neck is practically wrecked

from the whiplash. The weird feeling twisting through my gut that seems tied to the way he's looking at me doesn't help.

Austin clears his throat, and we both turn back to him.

"I should get back to practice, but I'll see you tomorrow for breakfast, right?" I ask Austin hopefully. Every Saturday morning, we eat breakfast with his parents before practice, a tradition I hold as sacred as Nadal does his water bottle ritual.

"I'll be there."

Nic has begun picking up balls on her side of the court, so I play catch-up on my side. At one point, I think I hear Austin say my name, and when I turn, Matteo is already watching me. I snap back to grabbing balls. A minute or so later, Nic finishes her side, joining me.

As I add a seventh ball to the flat face of my racket, Nic mutters beside me, "How does someone even become the bad boy of tennis? It's a noncontact sport and mainly for people who come from money. He slams his racket, sleeps with models, curses at officials and umpires, and suddenly he's bad?"

Right as I begin to respond, that same gravelly voice beats me to it. "I also think it's dumb, but I guess I did it to myself." I startle hard enough that I lose my grip on my racket and all the balls I picked up topple to the court.

"Didn't mean to surprise you." Matteo holds up a ball, pointing in the direction of the fence. "This one was stuck in one of the holes. Figured I'd help." He bends down to place it on my racket, then adds a few of the ones I dropped and passes the racket back to me, his hand brushing mine in the exchange. His eyes dart to the point of contact, and when he notices me watching him, his hand falls away.

Once I've recuperated, I answer, "Th—thank you."

"Of course." A pause. I'm too confused about what's happening right now to do more than stare back at him. "It sounds like Austin talked to you a little about us playing mixed. I know it'll be an adjustment, but... I'm in."

He seems so genuinely earnest, so completely incongruent with the picture of him I've built up in my head over the years. "Why?" I'm shocked when my mouth moves before my brain can.

"Why?"

Knowing my question may have come off more aggressive than I meant it, I tease, "Yeah, especially after you spent this week doing your level best not to talk to me. I guess I'm just wondering why me?"

Something shifts in his face, his eyes bouncing to Nic and back to me like he's uncertain how he should proceed. Gruffly, he says, "I apologize for the way I've acted this week. It's been...different, and I had a few...disruptions come up. I feel partially at fault for what happened to Austin. I shouldn't have kept playing after he dropped the ball. I should've made sure he picked it up before we continued the point. So I want to make up for that."

"By playing mixed doubles with me." It was meant to be a question, but there was no lilt at the end of the sentence. His answer is a half truth. I cannot fathom why he wouldn't just pair up with a more experienced and successful player; it makes me feel like I'm missing something, like I'm a pawn in a game with rules I'm not allowed to know. I almost say as much, but he bends down and grabs three more balls to stack onto my racket, and the gesture is nice enough that I bite my tongue.

When his eyes meet mine again, they're back to a honeyed brown, no longer shadowed by whatever his real motivations are. "Think about it. Please."

He walks back to his court before I can respond.

"I'm sorry, what just happened?" Nic asks, dumbfounded.

"I…don't know."

And I can't help but notice Mount Matteo has yet to erupt.

four

That evening, I lie on my back on our couch, my socked feet propped against the wall between the water lilies print and a menu from a restaurant in an old Wyoming ghost town. Beside me, Nic stares at the credits rolling on the second to last episode of a season of a reality show she pretends she hates, her arm against the back of the couch, palm resting on my shin. Despite her distaste for contact, thirty seconds of my moaning about needing physical touch was all it took before she slapped it there.

More than vexed by the show, she says, "He asked her in about twelve different ways what she looked like in episode one. She's just now seeing all the red flags?"

"Maybe she thought he was bad at making conversation. I don't know that I would do better in that situation."

Nic glances at me in disbelief. "Surely you would recognize he's a tool." When I only blink back, she sighs. "I know my dislike for the male species as a whole is further along the spectrum than most, but you stretch the meaning of giving someone the benefit of the doubt."

I chuckle. "Maybe." But I'd rather that than accidentally hurting someone who's dealing with issues unseen or unknown.

After the intro music of the finale ends, Nic pauses it. I sit up on my elbows, glancing at her. "What happened? Bathroom break?"

"No. I was waiting for you to bring it up, but you haven't, and now I suspect you're not going to." When I don't respond after a couple of seconds, she crosses her arms, a dark eyebrow raised. "Matteo?"

Ah, *that*. "There's nothing to tell. Like you heard, I guess he feels bad about what happened to Austin, so he's trying to make it up by playing mixed with me." And there's something else he's not admitting. I've been thinking about what it could be all day and have come up with zilch.

"He seemed more interested than a guy doing someone else a favor."

I shrug. "I don't know. All I know is, with my new endorsement deal, I should be fine this season without doubles, especially if I work my butt off at singles." My mind drifts to the warmth of Matteo's palm in mine when we shook hands and the expression I couldn't decipher after our hands brushed while we picked up tennis balls. Another shrug. "I'm sure he'll forget all about it in a couple of weeks, and then once we're on tour, I'll hardly see him."

The men's and women's tours only overlap during select tournaments. There are the well-known slams—

Australian Open, Roland Garros or the French Open, Wimbledon, US Open—and some lesser known (at least outside of the tennis world) tournaments. It's not like we're together all the time. I'll likely see him about as much as I saw him last season, maybe less, since Austin will be out for a few months.

"And you don't want to play with him?" she asks, then quietly says, almost to herself, "His strokes are a lot like Austin's in many ways."

"I'm just…not sold, I guess?" A divot forms between her brows, so I continue, "You know how doubles is. There needs to be good chemistry. He doesn't know anything about me, and I don't get the impression he cares to learn. I'm not sure I want to risk some of my singles time when it could go poorly. Plus, I have the bigger Stratosphere deal now." I raise a shoulder like that's answer enough. I went over the contract with Nic when it first came through, since she has a couple of big deals of her own.

So it's no surprise when she hits me with, "But don't you get more money if you make it to quarters in both? A good bit more?"

Nic's pushing harder than expected, but the biggest reason I'm wavering is one I can't voice. Not because she wouldn't support me, but because she wouldn't understand. I've built almost everything I have myself. If I were to count the number of people I can rely on for a stream of income, I wouldn't make it past my right hand. Playing doubles with Austin was always about having fun with the added bonus that I *might* make some extra cash from it. Nic and I worked together so well, and she was always so serious about it that I felt comfortable depending on it to supplement my singles income.

Sidestepping the question, I ask, "Who is this glass-half-full woman, and what has she done with my best friend?"

Nic cracks a rare smile. "Guess I'm used to one of us being optimistic about everything. But you're right, playing with Matteo might land you with a fine or worse when he inevitably loses his cool."

I'm not sure I agree with that now that I've seen him on court the last few days. Even near the end of the season, he'd calmed down. I hum in response, and Nic plays the episode. It's the last time we'll talk about it unless I bring it up again—something I appreciate about Nic immensely.

I flip around to face the TV, and as I laugh and she scoffs at the ridiculous antics of the people on screen, I remember the real reason I'll miss playing with her so much. The money was good, but more than that, it was the only chance we got to spend this much time together during the season. Next season, we may not even play in the same tournaments.

Our friendship bloomed so quickly. It was mainly because I wouldn't leave her alone the first couple of months—adding her to conversations she rarely seemed interested in during rest day walks around the track with Sahar, Harper, and Maya, finding her eating at the players' restaurant and sitting with her, jumping at the chance to pair up for singles work when she didn't have someone to hit with—but she seemed so sad and lonely on the outskirts, and that's always been my kryptonite.

Once Maya left the tour, and with Sahar and Harper as close as they are to each other, I naturally drifted more toward Nic. While she tried her best to keep me at arm's length, I tried *harder* to be let in.

We'll still see each other, get dinner a few times a month, and *maybe* get to spend an evening watching a movie here and there, but it won't be the same.

Right as a couple threatens to end their relationship at the altar, my phone flashes with a call. When I realize it's my brother Chase, I fumble to grab it, already answering as I say, "Sorry, sorry. I'm going to take this." Nic nods her understanding, and I disappear into my room, closing the door behind me.

"Chase? Is everything okay?" I'm so used to being the one who calls him, seeing his name on my screen sent anxiety slashing through me.

"Hey. Something's wrong with the car, and it's going to need some work."

I blow out a breath. Every time I think I'm going to be able to make things work, another obstacle crops up. "Oh. Alright. Did you get a quote?"

When he tells me the amount, I clutch my bookshelf, the vases full of fake flowers swaying. I take stock of the repairs I've paid for over the last year and try my best not to feel upset with him. Though I haven't been able to spend more than a few days at a time with him in years, I've never known him to be reckless. I'm sure it's just wear and tear.

"Okay. That's fine. Obviously the three of you need the car, so we should definitely get that fixed."

He doesn't answer right away, and as I begin to ask

him how he's doing, Chase says, "I got accepted into FSU. I'm thinking about transferring."

My heart leaps at the words, and now I'm clutching the bookcase for a completely different reason. "Chase! That's amazing. Have you talked to a counselor at the community college? Everything looks good for a transfer?"

"Yeah."

Sandpaper bites the back of my throat, happy tears filling my eyes. This is all I've ever wanted for him. And for the twins. It's why I chose to go straight to the tour—to make money immediately rather than trying to work a job while playing collegiate tennis, even though college was something I'd always wanted to try. I want them to find something they love, to get the education they need so they're set up for the lives we deserve.

And Chase is doing it. He's putting in the effort to get good grades and he's *doing* it.

For a moment, I think about the cost but immediately hate myself. We'll make it work. "I'm more proud of you than you could ever know, Chase. Truly. I—" My voice breaks, and I pull my hand from the bookshelf, shoving my nails into my palms to keep the tears at bay. I'm the eldest. The strong one. I don't cry. "I'm really proud of you. And so excited. Tell me how much you need, and I'll transfer it into the joint account so you can pay tuition, okay? This is the best news."

"Okay," he answers quietly. I would hope for more enthusiasm with news like this, but this is just Chase. The moment he found out he got accepted, he probably took a nap because it was so mundane and unimportant to him.

He doesn't give me anything else to work with, and

because it's been almost a week since I heard his voice, I ask, "How's everything at home?"

I think of my last text from Dad, telling me how proud of me he is and asking about Nic and Austin. That was weeks ago, but it was nice. Made me feel like he was paying attention. I wonder—is it a sober or drunk week for him? And what does that mean for the twins? Are they having to do more of the caretaking I tried so hard to protect them from?

"Dad's passed out on the couch. The usual. The twins are fine."

A drunk week, then. I walk the few feet to my bed, settling against my pillow and staring at the popcorn ceiling. Mindlessly, my free hand reaches for my nightstand, pulling a small photo from my wallet.

It's worn and faded, creased where I keep it folded. Mom sits on the floor in our old house, her belly almost imperceptibly starting to swell with the twins. I sit between her legs, seven years old, the biggest smile I could possibly give the camera on my face. Beside me, Mom holds up a chubby two-year-old Chase, his feet planted on her leg, his arms reaching for me. He's treading a fine line between enthralled and excited, and I can imagine right after the photo was taken that I swooped him up in my arms. Behind the camera, I'm sure, Dad is waving wildly, a goofy grin on his face.

"And how are you?" I murmur.

"I'm fine."

I sigh. He's been like this more and more since I left home. Short with me, rarely reaching out even when I try my best to keep in touch. He might be upset with me for leaving him behind, leaving him to take care of the twins, but I can't be in two places at once. This is where I'm able to make money. As much as I wish I could be there for them financially *and* emotionally, this is what I can do right now. I hope one day he understands that and forgives me.

I care most about him finding something he loves that will make him enough money to go out on his own. The last thing this family needs is another Mom or Dad.

We just have to get through a few more years of this. Chase will finish school and get a job soon. The twins start college next year (I hope), and then, in roughly five years, the bills will stop coming out of my ears and I'll focus on saving for myself. Maybe go to college. I don't know what I'll do if not tennis, but it's nice to believe I'll have the option one day.

"Del, I've got to go. I have class. I'll let you know how much everything is. Will you be coming home soon?"

"Yes, I'm definitely going to try." They're right outside of Tampa, only an hour and a half or so away. The problem is getting there when the one car we have is with them. But I'll figure it out on one of my off days. I always do. Thanksgiving is in a couple of weeks anyway, and I'd love to spend it with them.

He lets out what sounds like a scoff. "Okay, see you whenever."

"W—wait! The twins, how are they? How's school?" I talked to Hazel a couple of days ago, but it's been longer than that since I spoke to Finn.

"They have phones too, you know. You can call them."

I sigh again. I know that, but I also know they're busy,

and I don't want to bother them. "Right. Yeah. I'll do that."

"Bye."

"See you soon. I lov——"

He hangs up before I'm able to finish the thought, and once again, I have to push away the frustration. It's not his fault. We're all dealing with a lot.

I'm five years older than him, but sometimes I feel like a young mom with an unruly teen. When we were younger, before Mom left, Chase and I were inseparable. The best of friends. I'd go to school while he went to daycare (on the weeks we could afford it) or a neighbor's house, and when the bus dropped me at home, Chase would come running to hug me. He'd spend all evening with me, from cleaning the house, to cooking when Mom had a late double shift, to watching cartoons on our decrepit TV while I did my homework.

But then the twins were born, and Mom…struggled. The limited free time I had went toward wrangling the twins, figuring out how to mix formula and feed babies when I was a young child myself. Learning how to change diapers. Putting them to bed and waking up in the middle of the night when one of them woke the other. Figuring out what their many different cries meant. Dad only helped a quarter of the time, if that, so even when I could be physically present beside Chase, my attention was no longer on him as much.

As we got older, going to school became my reprieve. There, I had Austin, and tennis, and my teachers, almost all of whom I loved. But at home, life became learning first aid, memorizing important addresses and phone numbers of the adults in our neighborhood, packing lunches, signing report cards when Dad was too drunk to, helping with homework, and taking care of them when they were sick.

I tried my best to be the one to bear it all, not wanting Chase to lose out on his childhood when I'd had eight good years with Mom before things had changed. I felt guilty. Chase and the twins deserved someone raising them too, rather than having to raise themselves.

Then I started playing tennis, training harder and harder. Going to tournaments so I could go pro when I turned eighteen. A lot of that work fell to Chase. I should've done more, but all I can do now is take the luck I was afforded—befriending Austin, being taken in by his parents, being coached up to the pros by them and their tennis friends—and turn it into the saving grace we Andersons needed to break the cycle of neglect.

Maybe I *should* play mixed. With the new deal, getting into the quarterfinals could give me enough money early in the season so that I won't have to stress about Chase's tuition. If even *Nic* thinks it's a good idea to try, I should seriously think about it.

I need to talk to Austin.

five

By 6:15 the next morning, I'm in the Wards' kitchen helping Lilian, Austin's mom, make protein pancakes for us as Eli, Austin's dad, makes eggs and bacon. I have a practice match against Lina Maes, another woman on the tour, this morning, so I'm going to have to walk the precarious line between eating enough to feel properly fueled and not eating so much that I throw up on court.

Lilian interrupts her humming to ask me, "Sweetheart, would you mind flipping in a minute or two? I'm going to use the restroom."

"Of course!" I slide beside Eli at the stove, mouth watering at the smell of the nearly done bacon.

He nudges me. "Practice match today?"

"Practice match today," I agree, nodding.

"Feeling good?"

"I think so. Francesca wants me to modify my serve, so I'm going to experiment with that today." When I have to make adjustments to my game during the season, it can throw off everything, and unless I'm only playing one tournament every couple of months, there's not much room for error. The offseason is the best time to try something new. "She also wants me to go to the net more, but you know me."

Eli smiles down at me, the lines beside his kind blue eyes carved deeply. His salt-and-pepper hair has gotten shaggy, so he's donned the headband we make fun of him for using when he cooks. "I do know you. Not an aggressive bone in your body."

Austin snorts from the breakfast nook across the kitchen, where he sits on his phone. Usually, he'd be helping us, but Lilian insisted he stay seated because of his ankle, and Austin was more than happy to comply. Being here with them every Saturday in the offseason is cozy and healing in a way I can't put into words, especially with how much time Eli and I spend apart from Lilian and Austin the rest of the year.

Describing the Wards as a second family wouldn't do justice to our bond. When I was eight, right around the time the twins were born, Austin and his family moved to Tampa. Austin, whose glasses took up half of his face and whose two adult front teeth were growing in, struggled making friends at school. We sat beside each other in our third-grade class, and through conversations about SpongeBob (the only cartoon I got to watch) and Legos (which I managed to get my hands on thanks to the hand-me-down gifts brought to us by our neighbors), we quickly became thick as thieves. The Wards took me in, adding an extra thirty or more minutes to their morning and evening routines to give me and Chase rides to and from school when the bus perimeter changed so that we no longer qualified.

Both Lilian and Eli played professional tennis for years, so naturally, Austin had begun learning long before we met. Soon after we became friends, they brought me on excursions to the courts. From the moment I stepped onto the painted concrete, my life changed for the better. For an hour here and there, they coached me until I was good enough to play in USTA tournaments on the weekends. One of them took me, while the other took Austin, since girls and boys tournaments are often in different places. Chase—along with Dad when he was coherent and available and neighbors when he wasn't—took care of the twins those weekends. Once the money from the state, Dad's occasional work, and the few paid chores a fourteen-year-old could get wasn't enough to feed four growing children, the Wards found me a coaching job.

Saying we're indebted to them is an understatement.

When Austin and I finally went pro at eighteen, Eli began traveling with me, sitting in my box and coaching me until I made enough to hire someone, and Lilian went with Austin on the men's tour. While they both were second parents to me growing up, Eli kept the isolation of the tour at bay in the beginning, before I made friends. He was the first real father figure I felt I could trust and rely on for emotional support.

The sound of Lilian washing her hands in the bathroom reminds me of the pancakes that need flipping. I slide the spatula underneath one, answering Eli's joke about not having an aggressive bone in my body, "Yeah. As Francesca likes to say, I need to make more enemies on court."

We share a laugh and begin plating food just as Lilian returns, all of us sliding into the homely nook. The sun hasn't risen yet, the sky barely hinting at dawn, and the quiet stillness of an early morning on their residential street wraps around us.

Eli pours syrup onto his pancakes and bacon. "Thank you for the food, Del."

I wave it away. It's the very least I can do. Years ago, when we first started this tradition, they were thoroughly opposed to the idea of me buying the ingredients, but over time, and since I never stopped bringing them, they seemed to have recognized that this is my small way of paying them back. Of not taking any more from them than I already have.

"It's nothing. Thank you both for cooking."

We fall into a contented silence as we eat. About halfway through my first pancake, Eli says, "I hear you're keeping Matteo waiting about mixed doubles."

Cutting into the sunny-side up eggs Eli made special for me, I answer, "I wouldn't say I'm keeping him waiting. I told Francesca I'm going to stick to singles." Even if my call with Chase yesterday made me rethink the decision for a minute.

Lilian's eyebrows twitch like I've startled her, but she doesn't show it beyond that. "Can I ask why?"

I wipe my hands on a napkin, dabbing my lips as I think through the jumbled reasonings that have been floating through my head. "I guess I'm struggling to understand why he chose me? I can tell he's not giving me the full truth about it, and I don't think that's any way to start a partnership. Plus, he's normally a top ten player, which I'm sure he'll get back to soon, and he has so many prospects. I'm failing to comprehend why he'd be interested in me specifically." I don't mention what he said yesterday about feeling partially responsible for Austin's injury.

"Don't put yourself down like that, sweetheart," Eli chimes in. "You are such a strong doubles player and an asset to any partner you have."

Lilian nods. "Absolutely."

I laugh. "We just agreed I'm not great at net. Austin is a beast up there. If Matteo is looking for that from me, he won't get it."

"You're not playing men's doubles with him, Del," Austin adds. "It's mixed. He's not expecting you to be a copy-paste version of me on court. He's obviously seen you play and thinks you're a good fit or he wouldn't have asked."

"And nobody agreed you're not great at net." Eli forks another pancake onto his plate. "All I agreed about was that you aren't aggressive enough sometimes to get yourself *to* the net."

I sigh, knowing they only want what's best for me. If they're pushing, it's because they think I need to give it more thought, and I'm not sure their judgment has ever led me astray.

"Are there other reasons?" Lilian asks gently.

Remembering what Nic said yesterday, I shrug. "I don't believe everything reporters and players say about him, but I can't ignore the fact that he has, in the past, slammed his rackets, and yelled at chair umpires. Gotten fined for those things." I turn to Austin. "I didn't see him play with you a ton this season. How was he then? Did you get fined a lot?"

"So many people on tour do those things," he says with a derisive chuckle, shaking his head. "I think they like to latch onto him and make him seem worse than he is, honestly. And no, he wasn't too bad during doubles, especially in the latter half of the season. The once or twice we did get fined, he paid it all himself. We had fun."

I don't respond after a few moments, and Austin must take this as continued hesitation. He sets his utensils down and clears his throat. "You didn't hear this from me, but you're wondering why you, and if it helps you make your decision, you should know." Everyone, myself included, stops eating, raptly awaiting Austin's next words. He draws out the silence, enjoying the attention, until I shove him gently. "Matteo's sponsors aren't happy with him. Neither are the Italians, who kicked him off the Davis Cup team."

The Davis Cup is a team event where the top men from twenty-six countries compete every year, with the winning country touted as the world champions. Matteo, who, from my understanding, holds dual citizenship for the US and Italy, plays for his home country. I know he played in it for the last few years, so I *was* surprised to see him here since the Italians are still in the running.

Maybe this is the ulterior motive I saw him hold back on yesterday.

"His behavior is catching up to him, and he's struggling to outrun it. His own countrymen are against him.

Half of his endorsement deals were pulled at the beginning of the year, and the other half have told him he's on
thin ice, no matter how good he continues to be. The way
I see it, he needs someone like you to work with him to
prove he's not as bad as he's seemed all these years."

Eli is nodding like it all makes sense, but I ask,
"Someone like me?"

"You know. You're the WTA's sweetheart. Everyone
loves you. No matter what country you're in or who you're
playing against, the crowd is rooting for you. I imagine his
team recognizes that playing mixed doubles with you at
the beginning of the year will help his image this season."

I ponder that for a moment. I'm liked on the tour,
sure. I have no enemies. The people I've beaten usually
become good friends, even if we don't often talk outside of
tournaments. But I didn't realize my reputation stretched
over into the men's tour. Certainly not to the point that
someone like Matteo might *need* someone like me.

"And you truly believe that it won't end negatively if I
train with him? And if we qualify for Aussie?"

"He's a hard-working guy. Like I said, in the second
half of the season, he seemed to mellow out a lot." Austin
shrugs. "I don't know a ton about his personal life, but I
support it."

"Do you think I should do it?" I ask, turning to Eli and
Lilian.

Eli answers, "Let me turn that question around for a
second. Do *you* feel you need to, or could you do without?"

I think of my freshly inked deal with Stratosphere, the
conversation with Chase about the car, and those univer-
sity tuition payments starting in January...it won't be like

community college. If I explain all that to them, they'll try to help me like they always do, and I can't allow that. Instead, I weigh the two against each other.

"I'm not sure yet." But even that's a change from my mentality from Tuesday, when Francesca first pitched the idea and I was certain the answer was no.

Lilian sets a hand on mine. "And that's completely fine. Take some time. Think it over. Austin's is just one opinion." The man in question makes an affronted noise, but Lilian talks over him. "At the end of the day, the decision is entirely yours."

I'm still deliberating as we clean up, the sun rising and bathing the kitchen in warm light. We hug goodbye, and I thank Eli and Lilian for breakfast. If I were to thank them for everything they've done for me, I might never leave.

If I kept a list of names of all the people I play for, everyone I think about as I put my blood, sweat, tears, and everything else into this sport day in and day out, the Wards would come in very close second place to my siblings. Nothing I do will ever be enough to thank Austin's parents for helping me get out of the life I was born into, and that's something that pushes me to prove I was worth their investment.

Despite the three times Austin reminds me that it's his *left* ankle that's injured and that he's perfectly capable of driving, I navigate his car to the facility, ruminating. I promise myself I'll take a couple of days and decide what my offseason will look like by Monday.

AFTER MY PRACTICE MATCH, I COOL DOWN ON A stationary bike in the players' gym. Francesca went in search of Aleks, our strength and conditioning coach, for some resistance bands. Or something like that. I'll admit I wasn't paying attention. Winning my match in straight sets despite Lina's dangerous backhand has left me extra confident and cheery. I open the group message that has been going off, making sure to continue pumping my legs slowly.

SHOTS FIRED

SAHAR

D, in case it helps you make your decision, here's a thirst trap of Matteo

She sends the link, and I stifle a laugh.

Oh my god, you kid

NOAH

This page has fan edits of all of you, by the way

Waiting for them to make one about me being a hot coach

AUSTIN

Wow, they got all my best angles

He proceeds to send every single video of himself, then the rest of us.

NIC REMOVED THEMSELF FROM THE CHAT.

AUSTIN ADDED NIC TO THE CHAT.

HARPER

Some of these are gold!

SAHAR

Oh Delilahhhhhhh

Did that help you?

The moment I bite the bullet and click on the original link she sent, swiping away the notifications from a video I posted a few days ago that went minorly viral, the door to the players' gym rattles.

If I thought I wasn't going to see Matteo until I made my decision, I was sorely mistaken. The Morozov Tennis Academy may be a big facility with many players, but a good chunk of those players have the same weekly schedule as I do. It really shouldn't come as a surprise when he appears.

There are a few other players in the large gym: Lina on a treadmill facing the track and field we use on rest days with her team whispering beside her, a couple of guys over by the weight racks, and Nic and another woman stretching in the free-weight area with their teams beside them. And yet, the moment the door squeaks open, Matteo's eyes land on me.

His hat is backward again, covering his wet hair. I imagine he just finished up a practice match too, though his coach is nowhere in sight. When he starts walking toward me and the bikes, I make a high-pitched noise I didn't know I was capable of and toss my phone to the floor.

Unfortunately, it lands face up, a video cycling through photos of him wearing only underwear interspersed with a few shots of him on the court, wiping sweat from his brow with his shirt.

I now know my fight or flight reflex gives me a third, less useful option: freezing. My eyes feel as wide as saucers as they meet his two bikes away.

"I—I. My friends…they—" I can't finish any of my sentences, apparently. Matteo's eyebrows twitch, but he says nothing. Mortified, I finally regain the ability to hop down and click my phone off, tucking it under the bike.

Matteo bends down, casually changing the settings on his bike, and I pray he saw nothing. The lights in here are quite bright. The glare would make seeing it from his angle hard, I bet. Plus, there's some distance between us.

Yes. I'm going to play this like it didn't happen.

Clearing my throat, as if that will shove the remnants of my embarrassment away, I joke, "I don't bite, you know."

Matteo's head snaps up so fast, he nearly slams it into the handlebars. I hide a giggle in the shoulder facing away from him before giving him a small smile. Maybe he really didn't see anything.

"I know," he grunts, like the joke went right over his head and he never had me pegged for a rabid animal.

It takes a few seconds—and I can almost see him doing the math on something in his head—before he moves to the bike beside me, changing the height and distance to his body's specifications.

"Did you win your match?" I ask him.

He nods.

"Are you always this jovial after winning?" The answer

is yes. I've seen the neutral expression on his face after dominating in a Grand Slam final. Still…

"I prefer to save my emotional outbursts for when I'm losing," he deadpans, and I have to look at him to figure out whether he's joking. I learn nothing. When I don't respond, he says, "You played well."

I'm shocked he noticed me from four courts over. Inexplicably, my cheeks—which have cooled considerably over the last few seconds of semi-normalcy between us—warm again. "Oh, thanks. Had a hearty breakfast or whatever it is they say you need these days to keep energy levels up."

This joke is far more subtle, and probably not my best, so it's no shock when his eyebrows tip toward each other for a second before he sets his hands on his handlebars and starts pumping his legs, the muscles in his calves and quads flexing. I have to look away.

"You're doing something new with your serve." Matteo leans back, setting a hand on his thigh. "Worked well."

I'm once again blushing but saved from responding when Francesca comes back with three resistance bands, her eyes bouncing between me and Matteo. She says something to him in Italian, and he responds with a couple of words. When I raise a brow quizzically, she smiles. "Just making sure he's not bothering you."

She doesn't let me answer, gesturing with the resistance bands toward the free weights. I slow my legs and hop off, wiping off the seat and pocketing my phone as subtly as I can so as not to remind Matteo of what he *didn't* see. When I throw him a smile, he simply blinks.

Though we don't speak for the rest of our shared time in the gym, our eyes meet more than I should let them. His offer, which has been resting in the back of my mind since I learned of it, pushes itself to the front every time they do.

Still, I have no answer.

six

Matteo is late on Monday, so I busy myself, taking cute pictures in my new Stratosphere practice outfit to prove I can keep my side of the deal. "Linger" by The Cranberries plays quietly from my speakers while I attempt selfies, my phone propped against my water jug on one of the picnic tables beside the outdoor hard courts. A couple of women from the tour pass by, jumping into the photo, and we share a laugh.

"Del! Do you need help?" Lina calls.

I shake my head, smiling. "Nah, it's too early for good lighting anyway." I'll get Nic's help later.

When they disappear onto the courts to stretch, Matteo rounds the corner, looking more frazzled than I've seen him. His curls are tousled, less like he just woke up and more like he's been running his hand through them for half an hour. His usual frown, which seems etched deeper today, softens when he spots me mid-photo, my foot pulled to my butt so I can show off my shoes in what can only be described as a ridiculous pose.

I drop my foot and grab my racket and phone, turning off the song. "Good morning," I chirp. "You're late." I smile so he knows I'm teasing.

He sighs. "I'm sorry. I promise I'm usually punctual." When I don't respond, too busy dissecting the weariness on his face, he asks, "How was your rest day?"

I blink, surprised. "Oh…It was good, thank you. But that's not why I asked to meet."

"You didn't ask Francesca to tell Alessio to tell me to meet you here so you could tell me about your rest day?" This is now the second or third time his words sound like a joke yet are said without a hint of a smile.

I bite back a grin, moving past his joke-but-maybe-not-a-joke. "I'll play mixed with you. Until Austin is back. But I have conditions." And they were entirely concocted by Nic, Sahar, and Harper after I mentioned in our group chat that I was thinking about agreeing.

Matteo sets his racket down, pulling a leg to his chest to stretch it out. "Okay. Shoot."

"I would prefer it if you didn't swear loudly during matches. Or slam your racket. Or hit tennis balls up into the stands." I squint, trying to figure out if there is anything I missed. "Oh, and ideally no yelling at our box or the chair umpire or me." I put a finger up with each entity I mention.

He looks away, tongue wetting his bottom lip before his teeth sink into it. I realize I'm watching him far too closely and look away too.

"I can't even swear when we win a point? No well-timed 'hell yeahs'?" Once again, is he joking? When I glance back, his face tells me absolutely nothing. Again.

He drops his leg from his chest. "And what about if fans *want* me to hit balls toward them after we win? What then?" he continues.

My head cocks. This is the most I've heard Matteo speak uninterrupted. His lips twitch, and I can finally, *finally*, tell that he's messing with me.

There's a small hiccup in my chest, an excitement that *I* was somehow able to get him to joke with me when moments ago he seemed so unhappy. I memorize that twitch of his lips, the way the brown of his eyes seems to dance, just a little.

I pretend not to be thrown by his sudden change. To go from a man who hardly glanced in my direction for over half a year—who didn't so much as say a word to me when he got here—to a man making jokes about knowing my name and teasing me about the rules I'm putting in place…I can't figure him out at all.

"I didn't know you had a bossy side," he says.

"I didn't know you knew everything about me," rolls off my tongue. Another twitch at the corners of his mouth. "And I'm not being bossy. I just want to make sure this is a good partnership for both of us." Jokingly, I add, "Wouldn't want to get hit with a fine, you know?"

His jaw clenches, the ghost of a smile gone, and suddenly, I feel chided. Isn't my entire motto not to judge people because I don't know what they're going through? And yet, here I am, making jokes about his behavior.

"You're right. I agree to all your terms, though if a 'hell yeah' slips out, I hope you'll forgive me." After a few seconds, he continues, "Anyway, I'm hoping your cool, calm, and collectedness on court will rub off on me.

You're like ice. Doesn't matter what's going on, you don't show your hand."

Him knowing this much about me is such a shock, I lose my grip on my racket and it clatters to the ground. He steps closer, bending to grab it and hand it back to me, even though getting it for myself would have taken fewer steps. I accept it hesitantly.

"You keep dropping your racket around me like this, I'm going to develop a complex."

My brain is lagging, processing his words about my disposition on court and adding it to the things he said to me about my serve like little building blocks. Except I'm only in possession of a few of them and have no idea what they're building up *to*. "How do you know what I'm like on court?" Or *anything* about my game, for that matter.

His dark eyebrows knit together. "Why do you seem so convinced that I know nothing about you? Is it so unimaginable that people might pay attention to someone like you?"

My thoughts stutter. *Someone like me?* What could he *possibly* mean by that?

Recovering, I say, "You're answering my questions with more questions."

He huffs, an almost laugh. The most I may ever earn from him. "I've watched you play, Delilah. Both with Austin and in singles. I've never seen you get emotional on court save for a 'let's go' here and there to get the energy of the crowd flowing. For someone who knows so much about my on-court behavior, you seem awfully shocked that someone else might know yours."

"Not *someone* else. You. You're you."

"And you're you?" he asks, confused.

"Exactly."

The word seems to stymie the conversation. I'm glad for it since it's gotten away from me. "Are you warming up with your team or someone else this morning?" I ask.

"Was planning to hit with my coach."

"Do you want to warm up together? To get a feel for each other's ground strokes?"

Monday is a singles day, but we'll begin training together Tuesdays and Fridays since neither of us are playing regular doubles. Maybe hit with each other in the mornings on singles days, especially since so many players are still on vacation.

"Good idea. Did you want to stretch first?"

I nod and follow him onto an empty court, setting my stuff down against the bench. We stretch for a few minutes, his expression solemn, and a part of me is left wondering if I made up the amusement on his face and in his words earlier. When we're ready to start, we face each other on the service line, a few balls in his pocket and a couple in my skirt. Francesca and Matteo's coach, Alessio, speak in rapid Italian by the bench, having joined us as we finished our stretches.

I observe Matteo's movements closely—his strokes, his footwork, the fluidity with which he hits the ball. I've seen him play plenty, but I've never been on the other end of the court from him. After a few rallies, we move to the baseline. He hits clean, deep shots, his forehand powerful as it slices through the air, his backhand less so but still strong and reliable. His footwork is sharp, never sitting still, which allows him to set up for each strike with ease.

It's a work of art. Despite him pulling his punches so that I can keep up, I can tell how stunning his game truly is. Only once does he miss a shot, and when it sails out, all I see is a tightened hand at his waist before he shakes it off.

When we're warm, we go our separate ways for singles practice, and I move through the day like any other. That evening, as I lie in bed, ready to fall asleep, my phone vibrates.

UNKNOWN NUMBER

Matteo Corsi.

I snort, adding him to my contacts before jokingly texting back my name.

Delilah Anderson.

Have you ever texted anyone in your life?

MATTEO

?

No "hi"? No "looking forward to playing with you"?

MATTEO

Hi. It's Matteo Corsi. Looking forward to playing mixed doubles with you.

I laugh at the entire text, down to the period he makes sure to include at the end.

I'm glad you don't play as stiffly as you text

When he doesn't respond after a few minutes, I click

my phone off, embarrassed. I shouldn't have said anything.

Only when I wake up do I see his response.

MATTEO

Once upon a time I thought you were nice.

I guess your meanness is rubbing off on me

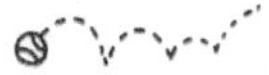

IF SOMEONE WERE TO DESCRIBE US AS OUT OF SYNC, IT would be the understatement of the century. A person who has never watched tennis in their entire life would be able to tell this isn't going well. Scratch that, an *alien* who just touched down from outer space would recognize how poorly we're doing right now.

This time, Matteo wasn't late, but he still seems completely out of sorts. I don't know if that's why we're struggling or if we're just not meant to be playing together. Our styles are mismatched. His shots are fast and aggressive, where mine are more measured and precise. He hits a forehand from the baseline to Alessio on the other side so hard that suddenly it's ping-ponged its way to me at the net in a matter of seconds. The footwork I'm used to while I'm at net isn't good enough to keep up with his pace. It's frustrating me, and I'm *sure* it's frustrating Matteo, even if the most he's shown it is with a couple of briefly tightened fists and a clenched jaw. Though those have only come after his own mistakes.

Francesca gives me feedback. Alessio too. I keep

trying, changing up the speed of my footwork so I'm more prepared to volley back powerful shots from Alessio, who stands at the other baseline, alternating between hitting to each of us.

Upbeat and trying hard to make it work on the outside, struggling and positive it won't work on the inside.

Finally, after Matteo slaps a shot like a whip to Alessio and it's sent back to me at lightning speed, my racket barely getting to the ball enough for it to be a shank, the shock absorber on my strings flies off.

I put on a smile, setting my racket against the net beside the ball I just missed. "I think I'm going to take a breather," I say, as if I'm not already two steps to the bench.

Matteo strides toward the net, picking up my racket and shock absorber and sitting beside me. He takes the small rubber absorber and artfully gets it back in its rightful place on my strings, his fingers moving quickly, hands flexing. It's so hot, I almost miss his words.

"It's fairly obvious we should switch you over to the forehand side." Matteo slaps the strings in the center a couple of times to make sure the dampener won't fall off again before he sets the racket down between us. "I thought it made the most sense before this drill, but Alessio and Francesca wanted to try it out this way to be sure."

I'm not positive this is recoverable, but I nod enthusiastically anyway. "That's a good idea. Your forehand is so powerful that the point will move too fast for me. If I'm on forehand, the pace will decrease a little with your backhand. Plus, I'm more comfortable on forehand."

My forehand may not be as powerful as his, or even in the top twenty-five most powerful women's shots, but it's damn good and very consistent. With me on the deuce side and him on the ad side, I do think we have a better shot.

Smile turning rueful, I half joke, "I bet you're regretting choosing me now. If we come up against any player with a shot as powerful as yours, I'm toast."

"No," he answers without hesitation. Like he won't give the words a moment of thought because he's so certain they're wrong.

"Del, let's get you on the deuce side!" Francesca calls to me. When I shoot her a thumbs up, she goes back to talking to Alessio.

"I'm not sure why you're acting like you haven't dominated in mixed doubles before," Matteo murmurs before taking a swig of water. "I've watched you hit winner after winner. Down the line, cross court. Against the man or the woman; it doesn't matter. Your awareness of where your opponent is at all times is something you wield well, Delilah. Credimi," he says, tapping two fingers against the bench between us. *Believe me.* "Power isn't the only way to win a point."

He stands, picking up a few of the balls that litter our court and hitting them over the net to Alessio so they can go into the basket for the next drill. I don't realize my mouth is open in shock until Francesca frowns my way. I snap it shut.

He's right. I know he is. The din of my inner voice telling me this might not work fades, replacing my negativity with hope.

seven

Our next doubles session doesn't go much better.

On Wednesday, we did singles drills together to continue getting a feel for each other's strokes. At one point, Matteo hit a shot so hard that I barely got my racket on it, shanking the ball so badly, it almost hit Alessio's head where he stood by the back fence. My shouted "Whoops!" was just enough to get him out of the way a split second before the ball thwacked the metal. I tried not to laugh, but a small giggle ripped through me, and Matteo looked at me like he didn't know what to do with me. No smile though.

Yesterday was a rest day, so I only saw Matteo in passing in the health and wellness offices. I tried *very* hard not to notice the gray sweatpants he was sporting. Despite my smile and excited "Hello!" all I got from him was a nod and a quiet "Hi."

I've been chasing the rush of that fraction of a smile since Tuesday, and yet I still can't say with any degree of certainty whether he thinks of me as more than an acquaintance he hits with sometimes. My friends have been no help, the group chat full of impractical tips.

SHOTS FIRED

I can't tell if Matteo hates me or not

AUSTIN

I highly doubt it

SAHAR

Pull the zipper on your practice dress
down more

I'm not trying to seduce him, S

SAHAR

Phew, I would be

NOAH

No. You don't have time for that

HARPER

He might just be very reserved! I'm sure he
doesn't hate you.

AUSTIN

Yeah, he's like Nic. Not very talkative

NIC REMOVED THEMSELF FROM THE CHAT.

AUSTIN ADDED NIC TO THE CHAT.

This afternoon is only our second time on the same side of the net, and once again, we're out of sync. Matteo's volleying balls back even when I say I've got it—though I might not be saying it early enough for him—and when I'm at net, I'm letting more pass me than I should. The gusts of wind hitting us sporadically don't help.

Checking in on his temper has become second nature. The smallest part of me is stuck on Nic's concerns like they're honey, but the worst of it comes when he misses a shot, stares after it, jaw clenched, then mumbles something in Italian and shakes his head.

"I do that all the time," I tell him encouragingly. "No biggie." Though I'm not lucky enough to be rewarded with a smile, I can almost see him rolling the words over inside his head. The next time he makes the same mistake, he brushes off the frustration and gets set for another rally.

A couple of hours later, when we play a practice point —me on the deuce side, him at the net on the ad side—we get a good rally going until I smack a ball a little too hard and it sails out. I tense, waiting for him to be upset or to tell me what I'm doing wrong. Instead, he shrugs and takes his turn at the baseline.

"Move your feet, Delilah. You're letting the ball get away from you," Francesca calls from the other side, feeding Matteo the next ball. At least she's giving me feedback. It's when she *isn't* providing advice that I know the situation is bad. This might just be salvageable.

I keep up my footwork, moving cyclically closer to the net to protect the alley, then back toward the service line as Matteo rallies with Francesca. When he puts away a ball down the line, I throw him a smile. He tilts his head in acknowledgement, then speaks in rapid Italian to Francesca and Alessio.

Francesca nods. "Get some water before you stretch

out." She continues talking to Matteo's coach, and by the pucker in her brow, it's nothing good. Are they worried we're not going to make it through qualifiers? Is it obviously my fault?

No, Francesca would never say a bad word about me to anyone *but* me, and that's reassurance enough.

I topple onto the bench, exhausted from a long day of tennis, and grab the last few sips of my water. Matteo lifts his shirt to wipe sweat off his forehead as he walks toward me. I have to cut my eyes away before I'm caught cataloguing the line down the center of his stomach and the subtle V of his Adonis belt.

He settles onto the bench beside me, sighing deeply.

"I'm sure we'll get better," I say reassuringly. "It's only the first week. It took me and Nic some time before we were able to fall into a rhythm. It's just a matter of time."

Matteo doesn't answer, staring out over the courts. He takes a long pull of his water, his Adam's apple bobbing, then sets it back down.

"How long did it take you and Austin?" I ask.

He shrugs. "Hard to say, but it seems like it took a while."

"But you pushed through. You guys were doing so well this season, especially near the end."

"Yeah, but…lots can change over the course of a season," he says cautiously. It makes me wonder what changed for *him* and if it's the reason he seems so different from the picture painted of him by everyone else. "How long did it take *you* and Austin?"

I think back to the first time Austin and I played mixed doubles. It was so long ago, sometime in middle school probably, that I don't remember. I tell Matteo as much. When he doesn't answer again, my eyes fall to my hands clasped in my lap. "We'll find our rhythm. We can stay longer on Tuesdays and Fridays if you'd like. Or we can make the full day doubles instead of doing singles work in the mornings."

Matteo shifts, and I meet his eyes. His eyebrows are drawn, but more in thought than frustration or regret. Or maybe that's me being hopeful. "I'm not sure it's just a matter of how much time we put in on the court. Though we would benefit from some practice matches."

"Sure. I can see if Nic is interested. Potentially Aleksandr and Anya when she's back since they played together until recently."

Matteo nods, and I worry I've lost him. I glance over to where Francesca and Alessio are talking. Matteo says something to them I can't understand, and the pair laughs.

I nudge him. "Now I know why you wanted to play mixed with me."

"Why's that?"

"Oh, come on. Clearly you just wanted to trash talk me with my coach without me understanding it," I joke.

Matteo gives me a real smile. Nothing big, no teeth, but both corners of his lips turn up and stay, his eyes lighting from warm chocolate to cool amber. I'm taken aback but not so much so that I can't tease him. "Quick! Hide it!" When he shoots me a questioning look, I gesture toward his face. "Your smile. If you're not careful, people will realize you're not a robot."

I'm rewarded with a quiet chuckle. Maybe the day

hasn't gone the way we'd hoped, but I still feel like I've accomplished something big. Something worth being proud of.

"You're ridiculous. All I said was we're going to need your highly accurate down-the-line shots to get us anywhere near the finals at this rate." His lips press together as if to subdue any further laughter.

I feel warm all over, and if I wasn't pink from running around, I'm sure I am now. Matteo seems to have no qualms about complimenting me, doling them out like Costco employees with free samples.

Francesca and Alessio amble toward us. They're clearly ready to be done for the day. Typically, we'd go through game strategy together, but until we're more in sync, that'll have to wait.

Matteo and I start our cool-down stretches. As I reach toward my feet, Alessio says, "We think that in order to make this work, and with less than a month and a half to prepare, it might be best if you two begin speaking outside of practice. Sometimes, when a doubles team is struggling, it's because they aren't on the same page off the court."

"What does that mean, exactly?" I ask.

"Walk around the track and talk about your child-hoods. Get a meal and learn about each other's fears. I don't care what you do as long as you push through this awkwardness and get personal."

I wait for Matteo to protest.

Nothing.

I guess it's on me. "I'm not sure we need to do that. Like I told Matteo, I can practice later into the evening. Or we can add more doubles work to Tuesday and Friday mornings. But I'm not sure getting that personal is a good idea."

Francesca shakes her head. "Alessio's being indelicate. Whether you 'get personal' or not is up to you, but get friendly. Two people who don't know the first thing about each other will never succeed on a tennis court together. If you can connect emotionally on some level, it might help how you move together on court."

I wait for Matteo to back me up, but he continues stretching. When I catch his eye, he shrugs. "Can't hurt."

I guess we're getting friendly.

AFTER I'M SHOWERED AND DRESSED LATER THAT EVENING, I check my phone hopefully to see if any of my siblings called. Nothing. I sigh, my fingers finding the worn photo of Mom, Chase, and me. I could—*should* call them, but so much guilt builds up in my throat when I get ready to. Guilt over leaving them behind. Wishing I could physically be there for them more than I have these last few years, desperate for the days when we're financially stable enough to pick up where we left off.

The fact that they're not calling either tells me they're probably busy anyway.

Grabbing both my bags in one hand, I keep the photo in the other, allowing it to act as a balm for that guilt, a representation of hope for the future.

When I step out of the locker room, Matteo is in the hallway, hands in his pockets. The scruff along his chiseled jawline is more prominent under the fluorescent lights.

"Oh…You didn't have to wait for me."

His eyes fall to the folded square in my hand, then to my face, concern etching itself between his brows. "I figured we could talk. If you're free."

It takes me a minute to remember what we agreed to earlier. "I'm free, but are you sure you want to do this tonight? It's Friday."

The lip twitch. "Is it? Well in that case…" He turns and starts toward the exit. Instantly dejected and a little shocked, I scramble to find a reason to keep him here. Luckily, when he gets a few feet away, he turns back. "I know it's Friday." He hooks a thumb over his shoulder. "Want to walk and talk?"

I peer down at my gym and racket bags. Before I've even responded, he's taking them both from me with ease and walking out of the building toward the rec area. "Wait! Where are we going?"

"Up to you. Courts, pool, track. I'm open to anything."

"Let's do the pool." There is something so soothing about the indoor pool at night, serenity in the chaos of the reflection across the large room. I tuck the photo into my sweatpants pocket and follow him.

The sharp tang of chlorine clings to the air outside the pool room, crawling into my nose as he swipes us in. Our sneakers squeak against the tile with each step. Matteo sets my bags down on a white slatted bench pushed against the wall, grabbing a white towel from the millions stacked in the closet near the bench and laying it on the ground inches from the overflow gutter, where water ripples peacefully. He gestures for me to sit, and I do, bringing my knees to my chest. A second later, he joins me at a respectable distance, leaning back against the bench.

It's quiet for a minute or so before I decide to break the ice. "Where did you grow up?"

"Florence, until I was six. Then New York City to be closer to my dad's brothers. Mom's mom followed, so most of my family was there. I still spent summers in Italy for a few years after that, but New York was home base."

"And what was that like? Moving your whole life to another country?"

"Easier for me, I think. I struggled to make friends, for sure, even with a couple of cousins near my age. Learned quickly how to mimic the American accent so I wouldn't be made fun of. Kids are brutal." I chuckle, though my heart breaks for the small boy who had to shed a piece of himself to feel he belonged. "But at the end of the day, I was young. I hadn't built a life somewhere else. The adjustment was harder for my parents."

I set my chin on my knees. "I can imagine."

"Where did you grow up?"

"Tampa. I try to stay nearby for my family, but, you know. Being gone nearly ten months out of the year is hard." The guilt I just managed to tamp down materializes in my throat once more. If Matteo notices, he doesn't say.

"Are you close with them?"

"My siblings? Yeah."

"Are they around the same age as you?"

"Chase is twenty. The twins, Hazel and Finn, are seventeen."

"And you're, what? Twenty-five?"

I nod. "You?"

"Twenty-eight."

I laugh quietly. "Sorry, I meant do you have siblings?"

Bowing his head, he admits gruffly, "I'm not good at this."

"At what?"

He shrugs. "Making friends? Being friendly? I'm not sure. But I suspect between the two of us, you might be the expert."

Though the words are spoken casually, there's a touch of woe that makes me want to reach out and hug him. I'm lucky to have the friends I do. I picture Matteo and how he might fit into our group chat one day, how my friends would act around him during game nights and movie nights.

It's odd how vividly I can imagine it, like proof he'd click with everyone.

"That's not true. You're great at talking to me. That one was my fault, anyway."

"You make it easy," he answers quietly.

This time I *really* have to stop myself from reaching for him.

"So, siblings?" I ask.

I can't tell if his eyes flash or if it's the reflection of the light from the pool dancing across his face like lightning flickering through dark clouds. "None that I'm close with."

He doesn't elaborate, so I guide us elsewhere. "When did you start playing tennis?"

"Pretty much the moment I was born. My whole family played. Nonno, my mom's dad, played professionally for a while, and her whole side of the family enjoyed it rather competitively. Didn't begin training hard until I was seven or eight."

"That's nice. I bet having family members who play made it more fun." Matteo doesn't respond, just looks out over the eight-lane pool. He doesn't ask, but he let me take the lead, so I say, "I didn't start until I was eight. Austin and I became friends and—I'm sure you know this—the Wards played professionally. They took me in like I was their own. Trained me, helped me with coaching. Got me to where I am now."

"You're not related at all?"

"No, no. Though the way they tell it, it might seem that way."

"Yeah."

Silence settles over us, and though I'm great at finding threads to pull in order to learn more about someone and gain their trust, Matteo has shared more with me today than I suspect he's shared with most others.

I can't be sure why.

"If you'd rather not do this, we can, like, make sheets with all our likes and dislikes and say we had the conversations they want. In case they give us a pop quiz or something." He begins answering, but I jump to finish my thought. "I don't want you to feel obligated to talk to me. I know how tiring these offseason days are, and I'm sure the last thing you want is to be spending an extra hour a couple of times a week getting to know me. You're already having to play with someone at a lower level than you. I don't want to cause any issues." I feel weak enough as it is when it comes to my family and our situation, the last thing I need is to feel powerless in this relationship too.

"You misread my silence as inattentiveness or disinterest. It's not. I just enjoy the quiet and, like I said, I am not the poster boy for making friends." When I look over at him, his eyes hold on mine. "And I think you forget that *I*, 'Matteo the Malignant Narcissist' asked *you*, tennis' golden girl, to play, not the other way around. *You* are the one who has no obligation to do this."

A smile blooms across my lips at his reassurance, even as something wiggles free in my head at the nickname he applies to himself so nonchalantly, like he believes wholeheartedly what others call him. Or at the very least has no interest in fighting it.

It makes me surer than ever that they're all wrong about him.

"I certainly don't feel an obligation either. I'm glad you asked." Surprise slips through me when the words ring true. "Maybe in a couple of weeks, we'll be able to win a point."

"Right. After we've gotten to know each other's favorite tennis stroke, color, foods, bird..." He trails off, but there's a ghost of a smile on his face too.

A laugh breaks free from my chest, light and easy. "Yes, after that."

We sit in silence for another few minutes, only broken when one of us thinks of a favorite to share. His favorite stroke is his forehand (shocking), and mine is my offensive slice. His favorite court is clay, since it's most common in Italy, and mine is hard court. He prefers to spend off days swimming laps at the pool because it's the place he feels closest to his mom, while I typically walk or jog around the track on my off days.

When the lights outside flick off and the facility starts to shut down for the evening, we stand. I toss my bags over my shoulder, and he drops the towel into a bin for cleaning.

"Will you be at game night?" he asks when we're about ready to leave. "At the Wards' on Sunday?"

"You're talking to the poker champion of the last two years," I answer, flexing my biceps. "Of course I'll be there. Have to keep those sharks away from my title."

Matteo blesses me with that muted smile that makes my heart dance victoriously. "Allora, I'll be there."

eight

The hard edge of my father's "Delilah" tells me all I need to know about the voicemail he leaves during Monopoly Sunday evening. I excuse myself from the game and move to the Wards' kitchen to listen to the rest.

"Delilah, Delilah, Delilah. Y'know I came up with that name? Your mom," he scoffs, "wanted to name you after some dumb flower."

Daisy. She told me that once, a couple of years before she left.

"Anyway, *Delilah*. Thanksforcheckin'in," he slurs. "I'm so glad your new life and family are *so* much more important than the one you were born into." Another scoff. "You really are 'zactly like her, aren't you? You couldn't just take her physical features, you had to leave us all behind too."

Every word is a lance tied with barbed wire and dipped in poison, shoving itself into my chest cavity. I put my head in my free hand, knowing where this is going. Where it always goes when he's in a particular mood, two, three, who knows, ten drinks in his system. But just because I know where this is going—know that this will be like the many messages he's left me before and will be followed in a few days or weeks with some kind of apology—doesn't mean that lance doesn't stick in the fleshy part of my heart.

The worst part is, he's right. I so badly wanted to be like her growing up, and now, in some ways, I am.

"Anyone can be trained tuh smack a ball with a racket, y'know? There's nothin' special about you or what you do. And clearly you don't have the talent to cut it since you can't even"—the sloshing of a bottle held to his lips muffles the last few words, but I get the idea. I wish after all these years that it didn't hurt, didn't make my chest clench painfully or pitch that baseball-sized guilt down my throat. But it does.

I can't bear to listen to the rest, sliding down the pantry door and setting my phone beside me.

Every word he said rings true, no matter how I try to outpace them with other thoughts.

I left to make money for them. I didn't abandon them and leave them with nothing. But what good is money if my emotional support leaves them wanting?

I clawed my way into the top fifty women in the world. Matteo wanting to work with me is proof I'm worthy of being here. My sponsorship *is proof that I belong.* But what if it's all a fluke? What if Matteo truly just feels bad about Austin's injury? What if playing with me is simply a means to assuage that guilt? And what if I can't uphold my end of the Stratosphere deal?

A sob notches in my chest, and I take deep breaths to

keep it at bay. In the other room sit three people who took me in like I was their own blood, plus my best friend and…whatever Matteo has become to me. More than an acquaintance, almost a friend. I can't let all of this overwhelm me right now.

A presence settles beside me. When I raise my eyes, I meet Eli's concerned blue ones. He picks up my phone and glowers at the screen, his jaw tight. I know he wants to know what my father said to me this time, but I shake my head.

"Please no." I don't know if it's because I don't want him to hear my shame, all the ways I've begun to feel small, or if I can't stand to let him listen to my father in this state. A solitary tear breaks free, and I swipe it away quickly, though not quickly enough.

Eli clicks the phone off, putting an arm around my shoulders and pulling me into him. "Do you remember the first USTA tournament you played? The very first match?" he asks quietly.

"Of course," I murmur. I'd been training with the Wards for months, but I'd never played against anyone besides Austin, and he always beat me. I was brimming with nerves when Eli and I showed up to the courts and waited for my name to be called over the speakers to signal the start of it all.

"I knew you were going to be something special the moment I put a racket in your hands, and that first match…I just wanted you to have fun. You needed it with all you were dealing with. You were shaky the first two games, but then you looked for me in the stands and something changed."

I remember it well. So much of my life until that point, I'd felt alone. Alone in taking care of my siblings despite both of my parents sometimes being around. Alone at school because I couldn't tell anyone about what was happening, and on the off chance I did, none of the kids my age understood. Something about turning to see Eli cheering me on, being there with me for this big moment in my life, felt like a cool glass of water after the hottest Florida summer day. All my nerves dissipated into nothingness.

He continues, "After that, you smiled the whole time, even after you lost the first set. I was so *happy*." His voice breaks on the word. "So honored to be there, watching you. Getting to be your number one fan when you won the next two sets, and then again and again every match you played. Even the ones you lost." He pulls away, grabbing my hands and meeting my eyes meaningfully. "I've never once wavered in that feeling, Delilah. You are so strong. So hardworking. And you pour everything you have into your family. Don't let that *man*," he spits the word out like he has a lot more, far less pleasant synonyms to use, "steal that truth from you."

More tears fall, and Eli smiles kindly at me while I dab them away with my fingertips. Sniffling, I whisper, "I'll try." There's nothing that can be done about it right now, other than to prove my father wrong.

"Do you want me to come up with an excuse for why we need everyone to leave? I'll give you a ride home."

"No, no. Let me wash up and I'll be back in." Game night is exactly what I need to put this out of my head and feel better. Compartmentalize like it's my full-time job.

Offering a watery smile, I say, "After all, I have a lot of fake money to collect from all of you and a few rounds of poker to win before the night is through."

Eli chuckles, giving my hands one last squeeze before going back into the living room. After taking a few breaths and splashing some water on my face, I text in my sibling group chat to make sure they're all doing okay despite the binge our father seems to be on.

When I come back, five concerned faces turn to me. Ignoring them, I beam. "Ready to lose it all to yours truly?"

AN HOUR OR SO LATER, WHEN THE GAME OF MONOPOLY has devolved into anarchy—as expected when athletes congregate for game night—and a bit of my earlier sadness has melted away, I belt (very poorly) the lyrics to "Dreams" by The Cranberries, which Eli so generously cued up for my benefit, my phone safely tucked far away. Out of sight, out of mind.

The board game is splayed out across the Wards' large oval coffee table. Across from me sit Eli and Austin. Nicola is to my left, Matteo to my right, and Lilian beside him.

"Wait, how are you buying a hotel?" Nic asks Austin suspiciously. Her question quiets the rest of us, who inspect Austin's stack of money. "You've only passed GO like two times."

I lean over to fake whisper to Matteo, "Austin loves to cheat during game night. Or do things that are cheat-adjacent."

"I do not!" he exclaims, offended.

"What is cheat-adjacent?" Matteo asks, befuddled.

Eli holds his money up. "It's when my son artfully 'forgets' when he owes someone money for landing on their property or raises out of turn in poker."

"I'm *not* cheating! I can afford a damn hotel."

Lilian scans the bank piles she's been meticulously keeping. "No, Nicola is onto something. This isn't right."

"That's it. I'm done for the night," Eli says, throwing his money onto the table playfully and standing from the carpet.

"Okay, old man," Austin responds. "We can pretend it's not because your joints are achy from sitting on the floor, I guess."

I snort, and I'm almost positive I see Matteo hiding a lip twitch behind the money he's counting.

"Feel free to say that the next time I'm whooping you on court," Eli responds, trying not to laugh as he heads to the main bedroom.

"As if!"

Nic tosses her money down. "Well, I'm certainly not playing if Austin's going to be like this."

Austin opens his mouth to retort, but Lilian beats him. "I'm out too. It's getting too late for me."

With a grumble, Austin begins putting his money back into the banker's piles. "Fine, but the four of us need to play poker. Someone has to beat Delilah before the new year, and Sahar isn't here to help."

"Oh ye of excessive faith," I respond. "You're talking an awfully big game for someone who had to steal from the bank just to lose at Monopoly." And Sahar only got close to beating me in poker *once*.

Austin rolls his eyes, and in a matter of minutes, we've managed to get the board game and its many pieces back into the box.

When Nic deals our first round, I peek at Matteo. He hasn't spoken much this evening, but that's not unexpected. After what he told me on Friday about struggling to make friends, I've made it my mission to coax him into conversations so he knows the rest of us are eager to hear from him.

"You know the rules of Texas Hold'em?" I ask him.

"I do. What are the stakes?"

Austin glances between Nic and me. "Dares? Or photos?"

My friends, forever the best people on the planet, make sure we never play for money. It's for my benefit, allowing me to have fun without stressing about what I could lose, and I love them all the more for it.

Matteo looks comically confused.

"We typically play for something like a dare for all the losers or embarrassing photos. Or sometimes for choosing a meal you want the others to cook for you. Stuff like that," I explain.

He nods his understanding.

Turning to Nic, I ask, "Photos, right? It's been a while since we did that." And I desperately would love to get my hands on an embarrassing photo of Matteo.

"I'm down," Austin says at the same time Nic says, "Sounds good."

The first couple of rounds move quickly. I win the

first, Nic wins the second. On the third, Matteo deals. I put in the small blind, Nic puts in the big, and after a few moments of pretending to inspect his cards then looking around the table suspiciously, Austin calls.

Matteo checks his cards briefly, then follows. Sliding my cards to my chest, I lean back against the couch and examine them. Four of hearts and five of clubs.

Easy, I think. I call, and we're off.

The first three cards Matteo puts up in the middle are an ace, a two, and a seven. I glance at Austin, and by the subtle shift of his lips from right to left, I know he's got nothing. Nic is usually good at hiding her tells, but I know her well enough to recognize that her refusal to meet my eyes means she's probably shooting for a pair or two.

Matteo is another story. I *don't* know him well enough to figure out what's in his hand.

"Del, stop watching everyone and go," Austin complains.

"Just for that, I'm raising," I respond, tossing in a few more chips.

Nic glares at Austin. "Thanks a lot. Call." She follows me. Austin calls too, though I know he knows he's going to lose.

Matteo stares intently at his cards, then at the center, his expression stoic. I shift closer to him, and he turns his cards so they face the far wall, where Lilian was sitting earlier.

"Go fish," I whisper. It's enough to make Nic snort and Austin chuckle. It's even enough to put a another smile on Matteo's lips.

"If you're not careful, someone might think *you're*

cheating with how close you're getting to my cards," he murmurs.

I gasp, moving away. "I would *never*."

He shoots me the smallest of smirks before raising triple what I raised. Nic groans.

With my eyes on Matteo's, I toss more chips in. "Call." Nic folds, Austin calls.

Matteo burns a card, then places a seven down in the middle. I bite back a grimace. I've already put a good bit into the pot and have a chance with the river. "Check."

Austin checks. Once again, Matteo raises, and I'm forced to follow.

"Oh, I'm liking this," Austin says, glancing between the two of us. "Delilah might lose her title tonight." He slides his cards away. "I fold."

Matteo burns a final card and then flips over a three in the middle. I could dance right out of my seat, I'm so excited.

I flip my cards over. "Straight," I say confidently.

Beside me, Matteo sighs, and I'm sure I've won. He flips his cards over. It takes me a few seconds to process his ace and seven.

Austin whoops. Nic inhales sharply in surprise.

"Full house," Matteo says, completely unnecessarily because I can *see* it.

My mouth drops open in shock. "*Matteo*, you've been holding out on us. I had no idea you had such poker prowess."

"My nonna was a feisty poker player. She taught me everything I know."

"It helps that your face doesn't move at all throughout the game," Nic mutters, running a chip across her fingers.

"Or is that just another one of my tricks?" he answers quietly, pulling his winnings toward him.

"I don't know. Delilah was watching you pretty intently," Austin says.

Matteo turns to me, something devilish in his eyes. "And? What did you learn?"

I grin. "I'll be keeping my secrets, thank you very much."

"Ah, so you've got nothing." I put a hand on my chest as though I'm truly offended, but he simply shrugs. "You have at least two tells."

Whipping to look at Austin and Nic, I ask, "I do?"

"Trust me that if I knew them, I wouldn't be losing," Austin answers.

Nic rolls her eyes. "Yes, you would."

My eyes find Matteo. It's like I'm seeing him for the first time. My expression must point to the wonder I'm feeling because he grants me a gruff chuckle.

"Do you want to know them?" he asks.

"Yes," Austin interjects.

I scoff. "Shut up. But yes, I do. Quietly."

"Austin, can you show me where to get a glass please?" Nic asks abruptly, standing. She grabs Austin's shirt and yanks him up, hauling him after her toward the kitchen.

"A glass?" he asks dumbly. "You've been here before."

She hisses something I can't make out.

Though they're gone, Matteo leans forward. Goosebumps rise on my arms, my breath stuttering for a moment, and I desperately hope he doesn't notice. "After the first three cards, you bit the inside of your cheeks just enough that I could tell you thought you had something good. You did that the first round, too. Then, when you saw the second seven, this corner"—he taps below the right side of my lips gently—"of your mouth tipped down for half a second. I guessed that meant you were playing for a straight, and knowing I had a full house, I kept betting."

He doesn't move away immediately, instead glancing at where his finger tapped, then back to my eyes. They're like honey right now, which, I'm learning, comes out when he's teasing me back. I worry that if I'm not careful, I might get stuck in them.

"And what's your tell?" I whisper.

"You'll have to figure that one out on your own." One last look at my lips, and then he moves back to his section of the table, that same winning smirk on his face. It's the most smug I've seen him.

I breathe a little easier now that he's not so close, though the distance feels like an ocean.

"Damn. Your nonna must be one heck of a woman."

"I never saw her lose," he agrees.

When Nic and Austin return, we play a few more rounds. The whole time, I hide my tells the best I can, but it's clear Matteo is too perceptive for me. Right before he wins it all, I joke, "Matteo *really* didn't want to show us an embarrassing photo tonight."

He shoots me another smile before flipping over his winning hand. When we each show him an embarrassing photo of ourselves—me flying off a golf cart when it stopped abruptly near my court at a tournament, Austin with tears streaming down his face while watching the 2005 version of *Pride and Prejudice*, and Nic with her hair tangled like a bird's nest because, of course, she never gets photographed doing embarrassing things—he leans back, arms crossed, my new favorite smirk on his face.

I'm so glad he's getting comfortable with me and my friends that I can't even be mad I lost my title.

nine

The two doubles sessions after game night went better. Tuesday we found a little more rhythm, and yesterday, we communicated better, even sharing smiles (or whatever his lip twitch is) after particularly grueling practice points.

I'll be the first to admit our three meetings at the pool after practice and poker night probably helped, though we've kept things mostly surface level. I don't know much about his family other than they're immigrants, but I do know that his favorite color is blue, he tries to steer clear of Italian food unless he's in Italy, and he *doesn't* have any cravings for things during the season that he's not allowed to eat.

Like ice cream. Which, right now, I'm desperate for. Going home Wednesday and Thursday for Thanksgiving and not eating within my normal guidelines reminded me of how good non-sanctioned food is.

Aleksandr's strength and conditioning sessions, I'm

finding, are significantly more difficult than those of the previous fitness trainer. Though I often felt exhausted after the latter's, Aleksandr is doing his best to make all of us puke. Luckily, none of us have. Yet.

When we finally finish our two sets of bleachers with a lap around the track to cool down, I pair up with Nic for some resistance band work. She holds the long band while I move from center toward the deuce alley, doing a shadow forehand before coming back to center and doing the same on the ad side. After three minutes, we switch. Next are medicine ball tosses, then ladder work, and finally, reaction time drills.

By the end of the hour, me, Nic, Matteo, Anya, and the few other players not on vacation are in various positions on the court, panting hard and wishing not so good things on Aleksandr (I assume I'm not the only one).

"I want ice cream. No, I *need* ice cream," I groan to no one in particular, though Nic turns on her side to look at me. Normally, she'd do strength and conditioning with her own performance coach, but Amelia's been out of town the last couple of weeks. "With everything on it," I continue. "Chocolate sauce. Caramel. Sprinkles. Oreo pieces. Reese's pieces." My mouth waters, and I have to stop.

Nic snorts. "Be strong. What would Francesca say?"

We do this sometimes when one of us is having late-night cravings, though I won't pretend I'm not 95% of the problem.

I recognize Francesca wouldn't genuinely care if I had ice cream, but I pay her so much money, it would be absurd not to follow her recommended diet. In the end, she's almost always right about this sort of thing.

"Ten-minute break, and then meet me in the player's gym for lift," Aleksandr says, grinning wickedly as he high-fives down the line. When he reaches Nic, she rolls her eyes and pushes to a stand, stomping past him to get water. His smile widens as he watches her walk away, then he turns back to me. I slap his palm as hard as I can—which is to say not hard at all—dreading the lift that will inevitably leave me feeling even more like a spaghetti noodle during my game strategy session with Francesca.

"Is this going to get easier at any point or will you be torturing us throughout the year?" I tease.

Aleksandr chuckles, picking up resistance bands and cones. "I saw what the last guy called 'strength and conditioning,'" he jokes. "It'll get easier. It'll also make those long matches less painful. At least that's the hope."

The strength session goes slightly smoother, and by the time I've talked through strategy with Francesca, showering feels like a chore. Thankfully all I have tomorrow is stretching, yoga, and physio.

I stagger out of the women's locker room after seven, glad I foam rolled while talking to my coach. Now I can figure out dinner and pass out.

Nic wasn't in the locker room, so she's likely back on court or in a meeting room working through her game strategy. I've waited up enough times to know it'll be a while, so I head out the door and start the few minutes' walk to my apartment.

Just before I cross the street, a dark car pulls out of the

facility parking lot and cruises beside me. I fumble for my keys, palming my pepper spray, but when the window rolls down and I see Matteo, I tuck them back into the pocket of my bag.

"Oh, hi! I didn't know you were still here," I say, pulling the strap of my gym bag further up my shoulder.

"Do you walk home alone every evening?" he asks so quietly, I hardly hear him over the purr of his engine.

"Sometimes Austin takes me when we finish at the same time or I walk back with Nic, but for the most part, yeah." At his furrowed brow, I continue, "It's only a few blocks down that way." I point in the direction of my building. "Doesn't take me long at all."

"I didn't realize. I would've dropped you home."

I let out a disbelieving laugh. "You definitely do not need to do that. I enjoy the walk, and like I said, it's not far."

"Do you still want ice cream?"

I blink at him, confused, until I remember he was nearby when I blurted my urgent need for the cool, lactose-laden goodness. Embarrassed, I duck my head. "I don't need it."

"That's not what I asked."

"Do *you* want ice cream?" I ask incredulously.

Matteo parks, turns off the car, and steps out, coming to my side and gently pulling my gym bag from my left shoulder. "Che cavolo." I know that one. *What the hell.* A favorite of Francesca's. "This is too heavy. What do you put in this? And why are you only wearing it on one shoulder? You're going to hurt yourself before the season even begins," he mutters, almost to himself. I let him take it, still shocked and confused. "We can make tonight one of our weekly check-ins. Alessio will love that we're making such an effort."

He puts my bags in his trunk, guiding me to his passenger's seat. When I'm comfortable, he closes the door softly. I take in the black leather seats and sleek dashboard, inhaling the rich scent of bergamot. I've never pictured what his car would be like, but if I had, this is exactly how I would imagine it.

"You don't like ice cream," I state when he gets in.

He gestures to the bag of what appears to be homemade trail mix on the center console. "I've got this," he says.

"And we haven't eaten dinner yet."

The right corner of his mouth moves, his eyes scanning my face. "Del, would you like me to drop you off at your apartment, or do you want to tell me a place where you can eat dinner and get ice cream?"

I laugh, caving. "Okay, okay. We can go to Hoagie's. There's probably something green and gross there that you'll like."

He huffs a laugh, typing the name into the navigation and taking the car out of park.

Hoagie's is a cute sandwich shop five minutes away with exposed brick walls and mismatched cushioned chairs tucked beneath wooden tables. Soft lighting turns brighter at the front of the shop, where chalkboard menus hang behind employees and ingredients are displayed in glass cases.

I make my choices and pull my card from my wallet, but because Matteo is ahead of me, he beats me to it. A flash of unpleasantness spears through me, my brain working five steps ahead to start a dedicated debt calculator. He doesn't seem to notice, setting a hand on my back and directing me to a table despite my gentle grumbling about being able to buy my own food.

"I know you can," he murmurs.

When we reach a far table and set our food down, Matteo looks around, confused.

"What?" I ask.

"They have ice cream here?"

I laugh. "No, no. Next door. I'm easing you into this. If you see me eat what I go for there, you'll run screaming before we can talk."

"Why's that?" Amusement dances over his features.

"I do not hold back. Everything goes on my ice cream. I've been told it's disgusting."

"I'm certainly intrigued."

Settling into our seats, we begin eating. After my first few bites, I say, "Told you they'd have something green for you."

"I'm not sold on this wrap."

"Well, Matteo, you didn't ask me for *nice* places. You asked me for places that have dinner and ice cream." I grin.

"Yes, and I'm not sure you abided by that guideline." Lip twitch.

I shrug. "Close enough."

His eyes scan my face. "You do that a lot."

"What?" I ask, putting my cheeks in my hands, a hint of self-consciousness cresting.

"Smile."

Laughing, I question, "Is that a problem?"

He shakes his head, eyes widening. "Not at all. I like it." Under his breath, he says what sounds like "Mi piace molto" but even if I were positive, I don't know what it means.

His previous words make me smile wider. "*You* don't smile much. And when you do, it's never a full one." Instantly, I feel like I've said the wrong thing, the air sucked out of the space between us. Matteo looks away, out the window, where his car sits in the parking lot.

"I'm not sure I've had much to smile about in a long time." The idea is so incomprehensible to me, it must read clearly on my face. Now he does smile, a small one I can tell is more for my benefit than anything. "Our outlooks on life are different. Very different."

"How do you mean?"

Matteo clears his throat. "I lost my mom."

Oh. An ache spreads deep in my chest for him. "Matteo, I'm so sorry."

"Years ago," he adds quickly, like that decreases the impact. "It was…sudden. Life seemed so harsh afterward. As if someone added a dreary, red-tinted filter that left me confused and angry all the time."

It strikes me then. His struggle making friends, when he was a kid and now. How nervous and uncomfortable he sometimes seems. The coaxing required to pull him from his shell. How much of that is because he's scared to get close to someone again? It was something I experienced right after Mom left, but with how overwhelmed I was and the support I got from the Wards, it passed me by quickly.

He shrugs. "I'd love to be able to change that, be happy all the time, but…"

"But it's not that easy."

"It's not," he agrees.

"Being happy all the time is unrealistic and overrated anyway," I say.

A raised eyebrow tells me he's probably calling me a hypocrite in his head, but he doesn't voice it. After we finish our food, Matteo balls up his trash and sets it aside. "I believe I was promised serving signals."

I giggle. Sometimes in doubles, the player not serving will hold a number or signal behind their back to give their thoughts for where the player serving should aim within the service box. More often, in professional tennis, we just talk between points and decide when huddled, but I find it fun, and Nic humors me.

"It's not only for serving. I like to use them to trash talk our opponents without them knowing." He chuckles, recognizing my joke for what it was, and my heart ricochets for a second. Matteo has somehow managed to laugh without moving his lips, and yet the sound feels an awful lot like victory.

"It seems like you have a lot of ideas, so let's hear them."

When I run through the numbers Nic and I use for serves sometimes, he asks, "Aren't you worried about me knowing these? Aren't they supposed to be private?"

I pat beside where his hand rests on the table. "First of all, she and I aren't playing doubles this year. And second, as long as you don't sell them off to other women's doubles teams, I think we'll be fine."

Matteo nods. "I solemnly swear not to tell anyone."

We slip into the ice cream shop next door, where I do, in fact, put every single topping on my ice cream. Matteo looks alarmed, but thankfully doesn't comment.

"Did you play in college?" I ask once we've left the parlor to walk around the small shopping area.

"No. I knew I could do well on the tour and didn't think it was worth it to tempt fate with an injury. You?"

I set the plastic spoon into my cup. "I wanted to try. Play with a team like in high school, find a subject I was passionate about. But despite having most of my tuition paid for with an athletic scholarship, I would've had to work a job or two to make sure my siblings were taken care of." The Wards offered to pay for any tuition not covered, but they had already done so much for me at that point, it would've been even harder to repay them. "I figured it was better to go straight into the WTA and make as much as I could to ensure they were taken care of until they could take care of themselves."

I try not to, but I think of my father. Of when I was younger, before alcohol became his greatest love, when he used to build forts for us to hang out in, blankets flung over the dining table and chairs. The little treats he would bring me from the store every few months after he'd disappear for two or three weeks, like an apology for being gone. The slow descent into total alcoholism and the calls I field from him now, some angry like the one I got only six days ago, others apologetic with words of affirmation that I'm a good player and that he's cheering me on.

Rarely, I'll get the third kind of call, where he asks me to send him money, and I do, even when I know I shouldn't. Even when I should be saving it for myself or giving it to Chase and the twins. Enabling him isn't something I want to be doing but I'm terrified that if I don't, one day, he'll just disappear and never come back. Like Mom. And though he's on the fringes of my life more and more nowadays and has been walking that path for years, I can't stomach being the reason for him leaving.

"What about you?" Matteo asks.

"What about me?"

"Are you taken care of?" There's a weight to the words. I can feel it moving from him to me, pressing against my sternum until I let loose a breath.

"I do okay. Once I pay everything off in a few years, I'll be able to truly start saving." I roll my eyes jokingly. "You know how it is with taxes and coaching and all the other stuff."

Matteo peers at me knowingly, and I shift in my seat.

"Anyway, I just got an endorsement deal that'll help a lot. *Especially* if you get us into the quarterfinals." Remembering his practice outfits the last few times we played together, I ask, "Strato sponsors you too, right?"

He nods, grimacing. "Yeah. Though they and the rest of my sponsors aren't very happy with me at the moment."

"Not big fans of the breaking of their rackets?"

Lip twitch. He hums. "Among other things."

I finish my *delicious* frozen treat, and we head back to my apartment, where Matteo takes my bags out and helps me get the straps on both of my shoulders in the "most efficient way."

"Are you sure you don't need help with this?" he asks

gruffly, glancing at the entrance of my apartment building.

"You're more of a worrier than I ever would've expected." I laugh at his offended expression. "I'll be fine."

Matteo doesn't move, eyes glued to mine and darker than usual, his pupils dilated, thanks to how poorly lit my street and building are. His eyes drop for a split second before they're back. Something I don't often feel in situations like this—want—shoves itself against my chest until I worry he'll notice I can hardly breathe. His fingers are still wrapped around one of my bag straps, keeping some of its weight off me.

I'm not sure how long we stand like that, but he breaks the spell, taking a step back and looking away from me. Rejection sinks its claws deep into my stomach, as if I've offered myself up to him on a platter and he's decided I'm not what he wants.

Which is dumb. We're only doing this so we can have a chance at a deep run in the Aussie mixed draw. I'm well aware of that.

Trying to make myself feel better, and to take back a bit of the power I lost today, I say, "Thank you for dinner, but I *will* be paying for myself next time. And for you." I mean it too. I'm no one's charity case.

Matteo's jaw moves for a second, like he wants to say something but is biting his tongue. Literally. He nods. "Good night, tesoro."

"Good night." I turn and hoof it through the door of my building, then up my stairs, so fast I don't give myself the chance to analyze whether that word means the same thing in Italian as it does in Spanish.

I may be learning more about Matteo Corsi with each day that passes, but I still don't know a thing about the way he thinks. And I shouldn't…no, *can't* want to. My focus has always been, and will continue to be, on making enough money to support my siblings.

It would behoove me to remember that.

ten

SAHAR'S BAD BERLIN BAGELS

MAYA

The village gossip is spreading an interesting rumor.

??

SAHAR

??

HARPER

?

MAYA

That Delilah's been seen with Matteo outside of practices more than twice.

If I'm the last to know, consider me HURT

NIC

He has yet to cross the threshold of our apartment so don't feel too bad.

HARPER

We have to do a group call ASAP so Sahar
and I can hear all about it!

AUSTIN

If it helps, I'm the person who connected
them and I didn't know

NIC REMOVED AUSTIN FROM THE CHAT.

SAHAR

How long has the "if it helps" guy been in
here?

You guys are so silly! We're just doing
what our coaches told us to do so we're
more emotionally connected for doubles

MAYA

Riiiiight.

SAHAR

I wish you could've seen the look Harper
and I exchanged. Even Noah is rolling
his eyes

By Tuesday, we're almost completely in sync. If I move one way, Matteo is covering the other side. If he's going for a cross-court shot, I'm ready to cover the alley. We hardly have to speak, moving like one entity during drills.

When Alessio tells us we can break, we plop beside each other onto the bench, breathing heavily.

"I wonder if there are any other sports where you pay someone to tell you what to do," I muse.

Matteo leans back against a pole, entertained. "Golf?"

I nod, feigning seriousness. "Mm, good point."

Francesca walks over and leans against the net post, practically beaming. "Allora, it's time for practice matches. You've made leaps and bounds' worth of progress in the last couple of weeks." Her eyebrows jump, her grin widening. "Guess your coaches know what they're talking about."

We laugh as I reach for my water bottle. When I do, I notice I've just missed a call from my brother Finn. A quick scroll through my messages immediately spikes my pulse. Five texts and two calls.

Chase is missing.

My eyes burn as I swipe to call my brother back, taking a few steps away from the bench.

"Del, hey."

"What's going on?"

"We're not sure. Chase has the car for school, so he usually picks Hazel up while I go to practice, but he never showed. We haven't seen him since last night, and he's not picking up his phone. Hazel's hanging back at practice with me, and we'll get a ride from one of the guys, but I thought I'd let you know."

Seasoned in stopping my tears before they fall, I bite down on the insides of my cheeks and nod, though he can't see me. "Alright. Keep an eye on Hazel and text me when you get home safely. I'll find him." I blow out a breath, trying to calm my nervous system. "If you're at practice, why didn't Hazel call?"

"She said she didn't want to bother you, but…"

But we know Chase. That's what he's not saying. Chase

missing an appointment or being apathetic about something big? Standard. Disappearing for hours and no-showing to pick up Hazel is different.

"Thank you for calling. I'll see you soon. I love you."

"Love you too."

Swallowing back the rest of my tears, I shake my head once, gather my bearings, and turn to the bench. Matteo stands, watching me, concern etched in his brow and clear in his eyes. I can't take it.

"Francesca, I have to go home." My coach looks at me, understands immediately, and nods. She says something quietly to Alessio, who has joined her by the net.

"Matteo, I'm sorry. I've got to go. I'll…" We're supposed to do singles drills together tomorrow, but I'm not sure if I'll be back in time for that. "I'll stay late Friday if you want."

He steps forward, his hand coming up like he wants to put it on my elbow, but he drops it. "Let me take you."

"No, no. It's an hour and a half away."

"So how will you get there?"

Typically, Sahar, Harper, or one of the Wards is more than happy to take me, though I always feel bad. Sometimes Chase comes to pick me up if he can spare the time. For Thanksgiving last week, I took a rideshare, but it cost an astronomical amount since the house is a good distance away. I could call Eli or Lilian, but waiting for them would add time to the trip.

Matteo is here now.

But I don't want him to see this. If he comes with me, who knows in what physical state we'll find Chase. Or worse, my father.

At my silence, he says, "I insist. This was all I was doing for the rest of my day, so I'm happy to take you." When I still don't answer, his voice drops to a whisper. "Please, tesoro."

I nod once, and we pack up. Matteo pulls off his shirt and throws on a clean replica, saying something in Italian to our coaches. Francesca smiles at him gratefully.

It only takes a few minutes to get to his car, where I enter our suburb in the navigation instead of the house address. At his questioning glance, I say, "I don't think he's at home. When we get there I'll guide you. I think we're going to have to drive around and look for the car."

Matteo throws the car in drive and follows the directions on the console. If he tries to talk to me in the hour and a half it takes to get there, I don't hear him. All I hear is the constant static in my ears and the sound of my heart beating faster than it should be. All I feel is the seat below me and the scarred skin of my cheeks between my teeth, ripped to shreds by my many anxieties.

When we finally reach the town, I direct Matteo around, searching for the car. "It's a silver Saturn Vue," I tell him, embarrassed. I can afford to buy them a new one instead of constantly paying for repairs on it, but the thought of dropping money on something new when our beat-up SUV is mostly functional physically pains me.

This is exactly why I didn't want him seeing this. He's never made me feel lesser than, never made me feel judged, but this situation will be on a completely different level. A level he shouldn't have to witness. One that will almost certainly change how he thinks of me.

Plus, this is my burden to bear. I don't want to add another item to the debt calculator hanging over my head.

As the thought crosses my mind, I spot it. "There!" I all but shout, stabbing a finger against the window. Matteo turns into the parking lot quickly, and I take in the building.

It's familiar. So damn familiar. I've been here countless times to pick up my dad. Mom too, once.

It's also hideous. Wooden planks peeling and cracked from years of neglect. Broken windows patched with cardboard and duct tape. A faded sign flickering weakly above the entrance, barely visible through a layer of grime.

Taking a breath, I say, "I'll be back."

"What? I'll come in with you."

"I'll be fine." I nearly choke on the last word. I need to get it together.

"Okay," he says gently. "But if you're in there for more than a few minutes…"

I smile at him, thankful, and jog to the bar's entrance. The front door hangs on rusted hinges, squeaking when I pull it open to reveal the dim interior.

Quiet settles over me when I enter, which makes sense for five o'clock on a Tuesday evening. There are a couple of people eating at tables, but it's the slumped figure at the bar who catches my eye. In a second, I'm beside him. His face is down on the bar, an empty whiskey glass beside him. His light brown hair, along with his arms, cover the rest of his face, but I'd know Chase anywhere.

"Chase." I shake him gently. He doesn't move, and I scan the bar. No one is paying any attention to us, especially not the bartender moving around in the back, disappearing out of view.

I have half a mind to say something to them for serving someone underage, but I don't know what kind of trouble Chase will get into if I do, and that's the last thing I need. What I *need* is for Chase to be okay.

I shake him again. "Chase," I say more forcefully. He stirs, mumbling incoherently. I pull his head up, turning him to face me, and that's when he blinks his eyes open. They're darker than usual, exactly like our dad's when he drinks.

We're the echoes of our parents.

Chase's eyes, a stormy gray, carry the weight of our father's gaze while my blue ones mirror Mom's. We're recreating scenes from two decades ago. Mom helping Dad out of the dilapidated bar he drank far too much in, me doing the same for Chase.

"Del?" he mumbles. "Wharyoudoinhere?" I just make out what he's asking, and I have to look away for a second. All I see in him is the little boy who followed me around, who helped me change diapers and played with the babies while I scrambled eggs or made instant ramen or mac and cheese for us. This man, a copy-paste of my father; I don't know him. And I don't want to.

Chase yawns. I smell the whiskey on his breath. It sends me back to the times when Dad would talk to me from half a slumber before passing out cold, his breath teaching me the very sort of thing to stay away from for the rest of my life. Smelling it again now nearly makes me gag.

"We need to get you home," I say when I've recovered. "The twins are worried, and you need to sleep this off."

When I reach for his arm, he pulls it closer to himself, slapping the glass down the bar. It nearly topples to the floor. "Go 'way. What you're good at anyway."

An exasperated sigh leaves me, even as my heart rate drops a few beats a minute at the knowledge that he's okay. He might not be *okay*, but he's here. I see him, and I can get him home.

"Chase, come on."

"No," he answers harshly, thundercloud eyes turning stormier. "I'm fine. Leave me 'lone. 'm not hurting anyone but myself."

The door pitches open. When my gaze slips over, Matteo stands there, out of place here in a tennis shirt and shorts. He finds me and covers the distance between us quickly. Whatever he sees on my face pinches his own expression into one of concern with a hint of something else.

Softly, I say, "Please, Chase. Let's go home."

Chase scoffs. "Wha' do *you* know 'bout home? It's"— he hiccups—"not yours anymore."

My lips twist to the side, chest aching as if he's taken a sledgehammer to my sternum. "Don't make this harder than it needs to be." Now people *are* watching, and I shouldn't care, but I do.

Chase finally notices Matteo beside me, and the fight leaves his body. He glares at Matteo but stands, staggering off the bar stool and into our arms.

"Hey! He hasn't paid his tab." The bartender comes

rushing out, glaring at us as if *we've* done something wrong.

Matteo fumbles in his back pocket, producing a few bills and tossing them onto the counter. I note how much so I can pay him back later. He looks exactly like he used to before an explosion on court, jaw clenched, eyebrows pinched. Menacing. But he just tucks his wallet back into his pocket and puts one of Chase's arms around his shoulders. I do the same, and we walk him out of the bar.

"I'll take him in the Saturn," I tell Matteo. "Chase, where are the keys?"

"Pocket," he grumbles.

When we get him to the car, I pull the keys from his pocket and Matteo does all the work of getting Chase into the backseat.

"Do you feel like you're going to throw up?" Matteo asks gruffly. Chase mumbles something I can't hear. "I'll be right back," Matteo says to me, walking quickly back into the bar. When he reemerges a minute later, he has a paper bag and puts it in front of Chase. "Use this."

Bending Chase's knees so he fits, I pat his leg before closing the door. Matteo's already hopping into his car, ready to follow me. If his opinion of me hasn't changed, it will when he gets into the house. I grind my teeth, trying not to resent Chase for this.

I shouldn't be upset with him. It's not entirely his fault. Dad was the singular male role model Chase ever had, and he became what he is long before Chase's memories begin. And then, his only other role model, who once was such a bright light in our home, even when she came home tired from working double shifts, slipped into the same patterns, joining Dad at bars. Partaking in whatever drugs he had at the time. Then she left.

So it's not Chase's fault. I should have done a better job of shielding him, but *god* he isn't making any of this easy. And a part of me, a part that grows with every one of these situations, is very upset with him.

Then I feel bad for thinking that way.

When I check the rearview mirror and see Chase passed out, I allow the tears to fall for a second.

All I've ever wanted is to give Chase, Finn, and Hazel the best life I possibly can. To prevent them from becoming like either of our parents, cut that sort of thing off at the source. When Chase got into fights at school, I took care of his busted knuckles and black eyes and talked him down, helping him see how fraught with challenges that path would be.

Yet here we are.

I wonder about his classes. Has he actually been going to them? Is this a one-time thing? Or is this what he's doing now? Does he even *care* that this could impact his chances at a state school? I sigh, turning onto our street and swiping the tears from my cheeks.

"How did you get in there?" I ask quietly, not expecting an answer.

"Fake." That one word is confirmation that he's either done this before or has plans to do it again. What other reason would he have for getting a fake ID?

I swallow over a boulder as I pull into the driveway. The old house sits low, faded beige siding warped and cracking under the Florida sun. The stucco beneath shows through in spots, discolored from years of storms and heat. The small front yard appears smaller thanks to the overgrowth of weeds, and the front door sags crookedly in its frame, like it's been forced shut too many times. Or slammed.

We moved a few times growing up, but I spent nearly half a decade in this house and it's never really felt like home. Not in the way my little apartment with Nic feels.

Shutting off the car, I wrangle my emotions and shove them into a box somewhere deep in my chest.

eleven

Getting Chase into the house proves as difficult as getting him into the car was. He twists and turns, trying to get out of our hold. Luckily, Matteo is supporting most of his weight, and by the time we reach the rickety porch, Chase has gone almost completely limp.

The moment we pass the threshold, Finn, who must have recently gotten home, takes Chase from my arms and helps Matteo get him to the bathroom. Hazel nervously bites a hangnail in the foyer, and my first thought is to envelop her in a hug. Tension eases from her body almost instantaneously, her arms wrapping around me and holding tight.

"You okay?" I ask quietly. She nods before I hear a sob break. Smoothing a hand over her short, light brown hair, I say, "He'll be fine, Haze. I promise." Even if I don't know that for certain, I don't want her to worry.

She pulls away, wiping at her face. "I'm sorry I told Finn not to call, I just hate to have you come all this way to deal with this when you already do so much."

"Nonsense. I'm glad I could be here." I wipe beneath her eyes, then kiss the top of her head. "I'm going to check on Chase, but I'll be back, okay?"

Hazel nods, and I join the three men in the bathroom. As I pass through the living room, I notice my father on the couch, an arm slung over his eyes, two beer bottles knocked over beside the couch. It's the first time I've seen him since his voicemail, and not even an iota of surprise passes through me. In a strange way, it's like I never left.

I sigh, grabbing the bottles and tossing them into the overflowing trash can before I continue down the hallway to the boys, ignoring the clothes that litter the house.

In the bathroom, I find Finn leaning over Chase, who's on the tiled floor. Matteo stands a few feet away, face inscrutable.

"Thank you. You don't have to stay. I can take it from here."

Matteo gazes at me, then pushes a stray lock that's fallen out of my ponytail behind my ear, fingers lingering for a second before he pulls back. "I want to help."

"Finn can drop me off later. Really, it's—"

"Stop. Let's get him cleaned up and in bed."

Seeing Matteo in the bathroom where I used to get the twins ready is a jarring juxtaposition between my life before I left and after. The room, the whole house even, feels smaller, and that has nothing to do with his height and everything to do with the fact that I outgrew this place long ago.

His eyes remain on mine, earnest as ever, so I turn back to my brothers, instructing Finn how best to help

Chase once he's undressed. By the way he nods and interjects, it seems he's been through this plenty of times.

Like, since I left, the burden of dealing with our father has fallen on him.

Matteo and Hazel help me tidy up, and when Chase is showered and clothed once more, we get him to his and Finn's room. I have him drink water and get some crackers in his body before we turn him on his side, a trash can beside his bed and another glass of water on his nightstand.

I watch him breathe for a minute or two, thankful for the subtle rise and fall of his chest. When we were young and I wanted to distract him from what was happening outside the confines of his room, I'd crawl into bed with him and pull his sheet over our heads. To me, it was a poor man's version of the tents Dad used to create for me in the dining room, but to Chase, it was the place he could tell me about his day, his favorite toys, what food he liked at school, his friends, or even, on the rougher days, how seeing Mom or Dad made him feel.

Everything in this house is a painful reminder of the guilt I feel knowing I'm leaving behind my siblings and a father I believe is still in there somewhere. A reminder of a time I keep trying to claw myself away from.

When I can finally breathe easier knowing Chase is safe and will be okay in a few hours, albeit dealing with the painful consequences of his actions, I sit on my bed in the room I used to share with Hazel, facing the twins, who sit on hers. I told Matteo he could join, but he excused himself to continue cleaning.

"How many times has he done this?" I ask.

Hazel and Finn exchange a look. Finn says, "Never like this. He comes home after drinking a few sometimes, but never so badly that he can't take care of himself."

I put my chin in my hands. "And him?" I point my head in the direction of the living room, where our father hasn't so much as twitched despite the noise we've been making. "How long has this bender lasted?" It has to have been at least a couple of weeks, since that's when he left the message for me and he wasn't here for Thanksgiving a few days later.

"Couple of weeks," Hazel confirms. "But we have him under control."

I can't meet either of their eyes. The twins shouldn't be dealing with this.

Finn speaks, quiet but insistent. "Del, we can take it from here. I was just spooked."

"But you shouldn't have to." I shake my head, finally looking up. "Let's get you a second car. If you see anything used you like, tell me. With Chase transferring, you're going to need another one." I'll be getting my first payment from the new deal soon anyway.

"You don't have to pay for it," Hazel says. "We can work and pay for one ourselves. I have a friend who says there's an opening at the ma—"

"No. I want you to be able to focus on school. I'll handle the money." Frustration lines her face, lips curled down. "Only one more semester, and you'll both be onto bigger and brighter things. Just get through the next few months."

Hazel is the smartest of the four of us, at the top of her AP classes, which I never even took in high school.

She'll get an academic scholarship without an issue. Finn is a star football player for the high school, and I have no doubt he'll go anywhere he wants. Scouts are already recruiting him.

They deserve as normal childhoods as I can give them. They shouldn't have to work.

Hazel stands, the features that are so much like Chase's pinched. "We're almost adults, Delilah. In one month, Finn and I are going to be eighteen. We appreciate everything you've done to keep us going, but if today has made anything clear, it's that handing us money doesn't smooth *everything* over." Gentler, she continues, "You worked in high school to make sure we never went without the things we needed. Now it's our turn to take on some of the responsibility you've been shouldering for years."

The words feel like an accusation, and the implication nearly bowls me over. Is she saying that by paying for the house, school, and everything else they need, I'm enabling Chase?

I think that's the end of her speech, but like a punch to the gut, she finishes with, "It would be nice to feel like an equal instead of an obligation."

I blink. Then blink again. She leaves the room, Finn frowning after her.

"I...I don't..." I stammer. Settling a palm on the pain in my chest like it'll help get the words out, I say, "I just want you to have good lives. To have free weeknights to hang out with your friends and do fun things. I don't see you as an obligation."

But don't I? Isn't everything I'm doing because I feel

it's my duty? It's an obligation I love, but...

Are they my equals?

"She's just...she's mad at me for calling you. Don't take it too seriously," Finn murmurs.

We're silent for a few moments as I turn her words over in my head, then fold them up and bulldoze them into any dark recess I can find. There's nothing I can do about it right now except be more proactive about Chase.

"This might be a one-time thing for Chase, but if it isn't and he does it again, let me know. Please," I beg. Once the pattern begins, I'm not sure I'll be able to figure out how to stop him from becoming the thing we hated growing up. But if I can catch it early, stop him, make him see that this is the wrong path, that he's *so* close to the right one, maybe I can put an end to it before it really starts. "I'll call him and try to talk some sense into him."

Finn nods, a small reassuring smile splitting his face. When I get back into the living room and note how much cleaner it is already, I try not to break out into hives that Matteo has experienced the last couple of hours of this with me.

"Hey." He pulls another garbage bag closed, tying it off. "You alright?"

"Yeah."

My father is still passed out on the couch. When I shake him awake, he jolts up, and I back up into Matteo's chest. His hands land on my hips, anchoring me. I don't have time to examine the heat radiating from the firm touch to the rest of my body.

Hurricane gray eyes meet mine. Ones I'm more and

more glad I didn't inherit with each passing year, even if two of the people I love most in the world did.

"The fuck are you doing here?" The words come out like he has cotton in his mouth, and I don't know if he's talking to me or Matteo.

Seeing Dad like this is a distressing reminder that I'm partly to blame for his behavior. Gone is the man who cobbled together a homemade kite with newspaper, sticks, and string so we could try to fly it at the park. The man who, later that evening, made me a paper crown and declared me the "queen of the sky." The man who made tents for me when I felt down or when the rain was too loud. And yet, a part of me will always cling to the idea that he's in there somewhere. I know I shouldn't give him money every few months, know that he uses it to fund this lifestyle, but if I stop and he leaves…

I'll never get him back.

"Dad." I hope the word is enough for him to recognize who I am. "Why don't you take a shower and get to bed? Do you have work tomorrow?"

He glowers at me, and I sigh. Matteo's big hands on my waist have yet to drop. When I tap the right one lightly, he reluctantly lets go.

Hazel and Finn step forward and work in tandem to get our father taken care of, helping him to the bathroom the way we did with Chase. They're seasoned veterans, I see that now, and it breaks my heart.

It's only now, in watching their practiced movements, that I notice the old shirt Hazel is wearing. It's falling apart, stretched beyond belief, and there's a hole in the armpit that I sewed up and that ripped again when it was

Finn's turn to wear it. The hand-me-down is a black The Cranberries shirt from their 1995 world tour, given to me when I was five or six by a friendly neighbor. They did that often, bringing over clothes they or their children had outgrown or that others might have taken to thrift stores or thrown away. I can't even remember which neighbor it was, since they all banded together to help us however they could, whenever they could.

I wore it for years, their music becoming my security blanket when I resented my parents or my siblings—something I suppress deeply because of the guilt that overwhelms me when I allow it to fester. The unique voice and sound pointed to something more troubling than any of my problems, to a far-off war and to the suffering of so many others. It helped me recognize how lucky I was to be where I was.

When I outgrew the shirt, it briefly went to Chase, then to Finn, and finally to Hazel, like a rite of passage for the Anderson children. I didn't know she still owned it, but seeing it hammers home the message I always repeated when I was wrapped in it.

Hazel comes out of the bathroom, and I can see she's still not happy with me. I hand her the keys to the Saturn and give her another long hug.

"I'm sorry. I'll think about the job." She was stiff at first, but now reciprocates the embrace. "I love you so much."

"I love you too," she whispers into my shoulder.

I hug Finn goodbye, and then we're back in Matteo's car on the way to the facility. This is the first time anyone has ever seen my father like this besides Austin. My skin feels raw, like I've scrubbed it for hours, and I realize I bit the inside of my cheeks so hard throughout this whole ordeal that there's blood in my mouth.

Sure, the girls know about my family. Nic and Maya especially. But no one has seen it under a microscope like this until now. Until Matteo.

It builds an odd, painful sort of intimacy between us that wasn't there before.

The moment we get on the highway, the dam breaks, and I sob quietly, my forehead pressed against the window so Matteo doesn't see me.

"Tesoro, please," Matteo says, pained. I don't know what he's asking of me, if anything, but he takes the next exit and pulls over as soon as we get to a street where it's safe to do so. My tears keep rolling despite how quickly I swipe them away.

Matteo puts the car in park and takes my hand, tugging until I gaze at him. No judgment, only concern. And that makes me cry harder. "I'm so…sorry. I try so hard"—I hiccup—"not to cry in front of other people. I don't know why…I can't stop."

"Please stop apologizing," he whispers. "Nobody expects you to be the perfect warrior you force yourself to be a hundred percent of the time." Flipping open his center console, he pulls out a package of travel tissues and hands them to me. I take them gratefully, ripping the plastic open and dabbing my eyes with one.

"It was a car accident…that killed my mom." He clears his throat, and I set the package of tissues between us in case he needs them too, the ache in my chest yawning wider at this new knowledge. "My dad couldn't handle the grief. Sent me to live with my nonna, Mom's mom. The one who taught me poker."

We're still in park, but one of Matteo's hands tightens around the steering wheel. "Dad got married again a few years later and started a new family. Left me behind like I was trash, texting me on holidays and my birthday like that was enough to keep the relationship alive."

My heart sinks as I picture him waiting for his father to come back for him, right beside me, waiting for my mother. Did he linger by the mailbox too? Stay near the phone as much as he could in case he called?

"Then my nonna died a few years after I went pro. It felt like I couldn't catch a break. I was sad at first, but then I was *angry*. Everything pissed me off. I was mad at the world, at the unfairness of it all." He swallows, and from the brief moment our eyes catch, I can tell there's more to the story.

"It *is* unfair," I manage. Slipping my hand back into his, I squeeze. "I'm so sorry, Matteo, that you've had to deal with all of that." *Alone*. He's been so alone these last few years. Of course he's mad.

I'm still dabbing at my eyes when I realize—

Matteo understood how embarrassed I am about my dysfunctional family, and now he's presenting me with his. An exchange of the pieces of us that make us *us*. Not our favorite colors or courts or tournaments, but the life-shattering, world-stopping pieces.

He wants me to feel less alone.

"I feel that anger sometimes too. The resentment." It feels good to admit it. "Like the world is crumbling, and for some reason, *I'm* the one who has to make it whole again."

Matteo nods. "Has your dad always been that way?"

I sniffle. "No. He was a good dad for a few years. Tried his best, I think. He hid the drinking well in the beginning, but over time, it took over his life, and he fell into this cycle: weeks where he's good, finding work and buying a few more groceries for us than usual, and then the weeks where he's drinking, gone for days at a time or passing out on the couch because it's closer than his room."

A ghost who haunts the halls of the house but doesn't truly live among us anymore. Who drifts in and out whenever he pleases, disappears and reappears when it suits him best.

"Is he why you stepped away from game night?"

I nod. "One of the perks of his bad weeks," I murmur.

"And your mom?"

I think of the photo tucked away safely in my wallet. It's ingrained so deeply in my brain, it has its own grooves. "She was this brilliant, effervescent woman who worked so hard to make sure I was okay. Truly my best friend. She called me her little helper because it was my job to clean and cook and take care of Chase while she worked, especially if Dad was MIA." I laugh. "I wore that title like a badge of honor. She'd get home late, exhausted beyond belief, and she would smile at me over her tea while I cleaned the kitchen."

When my eyes meet Matteo's, I expect to see something warm at the picture I'm painting, but the furrow in his brow reads like indignation.

"What?" I ask.

"That's a lot to put on a kid."

Looking at my lap, I shrug. "I didn't mind it so much. It got worse when the twins were born. Mrs. Elliott—she lived right next door and tried her best to bring us clothes her grandchildren outgrew or casseroles made with any food she had lying around—always said it was postpartum depression that sent Mom running into Dad's clutches. Not that I understood what that meant at the time. All I knew was that Mom stopped going to work, began sleeping more, and went out a lot, and then one day, she was gone." I glance at him again, hesitantly. "That's when my world crumbled."

Can he see how much I wish I could run away and start over all on my own? The small part of me—though it swells by the day—that hates myself for feeling that way? I've never admitted it, desperately crushing the thought into the depths of my being, and yet I can tell Matteo sees it. More than that, he *understands* it.

He pushes my hair behind my ears, hands on either side of my face. We blink at each other, savoring this moment of mutual perception.

"I knew you were incredible, but I didn't even come close to recognizing how much so."

I blink again, almost missing the flash of regret in his eyes, like he said more than he meant to. Words confound me, even after Matteo moves away, putting the car in drive and getting us back on the highway. I try to let go of his hand so he can use them both, but he only grips mine tighter.

We enjoy the silence, fingers interlaced, until he pulls

up in front of my apartment. Neither of us move. I need to get into bed so I'm ready for tomorrow, but my body feels leaden, like someone placed paperweights atop my shoulders, the exhaustion seeping directly into my bones.

Matteo was beside me the entire day, his strength becoming mine as the little I had waned. No matter how many times I told him he could leave me, he refused to.

"Matteo?"

"Mm-hmm?" he hums.

I peer at him, making out his features in the light of the dashboard and streetlamps. He's gazing at the dark street in front of us, eyebrows knit. His right hand still rests in my palm, and his left strokes the scruff along his jaw.

"You're a lot nicer than people give you credit for." Myself included.

Matteo doesn't respond immediately; instead he gets out of the car, grabs my bags, and sets them on the sidewalk. I follow him, and just when I think he either didn't hear me or is brushing the words off, he pulls me into his body, taut, warm, and smelling of bergamot. His lips are featherlight against my temple, so much so that I convince myself I've imagined them.

"Thank you," he whispers.

"Thank *you*."

I reach for my bags, and he lets me go reluctantly, a hand still resting beneath my elbow.

When I get my building door open and hike up the stairs, I pretend he wishes I'd stayed.

twelve

"Matteo, get in here," I insist three days later, gesturing for him to come into the frame of my video from where he stands beside a picnic table. "Stratosphere will love it if we do a fit check together."

It's funny what time can do for two people. Before, I might have thought the divot in his brow was a lack of interest or a vague distaste for me, but now I recognize it as uncertainty, a sign he's nervous.

"Come on, it'll be fun." I grab his arm and lead him into frame, smiling when his grumpy face makes an appearance on screen, his dark turquoise shirt contrasting well with my light blue dress. "See? Now turn around." I do a small twirl, giggling, the flowing, pleated skirt of my outfit fanning out. Matteo sighs deeply before following suit. Beaming, I wave to the camera and click off the video. "That wasn't so bad, was it?"

He huffs a laugh. "If you say so." We grab our stuff and stroll onto the court.

It wasn't easy, but after our trip to Tampa, I made it

through Wednesday practice, some of the weariness lifting throughout the day. Even more so when Sahar and Harper knocked on our door after dinner, sparing no details from their Italian vacation.

Thursday, the four of us girls used our rest day to go for a three-mile walk before Nic and I went to physio. When I finally got Chase on the phone, he told me it was just a bad day and that it won't happen again.

"Has it happened before?" I asked.

"No. It was a one-time thing. Don't worry about it." But obviously I worry. When I said as much, he sighed. *"Even if it wasn't one time, I'm not hurting anyone but myself."*

I didn't tell him that seeing him that way made my skin crawl. That it felt like someone thrust a knife into my stomach and twisted because I'm gone and can't stop him from becoming Dad, if that's what's happening.

"It won't happen again," he reiterated, and that was the end of it.

I spent the rest of the afternoon pondering whether I believed that. Luckily, Thursday evening movie nights are back, so the girls came over for the first in almost a year.

This afternoon, I'm feeling better, excited to play our first practice match. Matteo and I warm up together, and there's a clear shift between how comfortable we were with each other during Tuesday's practice versus today's.

Across the court, Sahar and Noah talk strategy for the match. They played mixed together until he quit the tour to take over as her coach, and they're formidable when they're on the court together.

"You ready to kick ass?" Matteo asks me when we high five before he's set to serve for the first point.

I nod enthusiastically. "Sahar's been gone for weeks and Noah hasn't played for months. If we lose, we'll never live it down."

Matteo smiles, and I have to remind my heart, which has decided it's a racehorse, that we're about to play a match. "No pressure."

"So, so, so much pressure, Matteo. More than you've ever felt in your life," I joke, and he chuckles.

"I will do my best."

"Great. And I promise not to hit you in the back of the head when I serve. Or at least I'll *try* not to," I amend.

"Very reassuring. I look forward to resting my head on a large bag of ice instead of a pillow tonight."

Matteo's service game goes off without a hitch when he hits two aces and easily puts away two returns.

"I'm not sure you need me for this," I deadpan, and he rolls his eyes playfully, walking beside me to the bench.

"But then who would tell me where to serve?" he answers. We laugh, grab water, then swap sides.

The next few games go well, with us only dropping a game during Noah's serve. At one point, Lilian and Eli, forever my biggest supporters, sit at the picnic bench right outside the fence to watch.

During a changeover, Sahar comes over to our bench.

I point at her with my water bottle. "I don't think you're allowed to be here. This here's enemy territory."

"Noah's annoying me and I was gone for *weeks*. Will Francesca kill me if I hang out with you for a couple of minutes?" Behind her, Noah laughs, his head resting on the fence as he watches her.

When I glance at Francesca, she doesn't seem happy

but says nothing. She prefers that I take my practice matches seriously, but sometimes, when it's Sahar or Harper, it's hard. *Especially* when it's been a while since we've seen each other and we're still playing catch up.

Sahar leans against the net post. "You guys are getting good. How long did it take to play this in sync?"

"Two and a half weeks, believe it or not."

She clearly does not believe it, her eyebrows rising suggestively as she observes the two of us. It is in no way subtle. "Wow. You read each other like you've been playing for months, so I figured you started practicing together when you got here," she says, pointing at Matteo.

He and I share a look, one that Sahar catches. She sends me her *excuse me? we need to talk* eyes, and I stifle a laugh.

Matteo surprises me by joining the conversation. "How long have you and Noah been playing together?"

"That man has been terrorizing me in mixed since high school, but we've been friends for longer. We fell into it pretty naturally after years of reading each other's minds." Sahar laughs.

She's right. It's clear in every movement they make that they've known each other for forever. They manage to communicate with body language alone. I'm both jealous and impressed by it.

Francesca claps her hands, letting us know our break is over. During my second service game, I again manage not to hit Matteo once. During his, I continue my silly signals behind my back, which grow more ridiculous the longer the match stretches.

Playing with Matteo is nothing like playing with

Austin or Nic. With Austin, it's always fun—easy and familiar, like goofing off with a cousin you've grown up with (or at least how I imagine that would be). We have our rhythms, our inside jokes, and winning comes second to enjoying ourselves because we only get to play a few times a year. With Nic, it was the opposite—focused, serious, like every match was a test. I knew most of my shenanigans wouldn't be appreciated because winning was what mattered, and since we played at so many tournaments, I welcomed that grounding force because it meant more money coming in.

But with Matteo, it's different in a way I never expected. Freeing. He plays like he wants to win, but also like he wants *me* here, even with all my chaos. There's no pressure to be perfect beyond what I put on myself, just a strange, quiet sort of trust and the knowledge that he's having fun too.

It's another piece I was missing in the Matteo Corsi puzzle. Now I'm desperate for the rest.

We win the first set handily. The second set takes more work. Sahar and Noah are finally getting warm and back to their higher level of play, but we get the win after a hard fight. During the final point, I send Sahar's powerful shot perfectly down the line of the alley, the ball moving so fast, Noah can't get to it.

When Matteo looks at me, fondness seems to settle on his features, his eyes softening and the line I often find between his brows almost gone. And though he keeps saying he's the one who asked me to do this, I can't help but feel that, today, I proved to myself I belong on this court beside him.

NORMALLY, THE MEETING ROOMS WE USE FOR GAME strategy and film are small, but they're not too bad when it's only me and Francesca. When it's the two of us plus Matteo and Alessio? Another story altogether.

Alessio and Francesca murmur to themselves while they try to get the film set-up working on the small TV.

"I'm going to see if the tech people are around," Francesca says, like it isn't the end of the workday on a Friday evening. Alessio follows her out.

The little black leather couch Matteo and I are sharing in this closet of a room is probably meant for one person or two very *very* small people—something Matteo would not qualify for. My leg presses against his, and my pulse jackhammers in my throat.

After a few seconds, Matteo inhales deeply, looking pained, then stands quickly. At my questioning stare, he shakes his head.

"What?"

"You smell like honey."

I rear back. "Oh, I—I'm sorry?" It's the shampoo I bring for after practice. I like the smell, but clearly he's not a fan.

Matteo pulls his hat off and runs a hand through his thick curls. "I didn't say it was a bad thing," he says quietly.

Before I can respond, he begins messing around with the cords behind the TV. Moments later, the cover image of a tennis court pops up.

"Not just a pretty face," I tease, trying to get us away from whatever that was.

"I'm an engineer in another universe," he deadpans. He takes a lap around the room—which is to say he walks two steps in every direction—and then he sinks back onto the couch, careful not to touch me.

His movements are tinged with awkwardness, and I wonder if the fun we had today has worn off and now he's remembering what happened Tuesday.

"Hey, thank you again for taking me Tuesday. And for helping. I'm sorry you had to see all that. And that someone you hardly know broke down crying in your car in the middle of the highway over an hour away from home."

Matteo turns his head to face me, though I keep my gaze averted. "It's time you stop apologizing for things out of your control, Del."

"No, I just meant—"

"I know what you meant. You feel embarrassed that I saw your family in the state they were in. That I was inside your home. You're worried things have changed between us because of it, and I'm telling you they haven't." Under his breath, so quiet I barely catch it, he mumbles, "At least not in the way you think."

I chance a look at him, taking in his profile. Thick eyebrows, a strong nose, stubble down his jaw and around his full bottom lip.

"I don't regret telling you about my family, and I hope you don't regret showing me yours," he finishes.

And I realize that I don't. I don't *regret* that he saw it. I worried that he would see me differently because of it, but if he doesn't, then a small part of me is glad that I got to share a personal moment with him.

I like Matteo. He's got a tough exterior, and an obvious reason (and potentially some not-obvious reasons) for being the way he is. But to me, at least, he's very kind. And I appreciate the care he showed me and my family. I'm glad I listened to Austin about taking him up on his doubles offer, and I'm glad that, on some level, we can call ourselves friends.

I also hope that someday soon, people see him as something other than tennis' malignant narcissist.

When Francesca and Alessio return, sans a tech person, they're excited to see it's working.

"See, te l'ho detto." *I told you.* "It just needed a second," Alessio says, as if he were the one who got it up and running.

Matteo and I exchange an amused look, but he doesn't say anything.

I watch video-Matteo for signs that he's upset, whether at himself or at me—I lost us a few points today, so I'd understand—but I find nothing. No hands fisted or jaw clenched. Nothing but a small smile aimed at the back of my head when I lose us a point, despite my shoulders slumping. When video-Matteo pulls his shirt up to wipe sweat from his face and I get a shot of his abs, my body goes warm and I become incredibly aware that his leg is pressed against mine again.

I don't know if he's noticed it. If he has, he hasn't done anything about it. My other leg bounces as I analyze whether I should move away slowly.

Right as I begin moving, Matteo's calloused hand

lands on my bare leg and squeezes softly. "Relax," he says quietly, and my body nearly shuts down, perhaps taking his words a bit too literally.

I'm hyper aware of the point of contact for the rest of the hour we spend strategizing and analyzing, well after he's taken his hand away.

When Francesca and Alessio deem us done, about to dismiss us, Francesca adds, "Vabbè. One more thing." Alessio crosses his arms, and I get the distinct feeling whatever her criticism is, it's about to be directed at me. "Delilah, you have to take this seriously. I don't mind you saying something to Sahar in passing, but talking to her during every changeover to the point that you go over time on your breaks isn't going to help your game. It leads to you losing the sense that you're playing a *real* match."

Alessio takes over. "We shouldn't have to remind you that you have less than a month to practice together before the tour begins and you're in separate places. These are your last few practices before the week of the Australian Open, which will move quickly since you'll both be playing singles too. Practice matches *and* drills should be taken seriously."

I nod, embarrassment warming my cheeks, probably turning me bright red. "I'm sorry. It won't happen again. I'll be very serious."

"Not too serious, I hope," Matteo chimes in. He shifts, his leg pressing against mine more firmly, as if communicating something to me. "I find that her cheerfulness and joy on court makes me want to be cheerful too. Makes me play less angry and helps me focus on having fun, which, in turn, allows me to play better." He runs a palm over his leg, brushing mine. "So not too serious, I hope," he reiterates.

"You wanted them playing mixed for a reason," Francesca says to Alessio.

"Whose side are you on?"

Francesca smiles at me. "Delilah's. Always."

Matteo gives me that same tender smile as before. "Plus, we won. Easily. So we can find a better balance of fun and seriousness, but clearly, our tennis isn't suffering."

Alessio grumbles about it being three on one, and I smile. "How about I join your side and make it an even two on two? I'll take things more seriously. I promise. Today was just a bad day. Next week's match, I'll lock in."

He sighs but shoots me a smile and nods. "That's it then. Roll out before you leave," he says, more to Matteo than to me, but it's a good note and something I'd already planned to do.

Our coaches leave for the evening, and Matteo and I walk to the player's gym, grabbing foam rollers from the large bin, and lie beside each other on the rubber flooring.

"Excited for tomorrow?" I ask him.

The Morozovs run clinics for young kids in the summer and on weekends during the year but are short-staffed at the moment. They sent an email to the players, asking if anyone could help in the coming weeks, and I volunteered for tomorrow. I got a second email a few days ago thanking the three of us who agreed to help, and because I'm nosy and the Morozovs apparently don't know how to use the BCC function, I noticed Matteo would be joining me.

If he's surprised I know he'll be there, he doesn't show

it. "More like worried. I wouldn't describe myself as good with children."

"I'm shocked. I had you pegged for someone who loves kids."

He rolls his eyes playfully. "Yes, I'm sure that's the energy I give off."

"Why'd you volunteer then? The money's not *that* good." Not entirely true. The Morozovs are *very* generous when they're in a pinch.

Matteo lifts a shoulder as he pushes the left side of his lower body over the roller. "Figured it would be good to give back."

I grin. "I knew I was a good influence."

We talk for a few more minutes before I realize what time it is. "Shoot! I have to be up early, so I'm going to head out."

Matteo checks the clock on the wall behind him, standing and grabbing both our rollers. It's clear he's not going to let me go home alone; he hasn't since the first time he dropped me off at my apartment. "Before the clinic?"

"Yeah. Ward family breakfast on Saturday mornings."

That same muted smile he's been blessing me with more and more appears. "I thought you said you weren't related." After putting away the rollers, he guides me back to the locker rooms.

"Not by blood, no. They just like to include me in family things."

"I truly thought they were your family for a long time. I didn't realize you weren't their daughter until I looked you up after we all had dinner at the French Open and someone said something that made me think…" He stops when he sees me grinning. "What?" he asks.

"You looked me up?"

He scratches the back of his head. "Yeah. Only to see if you were Austin's sister."

"Can't imagine what you found when you searched for Delia and not Delilah."

He chuckles, and the sound vibrates through me. "Yeah…Except I knew your name…" he trails off again.

"What?"

He shrugs. I poke his decidedly hard pectoral, but he simply shakes his head.

We grab our bags from our respective locker rooms and make it to his car. "Can't believe you thought Austin and I were siblings. We look nothing alike!" I exclaim, still thinking about it.

Matteo shrugs, helping me into the passenger's side. "I didn't say I was smart."

thirteen

SHOTS FIRED

AUSTIN

Since nobody else has sent this…

SAHAR

OH MY GOSH! DELILAH! YOUR FIRST
FAN EDIT WITH MATTEO

AUSTIN

Did you read the comments?

HARPER

Aww, people want you guys to get
together so badly.

There are three other accounts with
different edits too! I can't stop watching.

This is…odd

Though I don't know what I expected
when I posted a video of us

AUSTIN

Delilah and Matteo sitting in a tree…

Really? Nobody is going to finish that?

NOAH

Some of these people are not being very
nice about him

What the hell do they know

SAHAR

WOAH! She cursed??

NOAH

S you owe me thirty bucks. I called it

AUSTIN

Is this real?

I would like to be told about these sorts of
things seeing as I INTRODUCED the two
of you

NIC REMOVED THEMSELF FROM THE CHAT.

AUSTIN ADDED NIC TO THE CHAT.

The next day, I make it to the indoor courts four minutes before eight, dodging kids varying in age from five to twelve. Breakfast with the Wards put me behind, which is my fault more than theirs since I insisted on hearing every single detail of Austin's recovery so far.

Tall ceilings and large windows allow plenty of natural light to pour into the building. Beyond the office, where I'm sure to find the coaches, two rows of six indoor courts stretch out. A woman with short gray hair and a big smile is escorting a group of children to different courts, likely based on their skill level.

I step into the simple office and find that I was right: a group of coaches stand in a lazy circle just inside the door. I see Matteo and sidle up to him.

The woman I assume is in charge of these clinics steps out from an area with desks and flier-filled corkboards, closing the door behind her.

"Good morning, everyone. Thank you for being here. As a few of you know, we're short-staffed for the next few weekends, so we're having players fill in. Today we have Delilah, Matteo, and Lina. Adam, you're moving up to intermediate," she says, pointing to a guy who can't be much older than me with long shaggy brown hair. "Delilah and Matteo can take the beginners group, and Lina, since you've worked with us before, you'll be with Adam and the intermediate group."

Everyone in the circle nods and begins to file out of the small building. "Delilah, Matteo, one second."

We fall back. "I'm Louise. Thank you again for helping out with camp today. There's not much to it, but in case you haven't done this before, you'll spend an hour or so working on form. Then you'll have them try hitting the ball over the net when you toss it from beside them, then when you tap it over the net to them."

"Is there a set time to break for lunch?" I ask.

"Nope, just whenever they get hungry. After, you can combine your groups and play games. They're big fans of bounce it, caterpillar, and target practice where they win prizes." She hitches a thumb over her shoulder. "We keep a few small swag items in the office if you want to do that, as well as dollar bills because they love the idea of money, no matter how small."

"What is a caterpillar in this context?" Matteo asks, bewildered.

I laugh. "Roll a ball down the court and have a line of kids make sure it passes between their feet. Get progressively quicker. It's good for footwork with younger groups. You never played?"

Matteo shakes his head.

Louise smiles, tapping her chin. "I think that's everything, but I'll be down the way with the advanced groups if you need anything. Unless you have any other questions, you'll be on courts one and two."

We follow Louise out and onto our courts.

The learning is slow-going. I fix the grip of a six-year-old with pigtails and she immediately changes it back to what she had before. I demonstrate how they should set their rackets to prepare to hit a ball, and they swing wildly—so much so, I have to make sure they spread out so none of them get seriously injured. When, finally, they sort of have a grasp of strokes, I stand beside them and toss them balls. Another hour while we get their swings to work so they land their racket on the ball. When they've (kind of) mastered that, I move to the other side of the court, tapping balls over the net.

Some of them are better than others. Some are able to get their rackets on the balls, some are even able to get the ball to the other side of the court. When I notice I'm losing a couple of the younger ones who are struggling to get their racket anywhere near the ball, I teach them how to play bounce it. They walk around the outskirts of the court, trying their best to hit a ball straight down onto the court multiple times. It's great for teaching contact points, and when they're more engaged, I bring them back to try again.

I've always loved this side of coaching. I did a lot of it growing up, and then recently, Maya started a charity to coach underprivileged kids, and the few times I've been around and able, I've helped her there too. Every time I do, I'm reminded of how rewarding just one session can be.

Beginners, while easily distracted, can make large amounts of progress in a short amount of time. By no means are they ready to move up, but by the end of the drills, I have eight mostly smiling faces excited that they've hit a ball over the net. Even if it did sail so high, I lost sight of it in the rafters (twice).

Each time I peek over at Matteo's court, I see him floundering. Responding in one- or two-word answers to their many questions. I bite back a laugh when he glances over at me like he's in dire need of my help.

"Beginners, listen up!" I yell. "If I hit Coach Matteo with a ball, you get a long water break."

Grabbing my racket and a ball from the large rolling basket, I make sure none of the kids are near me or him and tap the ball lightly toward him.

I hit it to the side of him, but instead of letting it go past, he moves right into its path. The kids cheer.

While they get water, I walk to Matteo. "You cheated."

"Needed a break. They're terrorizing me."

I snort. "How could such tiny children be 'terrorizing' you?"

"Why do they ask so many questions? And how am I supposed to answer 'Does God believe in tennis?' or 'Do the tennis balls have feelings?' They're going to go home to their parents with an explanation that could rock their belief systems, and then I'm in trouble."

"Ah see, that's where your love of answering questions with questions will come in handy." I keep an eye on all fifteen kids, and when Aditi asks to use the bathroom, I nod, watching her run to the ones beside the office.

"You're so good with them," Matteo muses.

"Product of growing up fast and taking care of the twins, I think. Plus I love them. They're so easily pleased. I might not be able to wow adults, but I can certainly wow children."

"What makes you think you can't wow adults?"

My breath stutters for a moment, and I nearly preen under the subtle compliment. "I don't know. Anyway, they're going to get to go home and tell their parents they met Matteo Corsi. That you *coached* them. This is a big moment for them."

"I guarantee you not one of these five- to seven-year-olds knows who any of us are."

"Maddox knows. He asked me very softly if you were *the* Matteo Corsi. Again, wow moment."

Matteo's lips move infinitesimally, and he stares down at me fondly. "You really do have a way with people, don't you?" The way he says it seems to have another meaning.

"Is that a bad thing?"

"I'm coming to find it's something I need more of in my life."

Before I can think, I ask, "Me? Or the ability to understand others?"

His eyes scan my face, his Adam's apple bobbing as he swallows. Anticipation builds like a helium balloon as I wait for him to admit something to me I'm not even willing to admit to myself. "The kids are getting antsy. We should get back to it."

I deflate, taking a few steps back and calling for my group to get back on the court. We do a few more rounds of them across the net from me, trying to get their rackets on the ball. Before long, they're hungry.

"Alright. If I hit Matteo again, it's lunchtime," I declare, loudly enough that he and his group can hear it.

He puts his racket into the large rolling basket beside him. "Let's see what you got, tesoro."

This time, I hit him without him adjusting his position. All at once, the fifteen kids cheer. Clearly, lunch is their favorite part of camp days.

After I make sure all of them wash their hands, they settle onto the court and begin eating, most from sack lunches, others from fancy lunch boxes. I sit on the bench in front of them.

Matteo hooks his thumb behind him. "Going to grab sandwiches from the office. Anything you don't eat?" I shake my head. When he returns, holding one out for me, I take it gratefully.

"Thank you."

He sits beside me on the bench as we field more questions from the little munchkins.

"How old are you?" one of them asks.

"Twenty-five," I say as Matteo answers, "Twenty-eight."

"Wow, that's old," another answers.

Then, "What time is your bedtime? Mine's eight," one of Matteo's kids pipes up proudly.

"Phew, that's later than mine. I'm in bed by seven." Matteo lets out a short laugh, and the kids talk over each other to tell us their bedtimes.

Just as I'm polishing off the last of my sandwich, one of them asks, "What is tezuro?"

Matteo looks at me, a flicker of alarm on his face before he glances away. "Tesoro means treasure in Italian."

I've been meaning to search it up, to see if it really does mean the same thing as it does in Spanish. Hearing it confirmed now from his lips reinflates that balloon in my chest. Is that hope? It's oddly warm as it travels through my body.

The same kid asks, "So are you boyfriend and girlfriend?"

My last bite gets lodged in my throat for a second, and I cough into my elbow, trying desperately to swallow. My eyes water as Matteo lightly taps my back.

"I don't know if the idea is *that* offensive," he jokes quietly, handing me my bottle of water.

I sip from it, wiping tears from my eyes when I can breathe again. "No, we play mixed doubles together. Do you know what mixed doubles is?" I ask, hoping to get the derailed conversation on a different track.

A few of them jump to answer, and after a couple more innocuous questions, we get back to training.

"We're going to play games for the rest of the day, okay?" Fifteen heads nod. "Let's do one practice round of bounce it, and then the second one, we'll play for real. Whoever wins gets a prize."

They each grab a ball from the cart and spread out. When I yell "Go!" they start bouncing the ball on their racket. Matteo chuckles beside me.

"What?"

"Nothing. This is just fun to watch. They shouldn't pay me because I'm only following your lead here."

"I have to make up for all the winning you're going to be doing for us at the open."

"With your lethal cross-court angles and down the lines, I'm not sure you should be giving me any of that credit."

One of the children loses a ball, and it rolls over to us, hitting my shoe. I pick it up and note that most of the kids are done.

"Who's ready to win a prize?" I ask. A chorus of voices overlap as the children scatter, leaving plenty of room around themselves so they don't crash into each other. "On your mark, get set, go!"

A frenzy of balls thwacking against racket strings fills the air. Two are out immediately, and one of them, Aditi, crosses her arms and pouts. When she comes up beside us, I pat her shoulder reassuringly. "You'll have other chances."

When all but one has lost their ball in one way or another, Matteo and I applaud the girl.

"What do I win?" she asks excitedly.

"You win…a dollar!"

She jumps up and down like she won the lottery, and I turn to Matteo. "See? Easily pleased."

He gives me a full smile this time, teeth and everything. It's still small by most standards, but to me, it's like *I* won the lottery. "Any time I have to interact with someone under the age of ten, I'm bringing you with me."

I curtsy, forever high on making him smile. "It would be my honor."

After a few rounds of caterpillar and one failed attempt at jail break, I say, "Last thing before you go home for the day. Everyone is going to get three chances to hit a target. If you hit a target, you win a prize."

"Should I grab cones?" Matteo asks. "I can set them up along the other side of the court."

I grin up at him. "I have a better idea." Turning to the kids, I say, "If you hit Coach Matteo, you win a prize. Everyone gets three chances! Go line up, and I'll bring the basket."

Matteo grabs his racket from the rolling basket and comes to stand right in front of me. "You're evil," he whispers. "You just want to see me get hit since you promised *you* wouldn't hit me during matches." He reaches out to tap my visor, and I swat him away. Matteo stops me with a hand around my wrist, tugging me forward an inch.

My forearm presses into his chest, our faces inches apart. I lick my lips, and his eyes fall to them, watching raptly before they come back to meet mine, pupils dilated. His other hand rests on my waist, his racket pushed gently against my side. Neither of us move. I take in the details in his face I don't often have time to appreciate. The little scar on his upper lip. A handful of freckles on the bridge of his nose. A hazel quality to his brown eyes.

"Maybe I do," I answer softly.

"What else do you want?"

My breath hitches, and he notices, eyes dropping to my lips again.

"Boys have cooties! Don't kiss him!"

The moment shatters like a glass on the kitchen floor, and we jump apart.

Matteo walks to the other side of the net, regaining his composure far quicker than I can. "Let's do this." And then, like I'm rubbing off on him and he's learning how to talk to them, he calls out, "You'll never get me alive!"

He lets all fifteen of them hit him and pays them their one dollar right then and there. And when three of them ask him to sign a tennis ball for them, then three more who don't want to be left out, and then the rest of them, he grabs a marker from the office and signs fifteen.

I can't believe anyone could ever think he's a malignant narcissist.

fourteen

After the kids leave, I'm in dire need of a shower, so I head to the locker rooms. Theoretically, since I don't have anything else to do today, I should go home, but the water pressure is significantly better here, and the fact that Nic and I both shower at the facility most days keeps our water bill to a manageable number.

I step out of the locker room feeling much cleaner, hair tied up in a loose bun. Searching through my bag for my keys and phone, I pull them out and notice a voicemail from my father. Rather than guess the contents, I listen.

"Hi, sweetheart. I wanted to say I'm sorry for the last message I left you and the way I treated you when you were here. I wasn't in a good place. You know how these things are."

I really don't.

"Anyway, I was watching highlights of one of your old matches and phew! You're a rock star. Wanted to let you know I'm thinking about you, kiddo. Hope you're doing well."

I wait for the ball to drop. For him to ask me for money. But it never comes, and the message ends. Which means I'll be getting another one soon unless he finds work fast.

The door to the men's locker room opens, and I glance up, then double take when I notice Noah and Aleksandr beside a shirtless Matteo. His sweatpants are slung low on his hips, the subtle V overshadowed by the trail of hair that travels below the waistband of his pants. A lean but defined torso. Toned biceps and forearms. Not quite bulky, but strong enough that he could lift me. His hair is dripping, and…

Wait, lift me?

Suddenly, my mind drifts to the press of his body against mine on the court this afternoon, to what it would feel like to trace the smattering of hair from his chest down, down, down.

I realize my mouth is agape when Noah smirks, so I snap it shut.

"You okay?" he asks teasingly.

I clear my throat. "I'm great." My eyes dart down to Matteo's chest, then back, my father's message long forgotten. "Uh, what are you guys doing here?"

Matteo's raised eyebrows and Noah's and Aleks' smirks tell me I've been caught. I have nothing to say for myself.

"Sahar and I finished game strategy early, so I got a workout in with Aleks. We're getting dinner at the players' restaurant," Noah answers.

"Oh."

Noah snorts, clapping Matteo on the shoulder in

goodbye. Aleks does the same, and by the time the guys walk away, I'm grinning.

Matteo is making friends.

"Byeeee, Delilahhhhh," Noah calls as he leaves, drawing out the syllables in a way that tells me we will be having words in the group chat tonight.

"Don't forget to bring your A game tomorrow," Aleks chimes in.

Sundays are typically my day off, but because I didn't play today, the rest day shifted. Anya and Aleks agreed to spend their free day playing a practice match against us. Since we only have a few more weeks to train together and Anya, who is so busy, was nice enough to agree, who am I to complain? Especially after the scolding I got because of yesterday's practice match.

"Are you going home for dinner or eating here?" Matteo asks like it's our routine.

I pocket my phone and keys, throwing my bag over my shoulder. He glares at the strap, so I make a big show of putting the second strap on my other shoulder.

"I've got a date with some pasta, chicken, and reality TV. You?"

He shrugs, taking the towel around his neck and wiping his dripping hair. "I can drop you off."

"Oh, no. That's fine. It's a quick walk." Nic didn't do the clinic today, so she's probably still in a game strategy session with her team.

"This again?" he grumbles. It's almost comical how much he dislikes when I try to leave the facility without him. "Then I'll walk with you." He moves toward the exit, and after a moment of hesitation, I fall into step beside him.

"Are you going to put on a shirt?" I ask without thinking.

"Sorry to offend. I dropped my bag off at my car, and since you insist on walking, I will have to manage."

I pat his bicep in what is meant to be a reassuring motion but is somehow erotic enough that I have to rip my hand back quickly. "I do insist. Luckily, we're in Orlando and it's sixty degrees, so I think you'll be fine." I certainly won't mind.

"It's my first December not in New York in a long time. I knew it wasn't going to be as cold, but yeah"—he chuckles—"it's much warmer than I expected."

"You New Yorkers. Always waving it around in our faces that we're *not* from New York."

"Do you want to be from New York?" he asks seriously.

"Heck no. Far too much hustle for my liking. Of course, the politics there are more my speed, but that's the price I pay for training at one of the best facilities in the world." And for being close to home.

"My mom loved New York. She preferred the city to most in the US because it was walkable. 'The way our ancestors intended,' she used to say."

"So true. We should be walking everywhere."

Matteo hums in agreement. Is he thinking about her? Or the rest of his family? Is his father's new family still local to New York or have they moved somewhere else?

He's shared so much with me, I feel bad prying, but I so intensely want to collect every piece of him until the puzzle falls into place and I can perfectly understand him. Know what makes him tick and what makes him smile. Though I pride myself on the fact that I seem to be getting better on the latter front.

When we reach my apartment, I turn to him, ignoring his glorious chest. "I had fun today. I'm glad you agreed to help out."

"I didn't hate it."

"Wow, what a glowing endorsement."

He smiles down at me. "It is from me."

"True. Translated from Matteo, you're basically saying it was the best day of your life."

Matteo takes a strand of hair that's fallen loose from my bun between his thumb and pointer finger, rubbing them together before tucking it behind my ear, his movements slow, his finger lingering.

"Big match tomorrow," he mumbles softly.

"Yes. I think we've got it though."

"I think so too." His eyes drop to my lips. *Is he going to kiss me?* I scarcely breathe, worried that if I do, I might shake myself from this reality. Slip into another where Matteo never asked me to play mixed with him. Where Matteo didn't notice me and never insists on taking me home. Where I don't get to learn about his family or the things that make him *him*.

I hate that reality.

A honk down the street jolts us apart, and he shakes his head, his standard unreadable expression back. "See you tomorrow."

"Good night. Thank you for walking me."

He doesn't respond, but when I get to my room and

peer out the window, he's still there, hands in his pockets, staring at the ground.

And when I get into bed a few hours later, after watching what Nic described as "an astounding amount of reality TV," all I can think about is my arm on his chest, his hand wrapped around my wrist, and the distinct warmth that flooded my body when I thought about him kissing me.

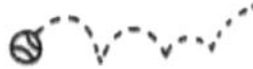

MATTEO

You left your visor in my car.

Keep it. You should wear it to our match today

MATTEO

Only if you wear my hat too.

You drive a hard bargain, but I accept your terms

Though I'll be wearing it backward in true Matteo fashion

Matteo?

MATTEO

I'm not sure you understand what the thought of that does to me.

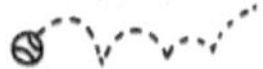

Sunday afternoons at the Morozov Tennis Academy are much quieter than the rest of the week. Even with players back from their vacations, the rec areas, gyms, and courts are almost entirely empty.

Except for Nic, of course, who's on the far court practicing her serves. This morning, she examined my practice match outfit before I left the apartment and said, "Well if you *insist* on playing today, I'm certainly not going to rest either," ignoring the fact that I had yesterday off when she did not.

After drills this morning and a break for lunch, during which I wondered if Matteo was picturing me with his hat on backward, he and I got warmed up and ready for our match, Alessio and Francesca monitoring us like hawks. The Wards, Austin included, settled onto the bleachers beside our court to watch.

I can't explain why, but this match feels more important. Like if we win it, we'll be elevated to another level. A doubles team worthy of winning matches at the Australian Open.

Matteo serves first, and we take the first game easily. The next game, I struggle with Aleks' serve, and after a few deuces, we lose. During my service game, I note Aleks' focus is down the row of empty courts where Nic is getting ready to leave. When I bounce the ball, he refocuses, but clearly not well enough because I ace him. It's enough to throw them off their feet, and the rest of the set goes easier. When we sit down after winning the first set 6–3, I try to keep my beaming to a minimum.

"Only one more," I whisper in awe. I don't want to jinx us, and I'm well aware that the siblings haven't played together in over a year, but we're playing better than ever. It's almost intoxicating.

Matteo chuckles like he can read what's running through my mind. I swallow over what the sound does to me, still new to hearing it out of him. "I don't know if I've ever seen you bounce this much, and that's saying something."

I still, not realizing I was doing anything. "Sorry."

"Not sure why you're apologizing. It's one of my favorite things about you."

Francesca and Alessio walking over to give us pointers for the next set saves me from having to answer. I desperately need him to stop saying these things mid-match because all they're doing is making me feel fuzzy and lightheaded, and now is *not* the time for that.

We battle hard for the second set but lose in a tiebreak. The mood on our bench after is somber, a stark contrast from after the first.

"They found their rhythm again," Matteo says while staring at a ball rolling slowly toward us in the early December breeze. He only lost his composure once, when he sent a ball long and lost us a game, but after I yelled an encouraging "It's all good! We'll get the next one!" he shut it down, the anger slipping from his face and turning to indifference.

"It's okay. We have another set in us. I'll go for more down the lines, and you keep going at Anya until her volley breaks down," I answer, knowing that Anya is probably telling Aleks the same thing about me. Matteo glances at me, his lips curving, eyes softening. "What?" I ask.

"Every day, you affirm my reasoning for wanting to play mixed with you." He walks to our coaches, leaving me speechless.

Once again, I have to brush off the words to prepare for the third-set tiebreak. A minute or so later, when Francesca has given me pointers, Matteo hands me a ball. "Ready?" I nod. "Slice out wide if you can. She's standing inside the baseline to intimidate you. Don't let it work."

Releasing a breath, I pocket a second ball. We get set, and I bounce it a few times before tossing it up and hitting it to the far corner. Anya barely gets her racket on it, and Matteo, who's up at net, positions himself perfectly for an overhead, placing it just far enough out of Aleks' reach. It bounces far too high for Anya to get it back.

Matteo smiles at me proudly. I tap the balls over the net so they can serve for the next two points while Matteo walks over. He stands close enough that I have to look up, his tall 6'3 frame not quite towering over my 5'9 one. "Told you," he says quietly, smiling before taking his place at the baseline.

We fight for every point, and by the end, we've pulled slightly ahead. It's my turn to serve again. I go for the slice serve one more time, acing Aleks.

We're one point away from the win.

Matteo strides over, offering me another ball. "Magnificent."

Normally, I'd brush off the compliment, so used to my father's hollow ones, given and then taken back with vitriol. But Matteo has consistently proven he's not like that, and with how good of a tennis player he is, the word is enough to make me believe I could truly be magnificent.

I haven't responded, so he continues, "Do it again. And if she gets it back, use the cross-court angle you're so good at."

The praise falls so easily from his lips, I could kiss him. Instead, I nod, ignoring the way his gaze travels over my face. If I let him take my focus off this final point, we might lose the little lead we have.

Match points don't normally rattle me. Like Matteo pointed out once, I'm as cool as ice no matter the score. Still, I take a breath and then another, bouncing the ball a few times. I toss it up and slap it into play.

Anya gets it back to me, then I back to her, and back and forth until Aleks steps up and volleys down the middle. I get my feet set and lob a backhand to Anya. She takes the bait, hitting a cross-court forehand that sends me to the alley, where I flick my wrist and send it spinning onto the far alley line, right inside the service line. Neither of them can get to it before it hits the fence. My racket clatters out of my hand in awe.

We did it. Whatever test was placed before us under the guise of a "practice" match, we did it. Not only does this prove we have what it takes to win at Aussie, but it's proof that agreeing to play with Matteo was the right choice. That my chance at some extra money is a very real possibility.

I'm so overwhelmed, I run to Matteo and jump into his outstretched arms. Whether or not he's caught off guard, he twirls me around like I single-handedly won us the match. His chuckle ricochets through my body, his arms holding me to him tightly. I laugh freely.

I can't believe we beat one of the top mixed doubles teams three weeks into playing together.

Remembering where we are, I tap Matteo's shoulder with my palm a couple of times, and he sets me down softly. We walk to the net to shake Anya's and Aleksandr's hands.

"Good match," we all murmur.

I skip to the bench, shoving my rackets into my bag. Matteo watches me. When I ask him, "Is this what it feels like to win a Grand Slam?" he shakes his head, smiling tenderly at me.

We thank the Morozovs, and Francesca and Alessio let us know we can go home. We'll go through strategy after our session Tuesday. The Wards say their goodbyes, and then my cooldown routine and shower go by painstakingly slowly, but about two hours after the sun has set, Matteo and I meet outside of the locker rooms, where he insists on driving me home.

"It's on my way," he claims. He doesn't talk much on the drive though, maybe lost in thought. I keep glancing at him out of the corner of my eye, anticipation swelling in my chest and setting my blood ablaze.

Anticipation of what, I'm not sure.

When we get to my building, he helps me with my bag, ever the gentleman. I'm not ready to say goodbye.

"So…" I start. Not sure what I thought he was going to be able to do with that.

"So." He clears his throat. "You played some damn good tennis today."

"The power I have when I take things seriously." I

chuckle, poking his shoulder. "And it helps that you're able to ace the heck out of everyone."

Matteo grabs the hand that still hovers near his shoulder, encircling my wrist like he did during the clinic yesterday. My breath hitches, and I think, *finally it's happening.*

"If we were to have an MVP today, it was you."

My mind has emptied enough that all I'm thinking about are his lips; the plush bottom one and smaller top one with the little scar. Moments stretch and pass us by. When it's clear that I'm, once again, reading this situation wrong, I laugh it off. "I'd better go if I want to make it home in time for curfew," I joke, pulling my hand away and walking toward my building.

Except Matteo doesn't let go of my hand. He tugs me back desperately, longingly. My body falls into his, and his lips press to mine, a warm hand cupping my cheek. We break away—just for a second, a gasp—and then his mouth is back on mine, and he's guiding me back, back, back. I curl my fingers in the cotton of his T-shirt as he slips his tongue into my mouth, and only when he groans do I remember that we're still very much in public.

I pull away, missing his soft lips and the scrape of his scruff already. Panting, I say, "You should come upstairs. Celebrate."

Matteo's eyes scan mine for a second before he nods.

And then, for the first time in my life, I sneak a boy into my room.

fifteen

The coast is clear—our bathroom door is closed, Nic's nighttime routine music drifting from beneath it—so I motion Matteo to follow me to my room. I shut the door behind us as fast as I can, tossing my bag to the side and toeing off my slides. He does the same, clicking the lock into place on the door handle.

I giggle before slapping a hand over my mouth. "Good call," I whisper, flicking the switch that turns on my bedside table lamp, illuminating him in a soft warm glow. He's giving me that look again, like I've amused him so thoroughly that it's become endearing. "What?"

He steps forward, hand slipping into my hair and bringing my lips back to his, as if he can't wait a moment longer. It's hurried, frenzied, rough kisses and bites until we pull away for air, and then more, sinking onto my light-blue-and-lavender floral bedspread.

We slow down, exploring the contours of each other's body. One of his hands cradles my head, the other gently strokes the line of my hip and waist. My fingertips drift over taut back muscles, slipping beneath his shirt to touch his strong abdomen and chest. Matteo groans at the contact, ripping his shirt off. The scent of bergamot that hits me is heady, but it's the kisses he places down my neck, chest, and stomach, the reverence in his eyes as he removes my shirt painstakingly, that shoot a thrill from my scalp to my toes.

He shifts a warm, calloused palm beneath the waistband of my shorts. I gasp and am rewarded with a sensual smile. A slow tug of my shorts from my body as he drinks in every detail, groaning something in Italian when he sees the cotton thong with a tiny bow in the front I've had for years. He doesn't seem to mind that I'm wearing a T-shirt bra, kissing slowly down my body like I'm the single most attractive woman he's ever laid eyes on.

I slip my fingers into his hair, dragging him toward me, wanting his lips back on mine. His grip on my wrist stops me. "It's only fair you give me a moment to take you in since you've already seen me like this."

Heat slips into my cheeks. So he did, in fact, see the video that was playing on a loop on my phone that one time in the player's gym. His grin when he sees my face is further confirmation, and I drop my hand in embarrassment, letting him have a moment.

When Matteo reaches below my stomach, his fingers circling along my inner thigh tantalizingly, he rumbles, "No need to be shy. I've been thinking about this for so long, tesoro. Months. You've been in my head more than you could ever imagine."

"Mon—" I'm cut off when his finger travels higher, nearing where I know he'll find me slick, my breath catching. Warmth sinks low, then slingshots throughout my body. "Months? We've been training together for a few weeks."

Matteo's eyes flick to mine, shuttering for a second. He chuckles, and I feel as though I'm on the outside of an inside joke. "Right," he murmurs. The fingers of his hand not touching my thigh trace up my body. "I love watching your blush spread from here"—he taps just below my collarbone—"up to your cheeks. It's one of my many favorite things about you." And then, with nearly no pause, he asks, "Can I touch you?"

I'm speechless, but manage a nod. He moves leisurely, taking his time kissing down my stomach until he gets where I need him, warm breath sending goose bumps skittering across my arms.

Slipping a finger inside the cotton, he asks, "Are you sure you can be quiet?" When I give another wordless nod, he shoots me the most charming smile I've ever seen. "I guess we'll see." My fixation on his grin is only broken when he slides a finger inside me slowly, his groan practically guttural. His thumb traces gentle circles on my clit, and when I gasp, he pulls himself up the bed to kiss me quiet. "Liar," he whispers against my lips.

My breath speeds up as he adds pressure to my center.

"Do you want another?" he asks.

"Please *yes*."

"So polite," he muses. Matteo adds another finger, and when it starts to feel a bit too much, he kisses me again, somewhere between frantic and feverish, his fingers picking up speed. Blood rushes in my ears, my heels digging into my mattress and my body writhing beneath him.

"Matteo," I whisper, closing my eyes and feeling the first rush of waves hit.

"Where you going?" he teases me quietly when I continue moving with his hand, chasing the sensation, begging for the wave to crash.

"Matteo," I moan again, louder, anguished. Needy.

His beard scrapes my cheek gently as his lips caress the shell of my ear. "Come for me tesorino."

So I do. His fingers hook gently inside me, and heat builds up my spine. His lips pressed to mine barely stifle the cry I let out as I clench around him, my head hazy.

When I can finally see again, I blink at Matteo hovering above me, his expression proud like *I'm* the one deserving of praise and not the other way around.

"I guess I can't be quiet," I murmur, eyes traveling to his sweatpants, where I can see him straining. I push the waistband down, taking his boxer briefs with them, smiling when he lets out another guttural groan. Spitting in my hand, I stroke up and down, enjoying the little noises he tries to stifle. His body moves in tandem with my hand, urging me forward until he's almost unhinged, his head dropped beside my ear, whimpering like he's at my mercy. After a particularly loud groan, I shush him, and he snaps to attention.

"Can I fuck you? Per favore, please let me," he begs.

"Do you have a condom?"

Matteo moves so fast, he practically trips over himself, pulling one from his wallet. "Is that a yes?" he asks gruffly.

I nod, pulling my thong off and biting my lip to hide

my smile. He's so eager and earnest, it makes my stomach flip.

Matteo rips open the wrapper and rolls it on, pulling off his sweatpants and boxers and crawling up the bed until he's positioned over me, his cock notched against me. He kisses me deeply, his hand pressing against my stomach, pushing me into the mattress, while his thumb circles my center once more.

Slowly, carefully, he slides into me, keeping his hand's rhythm the same. My body stretches to fit him, and I watch his eyes shut tightly, his breaths coming out in quick pants. He moves in and out a couple of times, still slow, still exploring until I can't take it.

I slip my fingers into his hair urgently. "I want more," I whisper against his lips. "I can take more."

Matteo's eyes fly open. He drags me to the edge of the bed, pulling my legs against his chest and using the hand against my stomach to keep me pinned down, hips drilling into mine as they pick up the pace. His other thumb slips into my mouth, my whimpers and moans quieter as I suck on it.

He's speaking Italian, the words melodic and beautiful, though I can't be positive what they all mean. "Sei bellissima. Perfetta. Ho bisogno di te." When he realizes I'm not understanding, he switches to English. "You're so beautiful." Thrust. "Perfect." Thrust. "I need you." Thrust. "Could. Do. This. Every. Day." He punctuates each word with a thrust. I cry out when I feel another wave cresting, and he shakes his head, a small smile on his face.

The bathroom door opens in the foyer, and Nic calls

out to me. My eyes widen, but Matteo doesn't stop. He simply pulls his thumb out of my mouth and nods. "Answer her," he commands me, and that alone nearly does it for me for a second time.

"I'm—" I close my eyes, trying to keep it together. "I'm here. All good. See you tomorrow." Every other word wavers, but it's the best I can do.

"Have you eaten?" she calls from outside my door. Matteo's smile tips into something devilish, like he knows exactly how hard he's making this for me.

His thumb continues working my clit, the rhythm of him pushing inside me barely slowing, just enough to stay quiet.

"I'm good, yeah. All good," I choke out, not remembering what she said. I hear her grumble something and walk away.

Matteo's expression is half wild, his thumb slipping back into my mouth. "Brava, pretty girl. Now come for me again so I can feel you tightening around my cock this time."

Like my body is made to listen to his commands, I do. His hand covers my mouth when I cry out, and a moment later, when his thrusts become erratic, he presses his lips to mine, hard, groaning into my mouth.

When he finally comes down, he pulls out, lying beside me on the bed and kissing my shoulder while our breathing slows. After we've had a moment to recuperate, he asks, "Do you have any towels in here?" He stands on shaky legs, pulling off the condom and tucking it and the wrapper into a tissue from my dresser. Grabbing our clothes, he stares at me expectantly.

"Sorry, no."

"Then we're going to have to go to the bathroom to get you cleaned up. That okay?" He pulls his boxers and sweatpants on, then throws his large T-shirt over me. I'm enveloped in his smell.

"Oh," I answer, my brain functioning at about a tenth of the speed it usually does, still reveling in what just happened.

"Del? Bathroom?"

"Oh, yes!" I stand, taking his hand, and his shirt falls halfway to my knees. Unlocking my door, I stick my head out. No sign of Nic. I turn back, drinking in his solid chest and abs before leading him out.

We tiptoe, but right as we're about to pass the kitchen entrance, Nic steps out. She blinks a few times, eyes flitting between Matteo and me. After a few seconds, she turns toward her room.

"Not my circus, not my monkeys," she mumbles, and I snort, pulling Matteo into the bathroom.

LESS THAN HALF AN HOUR LATER, WE'RE ORDERING AT A drive-through taco place I've been wanting to try. A chipper voice tells us to pull forward, and I grab my card from my wallet. Matteo's gaze finds me, and he frowns. "What are you doing?"

"Paying for dinner."

"No."

"Yes," I insist.

"Delilah, what kind of man do you take me for?"

"The kind of man who makes me orgasm twice and then lets me pay for dinner." The woman opens the window and reads out our order. Before Matteo can respond, I practically throw myself across his lap to give her my card.

We agree to eat at his apartment a few blocks away—in the complete opposite direction of mine despite him telling me it was on the way earlier—both because I'm not ready to talk to Nic (if she's even in a talking mood) and because I want to see where he lives.

Once we're on the way, he asks, "So are you going to explain or am I going to have to pull it from you?"

"Pull what from me?" I respond innocently.

"Delilah."

I sigh. "You paid for our last dinner and for Chase's tab, and I've been so out of it, I forgot to pay you back."

"I didn't do either of those things with the expectation that you would."

"I know. I know that. It would just make me more comfortable if you let me."

It's clear from his bewildered frown that he wants to push it. Putting my card back into my wallet, I pluck out the tattered photo. When he slots us into a parking garage and shifts the car into park, I hand it to him.

"Mom, Chase, and me." It's not an answer to his question, but I need a few more seconds to get my thoughts together.

Matteo runs his thumb over the corner, a small smile lighting his face. "You were very cute."

"Wow, is that your first time using that word? Good job," I tease. "And am I no longer cute?"

He hands the photo back. "I would not describe you as cute so much as…incredible. Stunning. Jaw-droppingly beautiful. Un tesoro."

"Oh." I fold it up and put it back into my wallet, face warm. "Thank you," I whisper.

I still haven't answered the looming question, but Matteo simply grabs the food. "Ready to go up?"

"Wait," I blurt out. "It's…I have this debt calculator that hangs over my head. Since I was, I don't know, eight or nine. It's a constant reminder of all that I owe the many people in my life. I refuse to become indebted to anyone else, because I don't even know how I'll pay back the people I already owe." Like the Wards. And the members of our community in Tampa. And the girls.

"Delilah…"

"After Mom left, we figured out how to get by. *I* figured out how to get by. I made sure we kept getting payments from the state. That Dad was presentable when he needed to be. I made money for the family when Dad was out of commission, and I cooked and cleaned up after Chase and the twins, even with school.

"I've been taking care of us for years, and I can continue to do so for a few more. I don't like accepting charity from anyone, even if it's only a meal. I've worked hard to get to where I am—to get to a point where I can almost comfortably afford living rather than scrounging two pennies together and practically begging at the grocery store." I swallow. "That helplessness, that feeling like it could all be gone in a moment and that I won't be able to take care of my siblings, it's what drives me. I'm so thankful and forever indebted to everyone who has helped me, but if my family is struggling, it's going to be *me* that pulls us out of it now."

I know I sound too proud for someone in my situation, but it's *because* of my situation and all that I've built that I *am* proud. My siblings have nutritious food instead of ramen and cereal, smart phones so they don't have to memorize numbers and borrow from others, a working TV instead of the beat-up one I had growing up that functioned twenty percent of the time. They have social lives and friends they relate to because I've been able to ease their suffering. So, no, I am not and will never again be a charity case for someone else, not after all we've been through.

Matteo steps out of the car and walks to my side. He bends down to plant a firm kiss to my lips, then helps me out of the car, wrapping my hand in his. "Thank you for dinner, then."

It's only after we get into his apartment, our food wrappers on the coffee table, an action movie on and a blanket around my perpetually cold legs, that he pulls me into his lap, my side pressed to his chest.

Brushing hair from my face, he whispers against my temple, "I've never met anyone like you. Without a shadow of a doubt, you are the strongest person I have ever known." He squeezes me. "But being strong and accepting help aren't mutually exclusive. Someday, soon I hope, your siblings are going to be out of school and find jobs of their own. The work ethic you're showing them will help them become independent adults. That said, they also need to see that it's important to take care of themselves."

Hazel's "It would be nice to feel like an equal instead of an obligation" ricochets through my head.

What good will I be to them then? It's a thought I've kept a hold on until recently. Will they still need me once they become independent? It was easy to ignore when it was years away, but the thought of it right now…

"Can we talk about something else?"

"Of course. Do you want to stay the night?" He checks the clock on the wall. "If so, we should probably get ready for bed."

I note the time and nod. There are lots of reasons for me to say no, to end this before it snowballs into something more, but much like the feelings I'm wrestling about letting my siblings free, I bury them.

I fall asleep with little encouragement, nestled in the comfort of Matteo's arms, where it's easy to pretend all my problems are nonexistent.

THE NEXT MORNING, BEFORE THE SUN BEGINS ITS ASCENT, I wake in a panic. All the concerns I tried to stash away are back with a vengeance. Particularly the ones that relate to us and this fragile relationship.

A relationship built on need; my need to have another stream of income, his need to have sponsors and countrymen see that he's not "Matteo the Malignant Narcissist." Us doing whatever this is, blurring lines that should remain unblurred…More than likely, it's going to lead to issues on court.

Whatever feelings I might have for him, I can't jeopardize the little stability I could bring my family. Chase needs to get it together and transfer to a better school, and I need to make sure we have the funds to do that. A cursory glance around Matteo's luxurious apartment—elegant, spacious, lots of light with panoramic views and pieces of furniture that each cost more than my rent—tells me money doesn't matter as much to him.

I have far more to lose.

Plus, my sponsorship isn't forever. If I want to keep Stratosphere interested in me, I need to be winning. And that means I can't let this be a distraction.

I leave without waking him, the pressure of my determination sitting heavily on my chest.

sixteen

SAHAR'S BAD BERLIN BAGELS

SAHAR

Delilah, do you have something you want to tell us?

MAYA

Pleaseeeee I'm desperate for gossip

SAHAR

Dellllll

NIC

Sahar you snake.

SAHAR

Hehe

HARPER

No worries if you don't want to talk about it yet! Tell us when you're ready!

SAHAR

Just tell us — was it as big as his energy makes it seem?

T hings are weird.

To be fair to Matteo, I'm sure it's mostly my fault. Monday was our singles day, so I trained with Nic—who has yet to ask me about the situation despite the group chat going off with questions (almost certainly brought on because she told on me). I saw him during strength and conditioning that afternoon, but I was able to prevent a conversation by surrounding myself with the girls—who made it very clear they want details soon. But it's also not like he's made much of an effort.

During practice Tuesday, Matteo wasn't particularly happy, and every time he made a mistake, he glared at his racket. Every time I made a mistake, he barely looked at me. The pride and fondness that always seem to slip across his features when we play together, even when I mess up on the court, were gone, and pretending it didn't hurt was a fool's errand.

Wednesday was more of the same. Singles training with Sahar, where I deflected question after question, then insulated conditioning.

Today, after my three-mile walk and physio, the time I've been taking to find the words to tell the girls is at an end. They accost me while they're trying on clothes at a boutique, and from the vaguely inquisitive look on Nic's face, the subtle excitement on Harper's, and the fake anger on Sahar's, I know it's time to come clean.

Sahar's honey-brown eyes flash with mischief as they meet mine in the dressing room mirror, a cowl-neck red dress draped across her body, tanned shoulders and legs on display. Her thick black hair is tied back into a ponytail, perfectly manicured eyebrows raised. "Nic tells us you had a friend over Sunday night."

"So much for keeping me out of it," Nic mutters, glaring down at a pair of jeans she's trying on. Her navy top makes her gray eyes appear darker, and she pulls her chestnut-brown hair away from her face, inspecting her outfit.

"What was I supposed to say? 'I was outside your apartment all night'?" Sahar replies.

Harper giggles, tucking a strand of dark brown hair behind her ear, still in the floral tennis dress she threw on after physio. Piles of clothes she wants us all to try on are slung over her tan arms. The dressing room is barely big enough for the four of us, and I'm glad I'm seated on the small stoop in the corner, watching them instead of trying clothes on.

"So?" Harper prompts me.

"What if I told you he was only over to discuss strategy?"

It's quiet for a beat, the three of them exchanging looks. Harper is the first to recover. "Oh! That's cool. How is that going?"

Sahar crosses her arms and interjects before I can figure out if I want to continue my deceit, "You are *so* lying. You were wearing *his* shirt and no pants and your hair was very telling."

"Sahar!" Nic grinds out, and I shoot her a disbelieving look.

"You told them everything?"

"I was asking them whether they thought I should bring it up. I wanted advice in case you needed it." She cuts a glare I wouldn't want to be on the receiving end of to Sahar, but Sahar's claws are just as sharp, and she waves Nic off.

"Del, if I don't get details soon, I'm going to assume it was the craziest, kinkiest night of your life."

I snort. "Okay, fine. Matteo came upstairs."

Sahar claps once. "Austin *and* Noah owe me. They were so wrong on the timing." Harper bumps her with her hip, and Sahar waves a hand. "Sorry, sorry. Was he generous? Did he make you come?"

My eyes widen, glancing under the other stalls.

Laughing, Sahar remarks, "Oh, please. It's not like he could be in here."

Realizing she's right, I nod somberly. "Twice."

"Uh-oh," she says, frowning. "That is not the positivity I was expecting from you, Del."

"Not that you're expected to be positive all the time," Harper reassures me, looping her arm through mine and pulling me to stand. "What did that tone mean? Are you regretting it?"

Spinning a bracelet Hazel made me years ago, I shake my head. "There's a lot for me to lose right now. My new Strato deal is proof I'm moving in the right direction, but in order to get that bonus, I have to make it deep into the draw. And if I want to keep the contract after, I need to keep winning. I'm not sure it makes sense for us to be anything, at least not right now. Not while we're prepping for Aussie. What if something goes wrong? He's doing fine, he'll *be* fine. But I don't know how that'll impact my season." And the last thing I want is to let someone else alter my year.

"Did he say he wanted to be more?" Nic asks.

Shoving away the fact that he's made no attempts to talk to me, I reply, "No, but I know I have feelings for him. Hooking up without knowing where we are is a bad idea." I mean, *god*, he's only the fourth man I've ever been with. Hooking up with *anyone* isn't my MO.

Sahar pulls the dress off and drops another in a different color over herself. "What does that mean for mixed? How have things been?"

"Not great." I pause and think about how terrible Tuesday's practice went. The dread I feel about how our practice tomorrow will go. "Really bad, actually. It's like when we first started playing together and knew nothing about each other, except…" I trail off.

"Except now he's been inside you and you've seen every part of his body." Sahar chuckles at her own joke.

"Right."

After we agree Sahar should choose the red dress, the jeans look good on Nic, and Harper doles out the choices she's made for each of us, including a pretty dress and a pair of white linen pants she hands to me, Sahar asks, "So, you like him? It's not just that he's ridiculously hot? Or that he's ridiculously mean?" She moans. "I bet he was *so* mean in *such* a good way."

"Sahar!" She laughs, pulling me into her body and folding herself across my shoulders, head tucked against my neck. "And that's the thing. He's not mean." We shift around so I can pull on the pants Harper handed me. "He's a sweetheart in many ways. Getting to know him the last few weeks has shown me there's so much more to him than what we've all grown accustomed to seeing."

I sit again, analyzing the buildup of emotion in my chest. It's similar to what I felt when I left him at his apartment. "I don't know. Maybe that's crazy. But yeah. I really like him. A part of me is glad we'll get to keep doing this through January, but another part of me wants Austin to get better soon so I can stop playing with Matteo and see where things go."

Sahar glances behind her, meeting my eyes for real instead of through the mirror. "Do you think he feels the same way? I mean, when we played last week, I definitely thought so, but I haven't been around long enough to read that mysterious granite wall."

I think of the affectionate way he often gazes at me when I'm being silly on court. The way his fingers always seem to linger when he's touching me in innocuous ways, like when he's setting my gym bag along my shoulder or pushing my hair behind my ear. How he took care of me and my family when we had to drive to Tampa. Of pressed legs on leather couches in too-small rooms, of smiles shared during drills and practice matches, of high fives exchanged between points and hand brushes as tennis balls are passed back and forth.

Does he feel the same way? "It's possible."

"He'd be an idiot not to," Nic chimes in, checking if a dress Harper brought her is too short on her tall frame.

Her kind words make me smile, even more so because of how rare they are. "For now, we'll just try to get through the Australian Open. Maybe once Austin is healed up and ready to play again, we can revisit whatever it is we're feeling."

They nod. "One problem, though," Nic says. "How are you going to get back to normal on court with him?"

Blowing out a breath, I shrug. "Who knows. Keeping my teasing to a minimum and barely talking to him Tuesday was a bust, so I might act like nothing happened? Go back to how things were before?"

Nic's eyebrows pinch, and even Sahar seems unconvinced. "Something tells me that's not a good strategy."

"Does that same something tell you what *is* a good strategy?" I ask, praying someone has advice, not that any of us can say we're particularly ready to dole it out. I've never been in a real relationship. Nic uses men for what they can give her, same as they do her. Harper's relationship ended a while ago, and she hasn't seemed keen to jump back into anything. And Sahar...well, she and Noah have things they don't even know they need to work through.

I sigh when none of them provide me with an alternative. "Then pretending nothing happened it is. If that doesn't work by Tuesday, I'll try a new tactic until we get somewhere."

"I mean, you could talk to him," Harper offers. "It might be better than pretending he doesn't know what you look like naked."

"Alright, that'll be my last resort."

We share a laugh. On our way out of the boutique, the three of them with small paper bags containing the clothes they chose, Harper declares, "I think tonight's movie night should be girls only. Agree?" Three nods. Austin and Noah will live if they don't get to spend *one* movie night with us.

Though I feel like I just endured a slightly cruel and incredibly probing game of twenty questions, I'm glad I was able to talk to them. Hopefully I'll find clarity on how to approach the situation with Matteo.

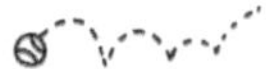

I WAS DELUDING MYSELF. NO CLARITY WAS FOUND. AND pretending nothing happened did not, in fact, work out. Friday's practice went as horribly as Tuesday's. Matteo was more withdrawn than usual, hardly speaking to me, and while I don't know Italian, I picked up on the frustration between him, Alessio, and Francesca the couple of times an argument broke out.

I didn't want to ask what about.

Even Eli appeared concerned when he sat courtside, though his words of encouragement kept ringing out no matter how we faltered.

Drills and court work went on for eons, and game strategy was no better. As we left that evening, Matteo reached toward me, mouth opening. I thought he'd offer to walk me home, but he just shook his head and walked away.

It was for the best, and yet my heart sank like I'd made the biggest mistake of my life.

Saturday's practice match against Anya went surprisingly well for me. Maybe a fluke, or maybe I really am as good as Matteo likes to tell me I am.

When Tuesday evening's mixed game strategy finally rolls around and we're beside each other on the couch, careful not to touch anywhere, Francesca shuts the door and crosses her arms.

"I don't know what has gotten into the two of you, but you're playing so poorly, Alessio and I have nothing to strategize with. I don't know if you're resting on your laurels after you beat the Morozovs or if you've had a huge fight and can't stand to look at each other, but this isn't working. La pazienza è finita."

The patience is finished. Francesca's way of telling me to shape up.

Alessio nods beside her, and when she turns to him, he jumps in. "You two need to get your shit together. You were playing well before, but now, not so much. You'll be lucky if you get to the first round at this rate. Are you prepared for the embarrassment that comes with losing during qualifying?"

It's a rhetorical question, clearly, but it's made more obvious when he and Francesca leave the room dramatically, shutting the door behind themselves. I stand, stretching my legs and pacing the few steps back and forth in the room.

Harper was right. Pretending hasn't worked. My last resort is coming into play.

And as badly as I don't want to lose out on money

from the Aussie Open because we're blurring lines, I don't want to etch a new line in the sand so divisive that we can't work through it.

Decision made, I sigh. Right as I say, "We should talk," Matteo grumbles, "Let's get food."

I can't help but smile at him faintly. He doesn't mirror it, but his face softens, his eyebrows marginally less pinched.

I nod. "Lead the way."

seventeen

The walk to the players' restaurant is devoid of conversation, though I'm sure Matteo has a different reason than I do to stay quiet. I'm the one making things difficult, but I can't quite figure out the right thing to say.

We sit at a table away from the hustle and bustle of the dinner crowd. Our waiter, a young kid who probably trains at the junior academy here, takes our order like he'd rather be anywhere else—probably because he waits on top-ranked players daily. Once he's been gone for a few minutes and I realize Matteo won't be starting the conversation, I steeple my hands and set them on the table. "So…we're not playing very well."

Matteo shakes his head but doesn't respond.

I glance away. "I'm sorry I made things weird. I've never done this before."

"Done what? Sleep with your doubles partner?" he asks, and my heart settles a little at the dry amusement in his voice.

"That too." I look back at him. "But no. I've only been with three other people, and I never saw any of them again."

He's silent for a beat. Then, "I guess what I'm more interested in knowing is why it has to be like this. What are you afraid is going to happen if we continue?" He clears his throat. "Or are you not interested in me for more than what we did?"

"That's…that's not it."

I'm *terrified* of lots of things happening if we keep going. I'm scared of not having any money, of going hungry. The fear planted itself inside me a long time ago, rooted deeper than almost any other emotion I feel. I'm scared of not being able to make payments on my family's house. Of getting injured and losing my income. Of not being enough. Of losing someone *because* I'm not enough.

Matteo leans back, crossing his arms. His beard is longer than I've seen it, but still scruffy. I remember what it felt like against my stomach as he kissed down my body, and my blood hums. His damn hat is on backward, holding his thick curls back. I wish I could run my fingers through them again.

I shake the thought from my head and clear my throat. "I think a relationship while we're trying to win a tournament could get messy. And I have a lot more to lose than you do."

"Can I tell you what I think?" The way he says it, nothing good can come next. Our server drops off our food, and as soon as he walks away, Matteo lowers his voice. "I think you're scared of being left behind, same as me. Because everyone who was supposed to be there for you failed you. So you're pushing me away before I have a chance to hurt you."

I blink. "Sorry, did you get a psych degree while we were apart?" There's an unintentional bite to the words—a reaction to feeling raw and exposed. I laugh to cover it, but it's already out there.

"No, I just have a therapist who's been helping me work through my abandonment issues, and I see some of the same signs in you."

The anger I was feeling dissipates in a cloud of smoke. He's doing it again. Giving me a piece of himself so I don't feel alone.

Clarity comes like a rug being pulled out from beneath me. I'm rotating along an x-axis with no end in sight.

Of course he didn't talk to me much after I *left* him Monday morning. He probably took it as a sign that I was done with him. Worst of all, he's likely scared of leaving things unresolved after how suddenly he lost his mother, and I all but made sure it stayed that way.

"I'm sorry I left without talking to you."

Matteo bows his head, tossing his salad around. "It's alright." He gives me a small smile fraught with dejection. I get an almost undeniable urge to reach across the table and steady his hand, but I have no right.

"It's not." I thought I was so good at putting other people's feelings first. Now I'm not so sure.

"I knew you were a flight risk, Del. I just took my chances." That almost hurts more than the rest of it. He gave me a shot, and I disappointed him.

As we eat, I imagine what it would be like to be with Matteo. To get on the court during shared tournaments and know he's cheering me on from my box. Getting to sit in *his* box with Alessio, encouraging him when he gets down. Offseasons together, mixed doubles, all of it. He saw my family and he didn't run. He understands me on a level no one else has, including what tennis means to me. I want it, *us*, so badly.

But I want my siblings to be okay a little more.

"Do I—" He clears his throat. "Do I have a chance? Sometime in the future? You said a relationship while trying to win a tournament could get messy, but what about after? Once Austin is back?"

"Yes." No hesitation. There's no one else I see in my future. "Of course you do. It just can't be my focus right now. Let's get through Aussie and see what happens."

Our waiter returns, brandishing our checks, so Matteo doesn't have a chance to respond. I scramble to grab one of my cards and lay it next to Matteo's, letting the kid know we're paying separately. He eyes us but doesn't say anything.

"Is that…Does that sound good to you?" I ask Matteo hesitantly when our waiter walks away. "Seeing where things go later? I don't want it to be weird between us on court. That's what I care about right now."

Matteo's expression is contemplative, his fingers tapping against the table. "I'm okay with that."

"Should we go back to the pool and spill about our favorite tournament on the tour so we can get back to how things were before?"

He huffs a laugh. "If you want."

Our server sets the check back down, hands my card back, and does a bad job of whispering to me, "Sorry, but this card was declined. Do you have another that I can try?"

My chest crunches like an empty soda can. The walls of the restaurant are closing in on me. When my ears start ringing, I grip the card tightly, feeling it cut into my fingers.

"I'm...I—are you sure?"

He nods.

Suddenly, I'm eleven again. Dad has found the money stash Chase and I were trying to ration and decimated it. All we have left is the ramen we've been eating for weeks and cereal. Maybe a couple of bananas, but I try to save those for the twins. Mom is gone and has been for a few days. She may even be with Dad. Deep, unrelenting panic settles in as I wonder what I'll have to do to keep us alive. If it might be better if I just called CPS and let us be split up. But then I think about not having little Hazel and Finn and snap out of it.

The waiter clears his throat.

I'm not out of money. I know because I checked my personal accounts not more than a few hours ago. Still, the idea that any card of mine might decline sends me spiraling.

Matteo sets his card back down. "I got it."

"No, no. I can pay for myself," I say, and I hear the harsh tone, the words bitter on my tongue. I can afford dinner.

When it was only the four of us, I found a way. I played tennis on empty, exhausted and starving after practice despite Austin sometimes bringing me an extra lunch and snacks. When Mrs. Elliott brought over a casserole every once in a while, I made sure to stretch it properly so we stayed fed for days. I felt the weight of failure so heavy on my back that I hardly ate any of it myself, especially when paired with the guilt of knowing I'd eaten more than my siblings thanks to the Wards.

"I know you can," Matteo answers softly. "You'll get me back next time, okay?" He nods to the kid, who walks away with wide eyes, suddenly interested now that the dynamic at our table has shifted.

That same feeling of failure seeps into my bones as I open my banking app and find the checking account associated with the card. It's one I rarely use, tied to an account I set aside for Chase and the twins for food, amenities, car payments, and all the other stuff I don't always have time to pay myself. I must have grabbed it instead of my personal one.

Didn't I check this one the other day? We haven't had anything due since then. There shouldn't be anything I'm missing. And yet, there it is, account wiped, cash withdrawal after cash withdrawal.

"Del, it's all good. I don't want you to stress about dinner when it was my idea. You'll get me back," he reiterates.

"I'm not stressed," I snap. It's a blatant lie, and the disbelief in his pinched brows tells me he knows it.

My body flushes with embarrassment. Having Matteo see my family was hard. Having him see *this*, the despair of so much money gone without my knowledge and it coming out during this dinner with him; the humiliation sears behind my eyes, and I have to bite the insides of my cheeks to keep the emotions at bay.

I need to call Chase. "Excuse me," I stand, my chair toppling over.

"Tesoro, ple—"

"I'll be right back. Promise."

I'm dialing as I dash past tables of people who look vaguely familiar, wiping at my eyes preemptively. When I get out of the restaurant, I lean back against the clouded glass wall and slowly slide down until my butt hits the ground.

"Hello?"

"Chase? Are you free?" I regret asking immediately. "I just need a second."

He speaks to someone he's with. There's movement, and then the voices on the other side of the call quiet. "What's up?"

"Have you been withdrawing money from the linked account?" Usually if he's making big purchases, he asks me first. Like the car repairs and the house payment.

"Oh, yeah." Something in his voice makes me uncomfortable, but I can't figure out why. "Sorry about that. I forgot to ask. It's for tuition and books and stuff for next semester."

Ire spears through me, more so than usual when dealing with Chase. Once again, he's making it harder for me to help him. "Why didn't you tell me we were overdrawn on that account? My card was declined."

"Sorry. I figured you would deposit more soon."

I bite back the words "how would I know to deposit more when I don't know you need it?" and sigh.

"I'm sorry for not telling you. I'll do better. I promise."

His words feel less combative than usual. Genuinely apologetic.

Still, all I can hear is *"It would be nice to feel like an equal instead of an obligation."* I haven't wrapped my mind around the idea of them getting jobs yet, but a part of me wonders if it would help Chase understand the sacrifice it takes to live the way I have. Help him get it together.

But I trust that he's trying in school, and I want him to find what he's passionate about without the stress of work.

I peer out over the grass courts downstairs, lights still on for a few stragglers practicing after dark. "I need to know what you're doing with the money. Call me or text me when you need to make big purchases."

He makes a noise that sounds an awful lot like a scoff but says, "Yeah. Of course."

"Okay," I respond uneasily.

"Thanks. I have to go. Talk to you later."

"Talk to you later." The call disconnects before I can tell him I love him.

Matteo comes out, eyes searching before he finds me on the ground. There's clear concern on his face, but he doesn't crowd me, just helps me up and sets a hand on my waist.

"It's Chase. Says he needed it for school stuff."

Something like skepticism skips across Matteo's features, and it's mirrored in my brain. Why would Chase need to take the money out in cash to make the payments? Why not pay directly from the account?

"Is that common? Him taking money for school without asking?"

I shake my head. "Uh, no. This was a one-time thing.

He forgot to tell me." The words scratch somewhere in my brain, similar to the ones I thought when we picked him up at the bar. *A one-time thing.*

Matteo's jaw clenches, his thumb adding a little more pressure to the divot of my waist. It sends warmth pooling between my legs until he says, "We're all good here. I paid."

The happiness that burrowed in me at Matteo's touch is shoved to the side. I step a few feet to my right, pushing my hair behind both ears and glancing away from him. This panic reinforces the fact that I shouldn't be doing this right now, as badly as we both may want to. We need to get back to how things were before, quickly, because we only have ten days until we're wheels up on the way to different cities in Australia.

Matteo reads me like a book, his hands slipping into the pockets of his pants. "Let's get you home. We have a big match Friday, and I need to memorize your serving signals so I don't mess things up."

The joke breaks the tension, and I smile at him thankfully. "Once you get them down, I'll make some up for mid-match."

Matteo chuckles, leading me out of the building and toward the locker rooms so we can pick up our bags. "Give me an example."

I ponder for a second, then snap my fingers. "Like when I yell 'lemon,' that means you move up to the net too. And if I yell 'guava,' we swap sides."

"Are they all going to be fruits? Because that might get confusing."

"I'm open to suggestions, but I think we both know I'm more experienced in this arena."

He gives me that fond smile, and I'm more than grateful he knew I needed this teasing to feel like we were okay. Already, the dread is subsiding.

I know there are things to work on, both with the Chase situation and with our doubles, but I feel better.

eighteen

We're all extra sore Thursday after the hellish workout Aleksandr put us through yesterday. Just walking around the track for my three miles today has every muscle in my body screaming for me to lie down.

Going to physio might kill me, but at least we're having movie night again tonight.

Matteo is stretching by the bleachers, his head down. I may be a ways away, but I can tell he looks mouthwatering, even if he is only wearing a short gray T-shirt and black shorts. Things have mostly gone back to normal between us, though we won't practice together again until tomorrow's match. Our last one before we leave.

When he reaches up, a strip of his stomach appears, and I almost joke with Nic that he's wearing a slutty little T-shirt like the ones she hates to love on Aleksandr, but if I draw attention to the fact that I've been gawking, Sahar will tease me incessantly.

I'm too late though. I watch the moment Sahar sees him. She smiles in a way that tells me she's about to do something I would not approve of, then yells, "Matteo! Over here!"

He scans the four of us walking side by side, his eyes landing on me for a few seconds. No response.

"Sahar," I hiss. "Leave him alone."

"What? I haven't had many chances to talk to him, and if you like him as much as you said you did last week, we have to vet him."

Nic mutters something about high schoolers, and Harper smiles kindly. "She's right though. I would like to meet him, especially now that I know he's not as scary as I thought."

As we pass him, I wave him over. He jogs up beside us, Nic moving to my left so he can walk next to me on the right.

"Hi." I smile at him, hoping to convey an apology for my friends and whatever they're about to say.

"Hey," he answers quietly.

"This is Harper," I say, pointing. "And you've met Sahar and Nicola." They each say their versions of hello. I glance at him. "I thought you liked to swim on your off days."

"Too many people at the pool today," he grumbles. "Which is frustrating since swimming works best for me when I'm this sore." I can't help but beam at him talking to my friends with more-than-a-few-word responses. He returns it on a micro scale.

"Right?" Sahar interjects. "What the hell is up Aleksandr's ass?"

"He's trying to get us ready for the season," Harper responds.

Matteo's shoulder rises. "Yeah, I don't mind. I like being sore on off days."

"Feels like the day off is deserved," Nic mumbles, and Matteo nods in agreement.

We continue walking, debating the best conditioning drills until we near the end of our three miles. Right when I think I'm in the clear and that Matteo will get out of this unscathed, Sahar turns with that same smile from earlier.

"Del, did you invite him over tonight?"

He coughs, and I attempt a glare at my friend.

"Matteo, we're having our weekly movie night at Delilah and Nic's apartment. You should come! Austin and Noah will be there, if that entices you at all." She pauses, then laughs. "And Delilah, obviously."

Harper looks at me worriedly, like she thinks I'll be

upset. I'm more focused on Matteo though. I watch him out of the corner of my eye, but when that tells me nothing, I turn my head fully. He meets my gaze, as if awaiting my permission.

"It's up to you. No pressure if you don't feel like it, but we have fun."

I can feel Nic about to say something admonishing about Matteo and fun. Just as she opens her mouth, I smack her arm, and she lets out a quiet chuckle.

"Only if you're free!" Harper adds.

Matteo clears his throat. "Yeah, uh, yeah. I'm free. I'll be there."

Sahar pumps a fist in celebration, wiggling her eyebrows at me and mouthing a "you're welcome." When we finish a minute or so later, I tell the girls I'll be right behind them and continue along the track with Matteo.

"There's really no pressure if you don't feel like coming. It maybe didn't feel that way with four sets of eyes trained on you while you decided, but I totally understand if this is a lot." I wave my hand around me, the words coming out of my mouth faster than I can think.

"Do you want me there?"

"Yes!" I say, perhaps a hair too emphatically.

The right corner of his mouth tips up. "Then I'll be there. Should I bring something?"

"Nah. Harper handles snacks. She usually brings *way* too much, so there will be lots of options. If you don't like typical movie night foods like organic candy and popcorn and whatever other healthy unhealthy food she might bring, then maybe bring something you do like?"

Matteo's eyebrows pinch. "Are organic candy and popcorn standard movie food?"

"They are for her, and I can't complain. They're not terrible."

"Hmm. 'Not terrible.' Not sure how I feel about that, but I'll bring my organic trail mix in case."

I laugh. "You'll fit right in."

It's time to go, to say my goodbyes, but as we grow closer to the start of the tour and to weeks spent apart, I find myself wanting to linger, to squeeze out every last drop of our time together so I miss him less. At least that's what I hope will happen.

"Everything okay with your siblings? And the bank?" We haven't talked about what happened at dinner a couple of days ago, focused on tennis the few times we've spoken.

My shoulder rises. "I'm torn about them getting jobs, Chase in particular. It could be a good idea, for him at least, but then I think about the fact that I was the only one who got our parents' good years. That they should get as much of a childhood as they can while I'm able to pay for things for them." That same skepticism from Tuesday flashes across his face. This time, I ask, "What?"

"I don't know. Not my place."

"Speak your piece," I say with two hand flourishes.

His eyes cut to mine. "I know people like Chase. I *was* like Chase. Getting a job is absolutely the kind of responsibility he needs. And the twins, well, they're going to do what they want soon, if they haven't already."

I wince. "Maybe."

His hand brushes mine as we curve around a bend.

"You know, them making money doesn't equate to you being dispensable. Even if, somehow, they manage to make enough with their part-time jobs to pay for the house and car and other things, you're still their sister. You're still the person they can turn to when they need a listening ear or a shoulder to cry on."

"Do you really think that?" I ask quietly. "That they would look to me for emotional support if I stopped paying for things? That I would still be…needed?"

This time, his fingers slip between mine, briefly squeezing before they're gone. "How could they not?"

"It's not a role I've had for a long while now."

"So it might take some getting used to. But you've got years and years for that. And with them all in or about to be in college, there will be lots for them to tell you."

Bumping his shoulder with mine, I smile once more. "Hey, you're not so bad at this. I could see you being a motivational speaker or a life coach."

"That would go poorly."

"It absolutely would."

I notice the girls waiting outside the gate, so I say my goodbyes, thinking of all the things I'll need to clean before he comes over.

Trying *not* to think about the last time he was in my apartment.

✦ ⌁ ⌁ ✦

SHOTS FIRED

AUSTIN ADDED MATTEO TO THE CHAT.

AUSTIN

I'm told The Menace is joining us tonight, so it's only right he's included in the group chat

The Menace? You're one to talk

HARPER

Hi Matteo!

NOAH

Matteo! Glad we'll have more guys tonight

SAHAR

Oh please

MATTEO

Hello. Are you sure I can't bring anything?

Just yourself!

AUSTIN

If it helps, they never want me to bring anything either

NOAH

Oh brother

SAHAR

Enchiladas do not constitute good movie food, Austin

Choosing a movie is proving far too difficult a challenge. Austin and Nic want an action movie, Harper and I want a romcom, and Sahar and Noah want horror. I

can't imagine what Matteo will want when he shows up, but we've been scrolling through every streaming platform imaginable for what feels like hours, though it's probably only been half of one.

Our apartment is small, but I love hosting. I made up the blue L-shaped couch with cozy blankets and pillows. Noah, Sahar, and Harper sit on it now, since they were the first to arrive, and in front of them is the wooden coffee table. To the left and right, I built mini forts for Nic and me respectively, with lots more pillows and blankets. Austin lies on his deconstructed fort at my and Nic's feet, right in front of the coffee table. Scattered about the room are bags of organic candy, healthy chips, popcorn, and cans of flavored water and a prebiotic drink Harper is a huge fan of. She also brought boxes of strawberries and blueberries that we washed and have been passing around in big ceramic bowls.

"Just pick something," I groan at the same time Harper sighs, crossing her feet underneath her and setting her chin in her palm, her elbow resting on the arm of the couch. Her brown eyes close, and I bet she'll be the first of us to pass out.

Nic gets comfortable in her fort, pulling a blanket over her head and another over her legs so she's completely covered, laying a pillow against the foot of the couch and resting her head on it. I'm the only one standing because I'm too nervous about Matteo joining us to sit quite yet.

Noah grins. "Great, I'll pick for us."

Scoffing, Nic glances across the couch to where Noah is spread along the L, his head resting on Sahar's hip. "I say we vote out having coaches here. It feels like my precious free time is being watched and reported on."

Noah rolls his eyes, and Sahar smiles down at him. He, Sahar, and Harper have been friends since grade school, and while he takes being Sahar's coach very seriously, he's a good friend to all of us.

"Someone tell the ice queen she's being dramatic," he replies.

Nic throws a piece of chocolate at his head, and it ricochets off the couch arm and hits Sahar. "Ow!"

"Sorry. Line of fire." Nic looks back at the TV, where Noah has settled on the horror movie he and Sahar wanted. "How do we manage to do this every week? Next year, we need a system in place for this."

Austin, who is lying near Nic's feet across the length of the room, closer to the TV than he probably should be, nods sarcastically. "Okay, Nic. We'll keep a document with all our movie recommendations, and we'll randomize it for the four or five movie nights we have next year."

Nic kicks him lightly.

"And you know what?" Austin continues. "I'm the injured party here. I should be on the couch."

"Why do we do this *here* again?" Noah chimes in, sitting up. "Austin's apartment could easily fit all of us, and we wouldn't have to listen to him whine like a baby."

"Shut up," Austin responds, whining harder.

Sahar elbows Noah in the ribs hard, and he bends over, cursing. "It's tradition. This apartment is sacred."

"More like haunted," Austin mumbles.

Nic shoots up, abandoning her blankets to rip the remote from Noah. "Everyone shut the hell up. Our apartment is perfect because Delilah is blessed with the ability to find interesting and pretty décor for cheap or free. Let's figure out a number system so someone picks before Delilah's loverboy shows up."

We're all momentarily speechless. Nic rarely talks that much.

Finally, I say, "While I think we can stop with the nicknames, I agree that we need to figure this out and everyone needs to be on their best behavior." I stare pointedly between Austin, Sahar, and Noah; the former two look away, and the latter appears offended at the idea that he might embarrass me.

"You don't have to worry about me. If you'll remember, he was *my* doubles partner first," Austin says haughtily.

"I'm only weird about it because he's *doing* Delilah," Sahar adds.

Austin opens his mouth to respond, disgusted, but there's a knock at the door before he can speak. I stand straighter, taking one last cursory scan around the living room and adjusting my shirt.

When I open the door, Matteo stands there, absolutely devastating, his hair out of sorts, like his hand has been a steady presence through it. His beard is trimmed, and he's wearing a Stratosphere shirt and sweatpants, a bag of trail mix and three small lavender-colored flowers in his hand. I wonder if, somehow, he's realized it's my favorite color.

He takes in my outfit, and I'm suddenly embarrassed by my thrifted gray cotton shorts and my disturbingly faded Sabertooths football cropped T-shirt.

Holding out his bounty, he declares, "I know you told

me not to bring anything, but my mom always said not to go to anyone's house empty-handed." His eyes shift up to meet mine, and I read the earnestness in them. "Also, this building is *not* safe," he says worriedly. "Someone left a rock to hold the door open."

I shrug. "Eh, it's a nice neighborhood." Matteo looks mildly horrified, and I laugh, taking the bag of trail mix and the flowers, gently putting the stems between my thumb and forefinger. "And thank you. They're beautiful."

Matteo's eyes flick over to the group of people who have gone quiet watching us. Even Austin sticks his head around the hallway wall, a dumb smile on his face.

"Come in," I say, ushering him inside. I set the bag on the coffee table and gesture around the room. "You know everyone. Couch is full, but you can share with Austin or me." I point to the pile of blankets Austin is crawling back to in front of the coffee table and my little area off to the side of the L.

Matteo says his hellos while I put the three flowers on my bedside table, scarcely containing my smile when I realize it's the first time I've ever gotten flowers. When I come back into the living room, he's settling into my area.

"Matteo, do you have a preference for what we watch?" Noah asks.

Matteo nods at the TV, where the horror choice still sits, ready to be played. "I'm fine with this if that's what you all agreed on."

Sahar and Noah high five, and he says, "That's three votes. This movie wins."

Nic groans, reluctantly pressing play, and I flick the

lights off, snuggling under the blankets, careful not to get too close to Matteo.

The movie starts the way they always do—with a happy family. I whisper commentary to Matteo, things like, "There's no way that's their baby," and "I bet the husband is the first one to go." The first time I lean in, my hand lands right beside his, our pinkies touching. When he doesn't move away, I keep it there.

Either he also likes to talk through movies or he's humoring me. He leans in more, his lips nearly pressing to my ear when he whispers things like, "Creepy creaky barn with rusty hooks, I'm sure that won't come up again," and "Oh! You were right about the husband."

The room laughs at things that are meant to be scary, and by the halfway mark, the right side of my body is pressed to Matteo's left, his arm resting on the floor behind me.

At one point, when it *does* get scary and grotesque, I have to turn away, my forehead resting against his neck. He tenses for a moment, then wraps his arm around me, pulling me close.

A minute or so later, he whispers, "That part is over. You can watch now." But instead of looking at the TV, my eyes find his. I know I need to pull away, know that it's going to make things more complicated and difficult later if I don't stop, but I can't bring myself to care.

I like him. So much. I'm the obstacle in our path, and I'm flailing.

He was right—if my siblings want to get jobs, who am I to stop them? It would take some of the financial stress off my plate. I'd feel fine if my only income came from singles and my sponsorship because they could cover the rest. Getting deep in the Aussie mixed doubles draw wouldn't matter.

Keeping things professional and safe wouldn't matter.

My eyelids flutter shut, and I lean in, brushing his lips. Just as it turns into a kiss, my friends begin yelling at the screen and we jump apart.

"The sheriff? You have to be kidding me," someone, I think Sahar, yells.

"That's bullshit," Noah agrees.

"I'm so confused. I thought he was dead," Austin chimes in.

"He's clearly a zombie," Matteo deadpans. It's silent for a moment, questioning glances tossed around before the room breaks out into laughter.

I giggle, shocked that he ever believed he wasn't good at making friends. When our gazes clash again, he gives me a full, real smile, and I'm certain I've won in all the ways that matter.

nineteen

Once the movie finishes, Austin and Harper say their goodbyes while Noah walks a half-asleep Sahar out.

"Are you sure there's nothing we can do?" Harper mumbles sleepily.

I wave her off. "Stop that. Unless you want the rest of your snacks back, we've got it."

She hugs me again before squeezing my arms. "The snacks are a gift."

Austin and I hug. He turns to Matteo, exchanging a strange handshake and pats on the back before he finally hobbles his way out of the apartment on his crutches. I give Noah a side hug and smile lovingly at Sahar, who murmurs her goodbye.

My heart squeezes, knowing this is our last movie night of the year. Next Thursday is Christmas, which most of us will spend with our families, and the next day, we'll all be flying to Australia to train a few days ahead of tournaments.

The girls and I will see each other plenty in the next few months, and the Wards, Austin included, will be following me out there to cheer me on until he's ready to be back on the men's tour, but it won't be the same. No matter how many friends, no matter the team, the tour is isolating. I'll go days without more than a quick "hi" from the girls, a week or more without hearing from my siblings, and while I love Francesca and Eli, the offseason is the only time we get this—the contentedness of late nights where we're all falling asleep watching a movie less than half of us want to watch.

By the time I shut the door, Matteo has gathered bowls and glasses, walking them to the kitchen. Nic and I pick up the trash littering the coffee table and toss it before folding our extra blankets and putting them in the basket by the TV, pitching the extra pillows on top.

When we're done, surveying our work, my eyes land on her, and a nostalgia for a time we're currently in builds behind my eyes. She notices, giving me a small smile, and though she hates to, opens her arms for me.

I close the distance in seconds, flinging myself into her arms. "I can't believe the offseason is almost over," I whisper into her hair. And without doubles together, who knows what this season will look like for us?

"I know," she responds quietly, tightening her rigid grip almost imperceptibly, like she needs this as much as I do.

Sniffling, I say, "Every tournament we both play in, we have to have dinner at least once. And at least one hitting session." We pull away, and Nic nods, eyes averted. To break the tension, I add, "Even if you beat the heck out of me. No takebacks."

She lets out a watery laugh. When I peer at the doorway of the kitchen, Matteo is watching us with a small contemplative smile. He points to the front door. "I should go too."

If I was on an emotional precipice, I'm falling now. I should ask him to stay, but when I try, my tongue sticks to the roof of my mouth. Instead, I manage, "Oh, yeah. Let me…" I trail off, making sure Nic won't mind if I walk him out.

Reading my mind, she shoos us off. "Go, go. My mom will be calling any minute." She gives Matteo a quick wave. I don't know if it's a made-up excuse or if today is the day she gets her "weekly" call with her parents, which seem to come once a month, but either way, she'll want her privacy after the moment we shared.

Closing our front door, I fall into step beside Matteo. "You okay?" I ask him as he opens the door to the stairwell for me, his palm hovering near my back.

His eyes dart to mine. "What do you mean?"

"You seem like you're frowning more than usual." He's not, but with all the time we've spent together recently, I can read the subtle language of his body: the shoulders that are slumped only a millimeter or two; the movement of his hands in his pockets, like he wants to wring them but also doesn't want to draw attention to it.

Matteo doesn't answer immediately. He opens the door to the ground floor, guiding me toward the covered spot in the alley between our building and another, where I told him he could park.

"I've never had anything like this. A friend group that wants to spend all their free time together and see each other *outside* of tennis."

"I'm sorry." And I am. I wish we could've found each other sooner.

"No, that's…it was, *is*, my fault. You know how I am. Everyone does."

I frown, looking over my shoulder at him. "I know what everyone *claims* you're like, and I know *you*. Those are not the same."

He shrugs, and I stop abruptly, so much so that he runs into me. His hands land on my waist and stay when I turn to him.

"No, Matteo. I'm serious. Now that I know you, not a single headline I've read about you got it right."

The corner of his mouth tips up, though his eyebrows stay drawn. His thumb rubs circles at my waist. "Maybe so. But I *am* the reason I haven't had friendships like yours. I just didn't realize why until tonight."

"Why?"

He pulls me into the alley, then leans against his car, eyes resting on our shoes. "My mom…the day she died, she was on her way to get me. It was the first summer we didn't go back to Italy. I was upset about it. Threw a fit at tennis camp. I didn't want to be there, so I called her and asked her to pick me up."

My heart comes crashing up my esophagus, anticipating where he's going. I slip a hand into his.

"Some guy on his phone blew through a red light and T-boned her at an intersection a few blocks away. Sometimes I think I can hear the crash, but I'm not sure if that's my guilt or if it really happened like that."

"Oh, Matteo." With my other hand, I cup his cheek, my thumb smoothing over his stubble. "I'm so sorry."

"I blame myself, of course. How could I not? If I had finished out the day, she never would have been in that position."

I open my mouth, ready to defend him, but he continues, "Dad thought so too. Couldn't stand the sight of me, even if he tried to hide it. Sent me to live with my nonna. And I kept playing tennis because it reminded me of the joy on Mom's face when she watched me. I grew to love the game too, but..." He sighs. "I was angry. So angry. Felt it festering, worse every day. At first, it was just at myself, but then Dad got remarried, had a couple more kids, acted like nothing happened, and then that rage grew to fill a never-ending pit inside me. I became volatile on court. Off court too. I pushed everyone away, for years. It wasn't until this season that I decided to do something about it."

"What'd you do?" I murmur.

"Started therapy." He shrugs like it's nothing. "Thought it was helping. Then, six weeks ago, my dad reached out, and it all came back."

Little pieces fall into place. His surlier-than-usual demeanor when he first began training at the facility. Him being late to our first practice together, and the cloud that seemed to hang over him the next time.

Like a broken record, I say again, "I'm so sorry, Matteo. I'm sorry that you lost your mother and that you or anyone else blamed you for it when you were just a kid.

It was *not* your fault. The only person to blame is the person who drove through the light." He opens his mouth, but I shake my head, my thumb swiping along his bottom lip. "It was *not* your fault. Maybe you dealt with the pain in a different way than some. Nobody can fault you for that. Even so, you've come so far so quickly. You're nothing like you have been in past seasons, and it's clear in every practice."

Matteo lets out a deep breath, rubbing his chest with two knuckles. "I just don't understand why he's reaching out now."

"He could be having his own revelations." I know the next thing I say may drive him away, but if our roles were reversed, I'd want him to say it. "I wish I had a parent who apologized for their mistakes. Made an effort to be better, even if it's years later," I whisper gently. Truth be told, I'm still the eight-year-old waiting by the phone. Waiting for my mom to come back. Waiting for my dad to come back to the man I remember.

Matteo scoffs but doesn't push away from me like I thought he would. "Even if it's to be better for someone else? Another wife and his other children? I wasn't enough for him to be better?"

Tears bite the edges of my vision. He's right. Our situations are not the same and neither are we. "Of course you are. *He* wasn't enough. And if you never want to speak to him again, you have every right to that."

His arms snake around my back, pressing me against his muscular body. "I wonder what life would have been like had I treated people better. If I would have had friends like yours. I wish I'd matured earlier, realized that none of what I was doing made me feel any better."

I sink into his embrace like it's quicksand, desperate to make him feel as comforted as he's made me feel these past few weeks. "Everyone's timeline for grief is different. Same for their reaction to it. So yeah, maybe it took you longer than some, but it probably took you less time than others. And maybe anger isn't every person's go-to in this situation, but it's what you felt. There's nothing wrong with that. Making mistakes is the human condition. That doesn't mean *you* are a mistake. You're owning up to yours." I tighten my arms around him. "Give yourself grace. Building friendships isn't something that only people of a certain age can do. You can make friends until the day you die if you want. And you're welcome to any and all of mine."

"How do you do it?" he murmurs.

"Do what? Make friends?"

"Be so happy and kind all the time." Quieter, he says, "So perfect."

I laugh, pulling back enough that I can see his face. "I'm far from perfect." He's not going to accept that answer, clear by the tilt of his head. I look away. "It's easier, I guess. I know many other people have had hard lives too. Even on the days I can't be kind to myself, I can be kind to others." Meeting his eyes again, I finish, "The least I can do is give others grace on their worst days."

His lips twitch up, and something tender slips into his eyes. "Your outlook on life is exactly why I wanted to play with you. Sure, I need to rehab my image so I don't lose out on sponsorships and other opportunities, but after meeting you this season and seeing how radiant you are—how easily you bring others into conversations and put them at ease—I knew I had to learn from you. My therapist called it a Band-Aid on a bullet hole but…" He raises a shoulder, laughing self-deprecatingly. "She's right, obviously. I haven't magically become someone new. I have a lot to work through, but sometimes, when I'm with you, I feel like I *am* capable of being someone new. Someone better."

"I hope you don't change too much. I like you quite a bit exactly as you are." He chuckles, though I haven't made a joke. "I'm serious," I insist.

Matteo's eyes drop to my lips, and it's a reminder of what we started upstairs. My body flushes.

He straightens, dropping his hands from around me. "I shouldn't have kissed you before you were ready. I'm sorry."

"Don't be. I…I've been wanting to do that since the morning I left."

A frustrated groan escapes him, his hand running through his hair. "Tesoro, please. You can't say things like that to me." The shadows cast by the streetlamp accentuate the torment, the absolute devastation in his eyes, and I can't take it.

My fingers find his T-shirt, fisting the fabric and pulling us back together. Our lips clash, desperation clinging heavily to the air around us. He flips us so my back is pressed to the car, his hand bunching my hair, pulling my head back enough for him to kiss along my jaw hungrily, the scrape of his beard against my skin soothed by his soft lips.

His other hand blazes a trail up and down my side. Right when I'm ready to drag him into his car, he pulls away, eyes wild. "I—" He pants. "I don't want to make your life any more difficult than it is. You said we should wait until after Austin is back, and I can do that for you."

But he doesn't look like he can do that. And I don't *feel* like I can do it. "I don't care about that right now."

This time, it's him surging forward as soon as the last word is out of my mouth. His kiss is demanding, like he's terrified this could be his last chance. Like I'll change my mind. When he lifts me, my legs wrapping around him, I feel him hard against my center, the pressure almost unbearable. His lips light a path down my jaw again, to my throat, heat bursting like fireworks all over my body in anticipation.

"Upstairs or mine?" he asks gruffly against my collarbone.

I hardly register the question, upping the friction until my fingers curl into his shoulders, desperate to get him inside me. When the words come again, stuttered and unsure, I knock a knuckle against his car.

Matteo pulls back, scanning my face until he's found whatever it is he's searching for. He rips the door to the driver's side open, tugging me inside after him so I land in his lap, straddling him. The moment I feel him pressed against me again, the desperation is back with a vengeance.

He says something in Italian that sounds an awful lot like he's swearing before placing a hand on my face, his lips back on mine. His other hand settles on my hip, guiding me so I'm grinding against him.

"Clothes. There's too many." I pant.

It's a mad dash to rip off my shorts and underwear while keeping every point of contact that we can. As he reclines his seat, I help him out of his pants and boxer briefs, rubbing the bead of precum dripping from his tip.

He groans. "Are you sure? I don't want you to"—he exhales choppily when I move my hand lower, pushing up on my knees and swiping him through my arousal—"regret this like last time."

I shift, leaning down to kiss him gently, trailing kisses down his jaw to whisper beside his ear, "I never said I regretted it. And I'm not going to leave this time. Do you have a condom?"

Matteo reaches blindly toward his center console. He unlatches it and I find one, ripping it open and rolling it on him. Just as I'm positioning myself over him, he grips my hip. "Come sit on my face."

"There is no way we're going to be able to do that," I say, gesturing at the limited space. It's already cramped in here; I wouldn't be able to bend that way.

His eyes narrow at my disobedience, but he puts a hand below my mouth. "Spit." The thrill of being told what to do zips through my blood, and I listen, gasping when he moves his hand down to cup me. "I'll have to make sure you're ready a different way," he states, then waits for my nod to circle my clit expertly.

It only takes a few moments before I'm whimpering, and he takes the sign to move to where I'm slick with need.

"*Fuck*," he moans throatily. "You liked rubbing on my cock, didn't you?"

Another nod.

That wicked smirk pulls at his lips. "You drive me to distraction all the time in those fucking dresses of yours. It's my turn to do the same for you." My head rolls back as he sinks a finger in, my heartbeat picking up. Lighting zings at the base of my spine, building hotter and hotter until I'm sure something as simple as a word will set me off.

Except, he takes his fingers out right before I come. I pout. Matteo uses his thumb to pull my bottom lip down gently. "I want the first time you come tonight to be around my cock. That okay?"

"I didn't take you for a tease, Matteo Corsi."

In less than a second, he's guided my hips to his, notching himself inside of me, pushing in slowly. My body bends to his touch, sinking lower and lower until I can feel every inch of him. "Delilah," he whispers, a slight hitch in his voice. "Look at you."

Our movements are slow at first, but the moment I adjust to him, it turns passionate and frenzied again, our kisses sporadic and messy.

"You take me so good, tesorino."

That first wave crests, my vision flushing black around the edges. "Matteo, I'm going t—"

The calloused pads of his fingers grip my chin carefully, forcing my eyes to meet his. "Touch yourself."

He hits the perfect spot just as I brush my fingers over my clit and shatter, losing all rhythm as I come. "*Matteo.*"

Picking up the slack, Matteo whispers praises and pulls my body over his so he can kiss me properly, his hands on my hips while he drills into me faster and faster. Moments later, his rhythm turns to a staccato.

"Delilah," he whispers against my chest, completely undone and entirely out of control.

When we catch our breath a few minutes later, we readjust, him lying on his back, me on my side with his arm wrapped around me. "I will beg on my hands and knees for you to come home with me," he murmurs into the hazy silence, finger swiping at a fogged-up window.

Beaming, I say, "As much as I would love to see that, there's no need." My fingers trace a lazy pattern on his chest. "I hoped you'd ask."

Us existing as we are right now is proof we can work through any issues that might arise and impact our tennis. We already have.

I'm done fighting this. If a week is all we have together before the season begins, I'm going to make the most of it.

twenty

I wish I could say travel gets easier with time, but after spending two months at home, the thought of the long trip to Brisbane makes my stomach turn. At least I'll have Nic with me for the first tournament of the season. Harper and Sahar are going to Adelaide, which begins in a week and a half and ends right before the Australian Open. I'm not a fan of starting a tournament the day after arriving, especially in a different hemisphere, but Francesca and I want to make sure I have a week off before the slam in Melbourne.

Anya, Matteo, and a few other players from the facility, along with our teams, are booked on the same flight to Dubai, where we'll go our separate ways. I've tried not to think too hard about not seeing Matteo for a couple of weeks, but it's the nature of this beast and we knew it was coming.

We've spent every night together for the past week since movie night, sensing the end of whatever phase of our lives we were in.

That first night, we went to his apartment, and when I pointed out that it is, in fact, in the opposite direction of mine, he said, "I thought that was obvious. I thought everything about how I feel about you was obvious," which in turn led to me jumping his bones for a second time that night.

Knowing all his family has either passed or is estranged, I invited him to spend a couple of days with me and my siblings. I couldn't imagine him by himself, and having him by my side in Tampa felt exactly right.

My family has never really celebrated Christmas with the big tree and lights. For as long as I can remember, our gifts came in the form of the neighbors chipping in to make sure we were well-fed, garage and attics pillaged to find us hand-me-downs. Sometimes, if we were lucky, Dad would sober up and bring us a treat from a bakery or a meal from a nearby fast-food place.

This year, much of our time in Tampa was spent on the couch watching reality TV with Hazel and helping Finn prep for a private lift with a scout from his dream school. Chase was standoffish, making an occasional appearance, but I couldn't be sure if that was because of me or the seemingly strained dynamic between him and Hazel—one she explained away by saying he'd said some rude things to her that she wasn't ready to forgive.

During Christmas Eve dinner two nights ago, with Matteo's hand squeezing mine beneath the table, I let my siblings know I have no issue with them getting part-time jobs as long as it doesn't impact school and Finn's football.

Dad showed up after dinner, barreling through the front door with a handle of vodka in one hand and a beer in the other. Just like old times. But the next day, in what I can only describe as a Christmas miracle, we all sat down for dinner. Dad seemed sober enough, and it was the first time, maybe ever, that we ate a meal together.

When Matteo and I got back from Tampa, we spent a few hours apart, packing and getting ready to be away from home for months. I spent the night at his apartment, though we didn't talk about what we're going to do during the season, and now that we're on our way to the season opener, I'm not sure we will. I hope I can handle whatever that means for us.

I find him as he gets his bags checked. As a group, we don't scream *understated* and *normal,* but I'm not sure people in this airport would recognize any of us besides maybe Anya and Matteo.

When he finishes, Matteo turns, eyes zeroing in on me waiting for him. He gives me his best imitation of a smile, though it looks more like a grimace, and I suspect he's not a big fan of flying either. Or maybe he'll just miss me as much as I'll miss him.

The thought makes me beam despite the cracking in my chest.

"It'll be weird not traveling with Austin. I saw him so often between tournaments and at airports," he says as he reaches me. We walk side by side, approaching the security line.

The Wards decided to hang back for a week or so since Austin won't be training. They'll join me in Melbourne, sitting in my box for each tournament until Austin is ready to get back on tour. I told them I didn't want them to spend so much money to come see me, that

I'd be happy to know they're watching from home, but they insisted.

"He'll be back in no time. He seems to be throwing himself into PT."

Matteo nods. We reach the back of the security line right as my phone rings. Finn's name flashes across the screen, and I frown, answering immediately.

"Finn? You okay?"

"Uh, yes and no. You know the private lift I have today?"

"Yeah…"

"Chase was driving me, and he…" Finn sighs. "I didn't realize he'd had a drink. I don't know when. He seemed sober or I would've insisted on driving."

My stomach sinks, crashing through the rest of my organs, so uncomfortable, I yearn for the travel churning I experienced before this call. Worst-case scenarios flash through my mind. Chase dead in a ditch, Finn injured. "What happened, Finn?"

"He tried to avoid a pothole and swerved too hard. Car scraped against the median wall. The front is messed up, and the sideview mirror is gone. It's drivable—the airbags didn't even deploy. I moved it to a side street, but I have to get going. I'm going to call a rideshare. I just…I don't want to leave him alone, and I'm not sure Hazel's going to be willing or able to come get him. They're not in a great place right now, and she doesn't have a car," he says, the words coming out of his mouth so fast, I can hardly process them.

Overhead, a final call for passengers of a flight to Los Angeles rings out. A couple runs past us, suitcases in tow.

"Is he okay? Are you?"

"Yeah, I'm fine. He seems alright, if not a little shocked. He's sitting on the curb with his head in his hands."

I sigh. At least they're safe. My mind's running faster than a bullet train trying to come up with a solution that doesn't involve me picking him up. If I screw up my training schedule for the Australian swing, I could lose all the money we're going to need right now, especially if the car needs repairs and with my plans to buy the twins a used car as a late Christmas present.

A balding man in a sweatsuit taps my shoulder impatiently and gestures for me to move forward. Smiling the best I can, I step out of his way so he can move ahead, scarcely conceptualizing the distance my group has moved through the maze of retractable stanchions.

"Are you in a busy area?" I ask Finn.

"Not really. I don't think anyone saw it, and like I said, the car is drivable, I just don't think Chase should be driving." When I don't answer immediately, his tone turns more panicked. "Should I leave him? I don't know what to do. I'm worried if I don't show or I'm late, I'll lose this chance. This is my top pick."

"I know."

Finn is so excited for this opportunity. The scout watched one of his teammates at the last game of the year a couple of weeks ago, and after seeing Finn play, he decided he wanted to get Finn in as soon as possible too, which is why it was scheduled during the holidays. I can't let him lose this shot.

I'm going to have to go back.

"Fuck," I breathe. Sweatsuit man has hurtled past my friends—who stopped ahead and now watch me with concern—as has another couple, who passed me while I was distracted. If I weren't so wrapped up in this call, I might have been embarrassed.

I'm simultaneously weightless and stapled to the ground, my head dizzy like static. "Dad's too drunk?"

"Yeah."

Rubbing my forehead, I say, "Alright. Can you put Chase on for a second?"

There's movement and then Finn's muffled voice.

"Hello?" Chase answers with the foresight to sound at least a little contrite.

"Are you injured anywhere?" I ask again, just to be sure.

"No. I'm okay. Look, I know you're mad—"

"Mad doesn't even begin to cover it."

"But Dad told me I was good to go. I was hesitant, but Dad said it'd been long enough and that I'd be fine."

I want to yell at him. Shake him until he sees how ridiculous it is that he's taking advice from a man who never drinks unless it's to the point that he can't see straight. A man who has at *least* one DUI.

Knowing I won't be able to stomach this conversation from miles away, I ask, "Are there any restaurants nearby that you can walk to? Somewhere you can safely stay until I get to you?"

There's a pause while he searches. Then, "Yeah."

"Then go there and *stay* there. Do not drive the car anywhere and stay out of any more trouble. Do you understand me?"

He mumbles a yes, and then the phone is handed back to Finn.

"He's walking there now. I'll make sure he gets inside and then call the rideshare, if that's alright."

"Of course. Send me the location and I'll get him."

"I'm really sorry to do this."

"Don't be. It's not your fault. I love you. Kick ass and stay safe."

Finn sighs with what sounds like relief, but I'm a long way from joining him there. "Thank you. I love you, too."

When I finally glance up again, the girls have pushed away from the group and toward me. "Del?" Harper asks quietly, her eyebrows pinched. Nic's eyes flick over my face, analyzing. Sahar looks ready to fight.

My vision swims for a second before I slam my teeth together onto the scars on the insides of my cheeks, willing the tears away. I smile at them. "All good! I'm going to have to meet you guys there. Where did Matteo go?" Trying not to feel disappointed that I'm losing a few more hours with him before we have to part, I scan our party.

Sahar points toward security. "He went to get your bags unchecked."

My heart is in a vice, an unfamiliar warmth wrapping tightly around it. I nod, giving them each hugs and texting Francesca. She was running behind anyway, so she'll likely hang back until I'm ready to fly out again. Whenever that may be.

I *just* loosened the reins with my siblings, and this feels like an instantaneous sign that I've screwed up colossally by doing so.

I walk quickly toward Matteo. "We won't allow bags to

fly without the passenger on board, sir, but I cannot get them for you right now. They're en route to the plane and will have to be stopped there," the woman behind the counter says to him.

"I will go down there myself to get them," Matteo grinds out, and her eyes practically pop out of her head like a cartoon.

"Uh…let me see what I can do." Her heels clack as she disappears through a door, and a few seconds later, the conveyor belt stops moving.

"Matteo, it's okay," I say breathlessly. "They'll keep them here, and I'll get them when I eventually fly out."

"We just dropped our stuff." He turns to me, and I take in the crease in his brow. Matteo runs a hand over my hair, dropping his forehead to mine. "They'll be able to get our bags."

I step back. "Our?" Shaking my head, I take another step back. "No, no, no. Matteo, no! You've helped me so much already; you don't need to come with me."

"I am *not* letting you go home alone right now."

"You don't even know what happened!"

"I don't need to. I know it's serious."

I swallow over the tennis ball in my throat, blinking a few times to clear my eyes again. "Matteo, you need to get to Melbourne to train. You have to be ready for Aussie." The men have no big tournaments before the Australian Open, but many are going early to get used to the summer heat.

"I'll be fine. It's over two weeks away. We could stay through the new year and still have plenty of time." Well, I can't. There's no way I'll play Brisbane at this rate.

My shoulders slump, knowing he's far more stubborn than I am. "I don't want people to have to help me deal with my family constantly. I can handle it." But my words are so quiet, so defeated, they don't carry much weight.

Matteo pulls me into his body, his chin resting on my head. "I know you can, tesorino. But you don't have to."

WHEN WE GET TO THE RUN-DOWN DINER, I JUMP OUT AND race to the door. Too-fried eggs, burnt coffee, and vinyl welcome me as I step inside, quiet conversation steady despite the panic and rage I'm positive I'm not hiding well. After a moment, I see him in a cracked red booth by a window, head resting on a table beside a steaming mug.

"Chase," I snap. Despite my anger, I give him a once over to double check that he was telling the truth. He lifts his head, and it feels like the bar all over again, except this time, he appears entirely sober. Standing before I reach him, he waves at a waitress and walks up to me.

I don't want to do this here, so I turn on my heel and walk out. I spent the whole drive to Tampa trying to figure out what I wanted to say, and yet now that I'm here, the script has disappeared.

Matteo, who was leaning against his car, stands quickly when we exit, menacing glare fixed on Chase. "I'll drive the SUV. You take him in my car."

"Are you sure?" I ask, glancing at where the damaged car sits on the shoulder of a minor side street.

"Absolutely." We play a game of musical keys,

Matteo's glare growing more thunderous when he gets close to my brother.

"Chase, get in." My voice brooks no alternative, no room for argument, and he listens, head bowed. I grab Matteo's hand, giving it a reassuring squeeze. "Thank you," I breathe. I don't know which of the many things I'm thanking him for—driving me here, making sure I take the safer car home, or any combination of the hundreds of little things he's done for me since we started playing together—and he doesn't seem to need any clarification.

He kisses my temple, grumbling, "Drive safe. I'll be right behind you."

Once he gets to the beat-up Saturn, I slump into his car, adjusting the settings until I'm comfortable. For a few moments, the drive is silent.

"We can't keep doing this, Chase," I declare finally when we get on the highway. When he doesn't answer, it drenches my growing ire in gasoline, and his prolonged sigh, like I'm in the wrong, lights the match. "Do you not understand what just happened? Not only did you do one of the dumbest things possible, you brought Finn into it. That is *unacceptable*."

"I didn't…" He sighs again, this time less angrily. "I didn't mean for any of this to happen. I felt fine. Sober. Dad said I—" A slammed fist into his thigh jolts me. "What does it matter? You don't care about us. You spend most of your life flitting away to other countries, leaving me behind to pick up the pieces and take care of the twins." The resentment is so bitter in his tone, I have to dig my nails into my palms, my hold tight on the wheel.

But he's not done. "You're so fucking lucky. You got out. Life has been so good for you compared to us. You left us when the Wards started giving you attention, and now we're completely abandoned."

"*My* life has been easy? Mine? The person who took care of you when Mom worked double shifts? Who taught you how to read and tie your shoes? Who went to school hungry to make sure you guys had food in your bellies? Or how about the person who took the very little luck this family was offered to make money? I work my ass off to make sure everything you need is taken care of, but my life is the easy one?"

"Nobody asked you to do that!"

"Are you *kidding* me right now?"

I'm so angry, I'm shaking, which is only making matters worse. I'm in a car I've never driven that's worth way more than I care to know. People are flying by like they're on the German Autobahn, and I need to stay in control of this situation.

Seeing Matteo, the steadiest presence in my life right now, behind me is like a security blanket thrown over me, dousing the flames of my rage. At least for now. Quieter, I say, "Let's calm down for a second. I need to get us home in one piece, and then I need to think."

We don't so much as breathe in each other's direction the rest of the way home.

twenty-one

The front door squeaks open to the scent of beer and Febreeze, piles of clothes pushed up against the couch and walls. An empty handle of vodka and beer bottles strain the top of the trash can in the kitchen, and Dad's legs are propped on the broken coffee table.

Rage is a surprisingly overwhelming emotion. I'm glad it's not something I feel very often. Still, it provides the courage needed to do something I should have done years ago. The moment my father is in my sights, I stomp toward him.

"Dad." He stirs. When one eye pops open, squinting, I put my hands on my waist. "You told Chase he was fine to drive Finn to his lift? After he'd had a drink?"

His other eye opens, but he doesn't respond. Matteo sidles up behind me. Dad looks him over, then frowns. "Wha…?"

"Did you or did you not tell Chase that he was safe to drive after allowing him to drink with you—something that is completely *illegal* by the way."

"It had been over half an hour. He was fine," he grumbles. He isn't slurring, which is a sign he's slept it off. At least somewhat.

"Get out."

Dad's head snaps up, scanning my face to see whether I'm being serious. "What?"

"Get. Out. I have given you a pass for *years* because I was so desperate for you to return to the person you used to be, but I am *done*. You are enabling one of your sons and putting the lives of all your kids at risk in the process. You may not care about that, but I do." My voice has risen, loud enough that Hazel comes rushing out of our room, eyes wide. Chase appears almost as shocked from where he stands against the sink in the kitchen.

"He was fine! Totally sober," my dad claims.

"Not sober enough because he scraped the car and almost took away Finn's chance to get out of this hell."

My father looks around. "Where is Finn?"

"Get up. Grab your things. You are no longer welcome to come back when it suits you, sober or not."

He shoots to his feet, a few inches taller than me. If Matteo didn't step right beside me, it might have been intimidating.

"You have no right! This is *my* house."

Hazel scoffs.

"Really?" I respond. "When was the last time you made a payment on it? Whose name is on the lease? Whose name has been on the lease for the last six years?" When he doesn't respond, I cross my arms. "*Mine*. Because *I'm* the person who takes care of us. *I'm* the person who wakes up every day with the knowledge that people are depending on me. So get the hell out."

He glares at me for a long moment. "Where will I go?"

"I don't care. I'll drive you to wherever you disappear to for weeks at a time and you can stay there."

Positive he has more to say, I stand my ground, staring up at him so he knows how serious I am. Rather than respond, he plods his way to his room, hopefully with plans to pack a bag.

I let out a long sigh when his door shuts, my body falling against Matteo's. It's only late morning yet I feel I've lived an entire day.

"Why don't you let me take him? You do what you need to here," Matteo says, nodding toward the kitchen, where Chase still stands.

"That's too much to ask of you."

"I won't do you any good here anyway. Let me handle it."

When I finally agree, I watch Dad reluctantly get into Matteo's car with a suitcase. I try to prepare myself for another reckoning, one with Chase, but I can't get a handle on my emotions. Desperate to get out of the house, I tell Hazel and Chase I'll be back, then find my way to my elementary school.

A distant monument of the part of my life where everything changed.

Tucked between two-story brick buildings and a line of trees sits the playground. It's winter break, but I can almost hear the little shrieks of laughter as kids run around and skid down the blue-green slides, getting stuck in the summer heat, the friction almost unbearable. Sunlight bounces off the metal bars of the jungle gym, the smell of mulch hanging in the air like they recently added wood chips for cushioning a few days ago.

Sitting on a creaking swing, my legs move back and forth, breeze rushing through my hair. I feel like a kid again, hands wrapped around the rubber-covered metal chains that attach the swing to the wooden frame. If I close my eyes, I can almost imagine what it was like when it was my sanctuary. The place I looked forward to going to every day to get away from all the chores at home. The place I met Austin.

The place where teachers worried about my home life because I was "too mature for my age."

That home life is coming back to bite me in the butt. I'm realizing that I don't know what I'm doing. Hazel asked to feel like an equal instead of an obligation, and I tried to give that to all three of them, so why does it feel like it backfired?

It's not Hazel or Finn, obviously. The problem is, and has been for a while, Chase.

Now that I've dealt with my father, I roll Chase's words from earlier over, hoping to glean what exactly he wants from me. Would he have traded the solidarity of taking care of the twins for starvation? Is the latter truly better than the former? And other than driving them places, it's not like he does much to take care of them now, so what's the problem?

It's infuriating knowing everything I've done for them, for *him*, is now being used as a vessel to show all the ways I failed.

I don't know how long I'm on this swing, but after the sun has moved significantly overhead, a head of light brown hair appears between two buildings. A few moments later, Hazel slides onto the swing beside me.

"Hey," she says quietly.

"Hey."

"Finn called. Said the lift went really well. He's on his way back now."

That's one thing to be thankful for, I suppose. I should offer to go pick him up so he doesn't have to take a rideshare, but I'm at my limit.

Hazel must recognize that because she continues, "Matteo got back a while ago, and only fifteen minutes later, he got in his car to find you. I convinced him you needed more time. Figured your first breakdown would probably last at least a few hours after years and years of keeping a lid on it."

Confused, I look at her. "Breakdown?"

She smiles teasingly. "Or are you here to enjoy the view?"

I snort.

"Can I say something and you not get mad?" she asks timidly.

"Sure. Why not? Pile it on."

She frowns before staring out over the playground. "You don't know everything that happened after you left. Chase did a lot of raising us while you were working, and since you left…" Her shoulders slump. "He changed when you left. Got more withdrawn. Finn and I were still young, so it took me a long time to realize it wasn't just the struggle of taking care of us on his own. He missed you. A lot. You were his best friend, and then you were gone."

All the fight building inside me whooshes from my lungs. One of my biggest insecurities with my siblings is that I can't be as present for them as I'd like because I'm so focused on the financial aspect of taking care of them. I assumed once they were set on the right paths, we could get back to how things were before.

But maybe Chase is right. I haven't let myself so much as *breathe* the last few years to keep them from dealing with what I did, but did they ever ask for that? Did I ever wonder what they might want?

"What am I supposed to do, Haze? Quit the tour?" Just because it's the thing I do to keep my family together doesn't mean I don't love it. Quitting would leave me with a gaping hole in my heart.

"Nobody expects that. But you could call occasionally. Tell us about what's happening in your life. Make us feel like you want us to be a part of it. When I said I wanted to feel like an equal, getting a job was only one piece of that. I want to feel like your little sister, not someone you have to take care of."

"That's a two-way street," I protest. "I'm always hesitant to call because of how busy you all are."

Hazel chuckles good-naturedly. "We're busy? Del, have you seen your schedule? Half the time, I only know where you are because I look at the tour schedule. I never want to bother you, and especially when you're traveling, I never know when to call."

Clarity slips behind the veil of insecurity I've clutched to myself for so long. I turn away from her. "It's so simple yet we've all been dancing around it for years, huh? Me not wanting to bother you all. You all not wanting to bother me." We share a laugh.

"I'm proud of the way you handled Dad. I know that was probably hard for you since you got to see him differently than we did."

Making my younger sister proud for something I probably should have done eons ago to protect all of us is odd, but it's also nice to hear. Like validation that I did the right thing, even if it was a decision driven by my heightened emotions. "Thank you."

We fall into our own thoughts, swinging slowly side by side.

A few minutes later, I say, "I'm sorry. I lived in the caretaker role your whole lives. I was terrified to step out of it for fear that once I did, none of you would need me."

Hazel smiles at me kindly. "We've always needed you. The way that we do has just changed over time."

The words are a comfort, especially after so long believing otherwise. "Yeah." Our legs move in tandem, pushing us one way, then pulling us the other. "I don't know what I'm going to do about Chase. Is he still upset with me?"

"When I left, he seemed more upset with himself than anything else. Before today, he was only hurting himself. I think knowing he could've ruined Finn's life flicked a switch in him. I also think seeing you finally handle Dad made him realize how serious you are."

I dig my heels into the pebbles to stop my momentum, standing slowly. I can't put this conversation off forever.

"We'd better get home then."

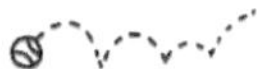

SAHAR'S BAD BERLIN BAGELS

HARPER

Del, if you need anything please let us know!

SAHAR

We love you!!

NIC EMPHASIZED "WE LOVE YOU!!"

MAYA

I don't know what's going on, but I'm in Charleston and your location tells me you're only an hour-and-a-half flight away. I can be there ASAP and I love you so much!

RIGHT AS I RAISE MY FIST TO KNOCK ON CHASE AND Finn's bedroom door, I hear two voices. I quickly realize it's Matteo talking to Chase, and though Matteo was visibly angry with him earlier, he seems to have calmed down. I don't know how long they've been at this, but their voices aren't raised and they almost seem…friendly?

"I know how easy it is to give in to the anger," Matteo states. "To lash out at others for the shitty hand you've been dealt. You might not know or care, but I've been in your shoes, and I promise you, life only gets harder the more you lean into that."

Chase, shockingly amenable, responds, "What do I do instead?"

"Find something that makes you happy, even on your worst days. Something that reminds you that there is good in this world, no matter how bad it's been to you. That you are deserving of lots of good things."

"What's that something for you? Ten—"

"Your sister." My breathing stutters along with my heartbeat.

Chase laughs quietly. "I should've guessed."

"Therapy also helps. I've learned—"

I back away from the door, knowing I've heard more than I should have, but the wood beneath my foot creaks, and a moment later, the door swings open. Matteo scoops me into his arms, burying his head in my neck.

"You okay?" he asks, panic sharpening the edges of his words.

"I'm okay," I breathe.

He sets me down. When I glance inside my brothers' room, Chase sits on his bed with his back against the wall, his shoulders slumped, eyes on his hands in his lap. Matteo kisses my temple and lets me go, disappearing into the living room.

I close the door as I walk in and settle on Finn's bed, across from Chase. My brother doesn't look up.

"How much have you been yelled at by people besides me today?" I ask, knowing Hazel probably gave him a piece of her mind in addition to what Matteo may have said to him.

"Probably not as much as I deserve."

"Have you been told how stupid it was for you to drive Finn?" He nods. "How screwed up it was for you to put his life, his *future*, on the line for a drink?" Another nod.

"How terrifying it is to see you going down this path when we saw what it turned Dad into?"

His eyes snap to mine. "That one's new," he croaks.

"How about this? I'm tired of bailing you out. I can't continue to sacrifice my emotional and financial stability to help you when you're not willing to help yourself."

The words stoke something in him. "I never *asked* for you to come back. Either time."

"You're right. You didn't. Next time, I'll let you rot away at Dad's favorite bar. What I will *not* do is let you jeopardize the well-being of the twins by dragging them down with you."

His shoulders slump more than before, head hanging low. "I know. I'm sorry. I never meant for anything to happen to Finn. I trusted Dad, and I shouldn't have."

Sighing, I shift over to sit on the edge of his bed. I know a white flag when I hear one. We could go back and forth like this for hours if we wanted. Instead, I say, "I get why you're mad at me. I do. I'm sorry I haven't been the best sister. I thought helping financially was enough, at least until you were all grown up. I spent so much of my childhood taking care of the four of us that it's been hard to separate myself from that role. But I was never there for you when it mattered."

"It's fine."

"It's not. I haven't called you to talk to you about how you've been. You felt abandoned when I moved out. That's important to me, and it's even more important to me that you feel you can talk to me."

He doesn't respond. There's an obvious wall standing strong around his feelings, but I have an idea. I hop off, grabbing the top sheet from my bed across the hall and throwing it over our heads when I return. A peace offering. It's immediately stuffy, but there's a lightness in Chase's eyes that tells me he remembers.

"Your turn to tell me how you feel," I murmur.

"We're going to suffocate."

"Then you'd better get on with it."

"I was pissed. I *am* pissed. I knew things were going to change when you left, but I didn't realize how much. You never called. Ever. I didn't mind taking care of the twins, especially after everything you did for the three of us. But you and I shared so much for years, and then you left and suddenly had nothing to say."

I nod, having thought through all of that after my conversation with Hazel. "What if we call a truce? We're not going to resolve this all today, and I don't expect you to forgive me anytime soon. But maybe you can tell me what I can do so we can move forward and make things right, and I can do the same."

Chase's face disappears for a moment, gasping for air outside of the blanket. I laugh and do the same. When we're both back under it, he says, "I don't know. Treat us like you care about us, I guess. Instead of acting like we're an obligation."

I smile, though it hurts to hear. Because I *do* care about them, so much. I just haven't been caring for them in the ways they want me to. "Okay. Let's plan for a sibling call once a week. We'll find a time that works for all of us and we'll update each other, even if it's only for a few minutes. Does that work?"

He shrugs. "Yeah."

"Great. And I want you to do things for yourself. I know I was focused on you going to school, but if that's not what you want, then get a job. Pay your own bills."

His head falls back until it hits the wall behind him. "There was never a state school opportunity. I dropped out. Months ago."

Bile rises in my throat. I swallow it, hard, schooling my features. "The money from the shared account? When my card got declined?"

"Had a couple of parties. Bought alcohol for me and Dad a few times. Drugs. Dumb shit I didn't need."

I so badly want to put my head in my hands and sob. To beg him to come off this path and join me as a productive member of society, but I can't do that. As I've learned with Dad, he has to want it.

"Then you need a job, whether you go back to school or not. You owe it all back to me plus the money for repairs on the Saturn. I'm planning to buy the twins a car to share, so you keep the Vue, if it's still operational. And if not, you find your own transportation."

His eyes meet mine. "I'm cut off?"

"One hundred percent. What you do with your life is up to you. I'm not going to be here to bail you out anymore. I can't be. But I can be a sounding board for things. Like figuring out what you want to do in life. Finding a path you're excited about. I want to be around for that."

I can't help but think of little Chase, following me around the house while I did chores. Asking me to watch him do somersaults in the tiny backyard. Learning alongside me the right way to hold up a baby so their small bodies don't snap. Sitting with me in the kitchen while I made breakfast for us before we wrangled the twins, or dinner after we put them to bed. The team our circumstances forced us to become but that I wouldn't have wanted any other way.

I must not be the only one reminiscing because he says, "I miss when Mrs. Elliott used to turn on her sprinklers for us a few minutes early so we could run through them and pretend we were at a water park."

I laugh. "Or when she pretended not to know we were the ones digging in her garden for carrots. Or stealing oranges from her half-defunct orange tree."

He snorts. "We thought we were so sneaky."

We trade more memories. Blankets knitted with love so we stayed warm in the winters. Potlucks the community put on at Mrs. Elliott's house that, the more I think about it, seemed to appear out of thin air when we were running low on money and hungrier than usual. And sadder ones: each of us waiting for Mom to come back and never telling the other, a hint of a thought of calling CPS before the guilt and shame ate us up and we knew nothing about getting separated would make the call worth it. The resentment that built between us when I started making money on my own and he had to step up more around the house. The guilt we felt for that resentment.

"We were lucky in our own ways," I muse. "Luckier than many. We had each other. And the community." And the Wards.

"And unluckier than many," Chase responds, the glass-half-empty counterpart to my glass half full.

"So, you're good with the truce?" I want us to fix this

the best we can, even if we can't make up entirely for the ways we've hurt each other.

Chase nods. "Yeah. And I'm sorry again. I really didn't mean for anything to happen to Finn. I never meant to involve anyone else in…whatever this shit is that I'm dealing with."

"I…I get it. You're twenty. You're going to make mistakes."

"You didn't."

I laugh. "I've made more mistakes in my life than I can count. I'm sorry if I ever made it seem otherwise. What matters is that you learn from them. And that you stop putting Hazel and Finn at risk."

Tears bite my eyes when the next apology forms in my head, but I shake it loose. It's not my apology to make. Sure, I wish he had the parents he deserves. I wish that for all of us. But saying it now, when we're all about to move into a new phase of our lives, would be pointless. So I allow it to sit in my chest for a moment before letting the hurt of losing the people who were supposed to protect me go.

I let her go too. The woman with the blue eyes to match mine and the unruly blonde hair who promised me a better life and then disappeared when the one we had got too hard. I let go of the idea of seeing her again. Of the idea that she might still turn up, wanting to see what we made of ourselves.

And when the thought brings a fresh wave of tears, I bite so hard on my cheeks that I taste blood. Hopefully, things will slowly get better between my siblings and me, but there's one person who I've given more credit than they deserve. A person I've been desperate to have back, who I've subconsciously known will never be strong enough to pull himself from his addiction. Or be pulled from it by someone else.

And while putting my foot down today may have gotten him out of the house for however long, I have no idea whether he'll try to come back as soon as I leave.

"I think it's time we talk about Dad."

twenty-two

Matteo's arms open when I step onto our back porch, his body dwarfing the old, banged-up patio furniture I found on the side of the road my junior year of high school. I sink into his lap, finally allowing silent tears to flow. I've never been so emotionally drained in my life. He presses kisses to my temple, wiping tears from my face and murmuring that no matter what happens, I'll be okay.

"You leave a message for your dad?" he asks when the well runs dry.

"Mm-hmm. Don't know if I'll ever see him again." While the four of us agreed on boundaries—him living somewhere else indefinitely, not contacting us until he starts a rehab program chosen by one of the twins, working for his own money—the call had to be made by me. I'm the one who has been enabling him for years. Plus, it'll be up to them to enforce the rules.

"But you gave him grace after everything. You're still giving him a chance to redeem himself."

"I hope he takes it."

To distract myself, we slip into mindless talk; the hard court season, which players we'd most like to play doubles against, whether we'll make it through qualifying. When we come to a lull, I gaze out over the small, unkempt yard, thinking of all the time I spent out here with my siblings over the years. The sun set long ago, but the back porch light casts enough of a glow on the overgrown grass to remember.

"It's all going to work out," he murmurs. "Your siblings love you. It's clear, even in Chase. Hell, everyone who meets you loves you, and how could they not?"

My eyes flick to his, my body leaning to get closer to him. "Everyone?"

He looks at me meaningfully, and I realize it's that same fond look he's been giving me for weeks. Eyebrows slightly pinched, adoration in his eyes, the tiniest hint of a smile. My heart ratchets up. "Everyone."

I plant a peck on his lips before resting my head on his shoulder. The pressure of the day releases its claws from my back, finally. "Tell me more."

"I can't even pretend it wasn't true the first time I saw you in Austin's box." His lips twitch like he's thinking of the moment. As if I exist in his head, a memory for him to return to.

I scoff playfully. "Yeah right. You couldn't even remember my name."

"Not true. That's just what I wanted you to believe."

"What?"

"I remember you sitting in our box during Indian Wells. I saw you beside Eli and Lilian, and I assumed you were their daughter." He shrugs. "I'm not proud of it, but a part of me resented you for the life of privilege I was sure you had as their child. So yeah, I thought you were the most beautiful woman I'd ever seen in my life, and I hated it. Didn't stop me from letting a ball roll onto your court so I could ask for it back. Or hanging on your every word after our quarterfinal match at the Miami Open, even if none of them were directed at me."

My cheeks have gone warm and, I'm sure, bright red. "Matteo, you called me Delia at dinner in Paris. We'd been properly introduced twice before then."

A wider smile plays on his lips. "You were wearing this lavender linen dress with straps that tied on your shoulders. Drove me crazy. We had barely spoken more than a few sentences before that, yet I kept thinking about what it might have been like to pull the ties off. Step back and watch."

Now I *know* my cheeks are red.

"I wasn't happy with myself for how entranced by you I was. I was dealing with so many of my own demons that being attracted to someone who brightened up every room and who was never going to think twice about me only made my life more difficult. That was also the dinner when Eli accidentally let it slip that you took care of all your siblings on your own and I realized you are so *good*. Your radiance came from lifting everyone up, and I'm… me. It pissed me off. Pissed me off more that it made me a thousand times more intrigued by you."

I'm flummoxed. Matteo nudges me, waiting for my response. "At Wimbledon…?" I manage to get out.

"You were getting ready to go on the court and I

didn't want to disturb you. Plus, we were pretty much alone and I hadn't talked to you without Austin present. I was worried I would spew something nonsensical and you would sense the crush I was harboring." He huffs a laugh. "Then I went and made a fool of myself at the US Open anyway. Could hardly take my eyes off you during our matches. I feared even Austin would notice that my concentration was slipping, which is not something that happens often." He rests his temple against mine. "Need you to stop looking so stunning when you're sitting in my box."

I shoot back through time, remembering each of our interactions this year. Putting those moments in a different light. In the light that *he* saw them in. "Why didn't you tell me? And what about that first week at the academy? You were standoffish and weird, and then suddenly you weren't."

"Tell you what? That I couldn't stop thinking about you despite having talked to you only a handful of times about very mundane things? Because I was certain you would have no interest, and I didn't want to make you uncomfortable. As for my behavior when I arrived, my dad had just reached out, and that, in conjunction with Austin's injury, threw me for a loop. But then he mentioned feeling bad about you losing mixed, and I couldn't help myself.

"It was a chance to play with you, spend time with you, maybe make you see I'm not the person everyone thinks I am. Maybe learn to see the world the way you do. But you didn't give an answer, and I figured that was answer enough. I tried to stay out of your way until Austin told me you were still thinking about it—the day you reintroduced yourself to me. Being that close to you was intoxicating. I wanted you to agree so badly."

I shift, my chest aching at the sight of him with his head bowed. Placing a hand on either side of his face, I press my lips to his before whispering, "I'm sorry if I made you believe I wouldn't have been interested in talking to you. That you felt talking to me would make me uncomfortable. I've loved getting to play with you. You've made this offseason fun. Made me excited to play mixed without feeling stressed about how losing will impact my life off court." I shake my head with wonder. "I can't wait to play with you in Melbourne."

Matteo's muscled arms wrap around me and pull me into him as he stands. I understand what he can't say. What the tightening of his arms around me means, my cheek pressed to the hollow of his throat. "That thing you said before," I say. "I'm almost there too. I don't know what the season will look like, and I'm not sure what I can give you right now, even without the stress of paying for everything for my family. But I want to try."

When he throws me over his shoulder, pure joy in his eyes like I've never seen before, I giggle. Maybe I *can* make this work. I've persevered. Got myself to the top one hundred, then to the top fifty. Got myself a great sponsor because of all my effort and dedication.

Hope for the future has never tasted so sweet.

twenty-three

I missed Brisbane by a day. Not ideal, but it's given me extra time to train ahead of Melbourne, both alone and with Matteo. Mixed doubles qualifying matches begin today, which means we're finally going to be put to the test.

As if that's not anxiety-inducing enough, our Stratosphere rep, who we were meant to be meeting a couple of days ago, got delayed and now wants to meet a few hours before we head onto the court.

I didn't do anything wrong by not playing Brisbane; the Australian Open was the first tournament my new contract says I *have* to play in. More than likely, they'll want to say their hellos and do a quick shoot in our game-day outfits for social media content. Still, not even the sight of the Wards—Lilian and Austin waving from the observation bridge above the courts, Eli with a wide grin and two thumbs up—is enough to calm the clip-clop of my heart as Matteo, our teams, and I exit a court in the village.

The Australian summer sun is absolutely brutal, though the air is nice and dry. Melbourne Park's grounds are bustling despite it being days before round one matches. Fans with various country flags amble about, pointing at players on the bright blue practice courts and *oohing* and *aahing* in time with the *whack* of tennis balls against strings.

Matteo grabs me loosely around the wrist once we break from the group, tugging me gently past the courts and to a quiet corner, tucked away from view. "You doing alright?"

"Just nervous. You know, match-day jitters."

He scans my face like he doesn't believe me, but other than telling him about the wave of foreboding that hit me like a slap in the face near the end of our practice, I have no better way to explain it.

"I'll be fine," I promise. "It's the start of the season, that's all. This would've happened in Brisbane."

His brows furrow, and he squeezes my hand. "I have no doubt that you're going to be amazing. Today and this whole tournament. The whole season, even." I give him what I hope is a convincing nod. "I'll meet you in the Strato suite?"

Another nod. His eyes dip to my lips briefly, but it would seem that our agreement not to identify exactly what we're doing means we're also keeping it under wraps.

We go our separate ways. I change into my outfit for the day—a lavender two-piece kit. The top is a tight tank with a short V-neck and a collar with a white stripe. The skirt is my favorite part: pleated and loose, with a thick white stripe across my waist and a smaller stripe above it, the Strato logo bold on the side.

Three and a half hours before our qualifying match, I meet our rep, Rebecca, in the Stratosphere suite, where Matteo stands against the wall with his arms crossed, brooding. His outfit matches mine, though the majority is black with small darker purple accents. Rebecca hugs me tightly.

When she pulls away, she's beaming, "Delilah! It's so great to meet you in person. So sorry to do this before a match, but hopefully it won't take too long and you can both be warming up in no time. We just want a few photos of you together plus a quick Q and A."

"Of course. Thank you so much for having us. We're excited to be repping Strato on the court," I answer. Matteo seems unbothered by my speaking for him, his arms uncrossing as he comes up beside me.

Rebecca claps enthusiastically, her energy infectious enough that any lingering foreboding is washed away. I match her smile, posing the way we're told: first with rackets in our hands facing forward, then back-to-back, then a few iterations of poses we might take during a match.

After about half an hour of posing, she pulls two chairs to the middle of the room so we can sit side by side. The videographer sets up a camera, and when he indicates we're rolling, she asks, "Can I have you both tell us your names, your home countries, and why you're excited about this tournament?"

Knowing Matteo would hate going first, I jump in. "I'm Delilah, I play for the United States, and I'm excited to be playing mixed with someone new this January." With a wink, I add, "Helps keep the tour interesting."

Rebecca laughs with me before nodding to Matteo.

He clears his throat. "Matteo, Italy…" He trails off. When his eyes meet mine, I smile encouragingly. "I'm excited to be in Australia for hard court season again."

"How long have you two been practicing together?"

"Roughly twice a week for a couple of months." I elbow Matteo lightly. "Not that he needed the practice. He's a natural."

"You were playing just as well when we first started." He turns to Rebecca. "If I could bet on it, I'd say she's the one who's going to win us the match today. Watch for her killer drop shot."

I can't contain my smile, and I only barely stop the urge to lean into him. His words and the twitch of his lips shake something loose in my head.

A drop shot, knocking someone off balance and sending them skidding in a direction they weren't ready for. Matteo, who came into my life and changed everything, catching me entirely off guard.

Rebecca asks a few more questions, then we play a quick game of favorites, where I'm able to accurately tell her Matteo's favorite pre-match snack (organic trail mix), favorite surface (clay), and his favorite recovery activity (swimming), among other things. Matteo is just as knowledgeable about my own favorites, and when the camera switches off and we hop to a stand, Rebecca seems more pleased with us than I could have hoped for.

"This was perfect. Thank you both so much for taking time out of match day to do this with us."

I wave her concern away. "We're happy to. Thank you for warming up our brains before we warm up our bodies," I joke.

Rebecca turns to Matteo. "And thank *you* for recommending her to us. You were right that she's exactly what we've been searching for." Her eyes back on me, she finishes, "Strato is so excited to be working with you in this greater capacity."

I'm untethered, floating in space. I nearly stagger back, my arms crossing reflexively and holding tight. I don't understand until, suddenly, I do.

The conversation with Francesca outside of the women's locker room, when she first posited the idea that Matteo would be a good doubles option. Him stepping out of the men's locker room and meeting my eyes before he disappeared out the door.

Stratosphere calling Shay, my agent, a few days later.

I feel so monumentally stupid. What I believed was a reward for how hard I work was instead handed to me. Once again, I got lucky. Just like when I befriended Austin, which led me to the Wards and all the other life-changing chances I've been given.

I've got nothing to show for my work, and after everything, people are still treating me like a charity case. Every time I think I can get out from under the thumb of debt, something gets added to the calculator hanging over my head.

I will forever be indebted to others.

Worse than that, Matteo went behind my back and has lied every day since. I thought I was angry with Chase a couple of weeks ago, but if that was anger, this must be incandescent fury. Or maybe it's the betrayal slicing away at the skin of my levelheadedness. I can scarcely think as I stare unseeing at Rebecca, whose eyebrows are drawn as she looks back and forth between us. She's speaking to Matteo, but I can't hear a thing.

It's not until she apologizes that I find words. "You have nothing to be sorry for. I do need to get warmed up though, so I'm going to have to step away. Hope that's okay."

I don't wait for her answer, turning on my heel and walking out.

"Good luck this week!" she calls.

I'm pacing outside when Matteo steps out, his head hanging, both our rackets in his hand. Snatching mine, I drag him with me until I find an empty room down the hall.

I turn on him, taking in his pinched brows and the eyes that glide over me affectionately. That only serves to make me more angry, more indignant that our entire relationship was born from a lie. At least on his end.

"Delilah, please." He reaches for me, but I move out of the way.

"You told Stratosphere to up my deal." I meant for it to be a question, but it comes out a statement. Strong and marked with a fraction of my frustration.

Matteo's arms drop to his side, and he backs up. "Not really. I talked to my old rep—"

"Why?"

"Wh—Why? Because I heard you were concerned and wanted to see if there was something I could do to help."

"I'm not a charity case, Matteo."

"Of course you're not. I know that. It wasn't charity. I had a call scheduled with them for something else and worked you into the conversation. Let them know how much you could help their brand."

"I didn't ask you to do that."

He runs a frustrated hand through his hair. "I know that too. I wanted to help."

"How did you manage it? Austin said, and you even admitted, that they were upset with you after your blowups on court." The words are barbed, and I see them land. Watch him realize he's losing one of the few people who saw him as more than the anger that fed him.

"They called to tell me I needed to get my shit together. I told them I was hoping you and I could play mixed doubles together. That playing with you, along with minimizing my outbursts, should help. It was a peace offering to them—I'll get my shit together and in exchange for them letting me keep the deal, here's this amazing player with a presence unlike any other who they were sleeping on." Anguished, he says, "Delilah, it was entirely up to them whether to follow through. I just—"

"Why didn't Shay know? She's on top of every single thing."

"I asked my rep not to tell her or you when I gave them your name. Figured it might make you feel like you had an obligation to play with me or something. I don't know."

"And now? Now that you know me, know how I feel about being someone else's charity case, why haven't you told me? Did you really think it would never come out?" I cross my arms. "Why would you not tell me as soon as we had that conversation the first time we hooked up?"

Another jab. This time, he flinches, opening and closing his mouth. "I…I guess I didn't think about it like that? It wasn't like I paid them to up your deal. I didn't know any of the particulars. I just pointed out that someone they sponsored deserved more. They must have done their research and realized I was right."

"But they took it seriously because it was *you* saying it. It wasn't me catching their eye." I remember the money I set aside in the bank account I now share with only the twins. The one they'll draw from to fund part of the used car they're buying this week. An eighteenth birthday and Christmas present from me. That money came from my first big Stratosphere payment, and that was brought on because of *him*.

He's shaking his head, desperate for me to hear him, but I'm done listening. Feeling that familiar bite behind my eyes, I say, "You should go. We can warm up separately."

Matteo steps into my line of sight. "Delilah, per favore. You have to—*please* understand. I've been doing everything in my power not to feel as weak and helpless as I did the day…" He trails off, but I can fill in the blanks.

The day his mother passed away.

Changing course, he says, "I heard you were struggling, and I thought I'd pass your name along. I didn't want you to feel the same way. You're such a strong player with so much potential. I thought I was helping."

I take a step to the right, trying to reach the door. Matteo sags against the wall with a loud *thump*, unintentionally cutting me off. He looks like he might fall to his knees. "Please, *please*. You seemed helpless that evening, and if I could…if I could just find a way to make that go away for you…I thought—"

"And do you see how, in doing that, you made me feel weaker and more helpless? *You* got me an increased deal, no matter what small part you played in this, and it's proof I can't even get a strong endorsement of my own merit. I work *so* hard, and yet it feels overshadowed by all the things I'm handed."

"I don't have the power you think I do. And it *is* your merit that got you the deal. I gave them a name, and every reason they listed for upping the deal was the truth." I move again, but he pleads, "Delilah, please. I pointed them in your direction, and you shined the way you always do. It's always you. Luck has nothing to do with it." He sounds as miserable as I feel, and I'm about two seconds from the dam breaking. "Don't do this. I love you. Please don't do this. I never meant—"

"I need to go, Matteo. Please." The waver in my voice finally does the trick. His shoulders slump as he steps out of my way. I'm out the door and in a bathroom seconds later.

I take ten minutes to cry in a stall before I splash water on my face and search for Francesca.

twenty-four

Francesca has a lot of questions, most relating to why I'm warming up in a different part of the players' area than Matteo. The complete opposite side, to be exact. I answer none of them, and my not-so-sunny disposition is enough to put her off asking any more.

In the tunnel, before they call our names, I don't so much as look at him, and when we step out on the court, all our emotions come to a head.

We lose the first four games quickly and without much of a fight. I flash no signals before or during points, nor do we talk during or between them. I haven't glanced at our box, sure that I'll see plenty of disappointment and confusion.

I don't need that.

It's after we lose the fifth game that Matteo finally turns to where I sit on the opposite end of the bench. I struggle with the cap of a water bottle before setting it onto the ground angrily. Matteo sidles closer, and I tense as he opens the bottle with a *crack*.

"I get being mad at me," he says quietly, "but don't throw away our shot at main draw right now. I don't want you to regret losing this. We can do it. I know we can. Even if we lose this set."

Anger still boils red-hot in my blood, but he's right. I would regret losing this, no matter what's happening between us. Standing, I wait for him to set the water bottle back down and follow me to the other side of the court.

Just before Matteo gets ready to serve, I ask, "Drop the set and try for the next or fight?" I already know the answer.

"Fight like hell."

So we play angry. I smash a down-the-line shot right at Volha Barazna, who ducks out of the way with her racket held above her head, missing the ball entirely. Matteo aces them twice, as if my speaking to him was enough to get his serve back to its former glory.

We win the next seven games that way, exchanging as few words as possible. The second set is bumpy, the momentum shifting back and forth. I hit a drop shot that turns a game on its head. Volha slaps a shot at me to get me back for the last one, and suddenly, they're up a game. The set slips from our fingers, and we're left with one tiebreak to decide whether we're out of the tournament or into the next round.

"She doesn't like when you serve down the T," Matteo murmurs with his back to them. By the way his mouth opens again, I know he has more to say; instead, he turns and walks to the net.

Begrudgingly, I listen to him, and it's a damn good tip. We win the first point. Then the second and the third, picking up momentum fast. All of a sudden, it's match point, and a well-placed forehand volley from me wins it all. The few people watching clap.

Normally, I'd run and jump into Matteo's arms. At the very least, give him a hug. We did something we've never done before, and yet I don't look at him, standing at the net awaiting handshakes from Volha and Dmitry instead.

I might not have gotten the increased sponsorship entirely of my own merit, but despite not playing my best, I proved that I belong here today. Pride roots itself in my chest.

After the post-match fanfare, I hoof it off the court, pretending I don't see the disappointed tilt of Francesca's head.

"Delilah," Matteo calls out right before I go into the locker room. "Please, can we talk? We need to work through this before we have to play a stronger team."

A few hours ago, if someone had cracked my sternum open and pulled out my heart, they would've seen countless tiny holes patched by this man, healing parts of me I hadn't realized needed it. Now though, it feels as if those words and caresses that stitched me up have been ripped away, leaving them bigger, darker.

More cavernous.

"I'm not ready to talk," I croak.

Later, after cooling down, when Francesca, Alessio, and Matteo start speaking in rapid Italian, I slip away. I no longer care what they could be saying.

A LOUD KNOCK ON MY HOTEL DOOR WAKES ME. IT'S SO dark, I can't see a thing, though whether that's because the sun has gone down or because my thick curtains are closed, I can't be sure. My eyelashes clump together, sticky with salt from the tears that kept falling while I tossed and turned.

I grab my phone to check the time and note that it's eleven. Text messages in the group chat with the girls pour in, some about the flight Nic is on, and others about Adelaide, where Sahar and Harper are currently playing their last tournament before the slam.

SAHAR'S BAD BERLIN BAGELS

HARPER

Also, Delilah!! Congrats on winning your first mixed qualifying match with M! So proud of you.

MAYA

SO PROUD OF YOU!!

SAHAR

Is everything good? You seemed upset in the few clips I saw

Nic texted me separately.

NIC

Just got in. Room 1512. I have two beds and a pint of ice cream if you need either.

It's the good stuff too. Won't even ask what's wrong.

That nearly makes me smile, typing out a *rain check* when the knock sounds again.

"Go away," I call miserably. I don't want Matteo begging me to talk to him again or Francesca trying to figure out what's wrong with me. That's an issue for tomorrow.

The knocking becomes more insistent. I stand, wrapping myself in a hotel blanket like armor and padding to the door. When it swings open, I'm ready to say the words to their face, but they die on my tongue when I see who it is.

Eli Ward.

If I thought I was done crying, boy was I wrong. I burst into tears again, and he comes in, pulling me into his arms and smoothing my hair down, whispering that everything's going to be okay.

"Can I"—I hiccup—"get you some water?" I ask.

"No, sweet girl. Let's sit down, okay?" I nod, and he guides me to the small couch in my room, settling beside me until the faucets slow.

"How did you know something was wrong?"

Eli smiles, taking my hands in his. "I know you quite well, believe it or not. I knew something was wrong the moment you stepped on the court." He squeezes my hands. "Lilian convinced me to give you a few hours to sit with it, especially after Matteo talked to Austin, or I would have been here sooner."

I sniffle. "So you know about me getting handed the Stratosphere deal? I thought I earned it, but it turns out I was just lucky." For some reason, this makes me feel embarrassed. He worked so hard to give me the opportunity to be on tour, and my biggest accomplishment was orchestrated by someone else.

"I'm not sure luck had much to do with it." At my frown, he says, almost to himself, "You never were very good at accepting help after Lillian and I came along, were you?"

"What do you mean?"

He clears his throat. "You know, back then, we wanted to adopt you. Help take care of your siblings. But you told us you had it covered."

"There were four of us. You'd already done so much for me. I felt bad. I didn't want to take anything else from you." That, plus I'd always held out hope that Mom might come back. Or even Dad. But I can't tell Eli that. It's too mortifying.

"When you were getting scouted for college programs, we offered to pay anything your scholarship missed and make sure Chase and the twins were taken care of, but you 'had it covered,'" he reiterates. "You chose to go straight through to the WTA tour instead. I know that's something you regret."

Emotion sticks in my throat, but I seem to have cried myself dry. "It didn't make sense. I got so lucky that you guys gave me all that you did. I couldn't keep taking from you and potentially squander it by getting injured in college. Or getting burnt out."

"There you go with that word again. Luck." Eli squeezes my hands once more. "Luck may have played the smallest of parts in your life, Delilah, but everything else was you."

He smooths the crease in my brow, continuing, "You befriended Austin because you saw he was struggling and you're like sunshine to everyone you meet. It was *you* who made the relationship work, who brought him into the fold, and it was *you* who Lilian and I fell in love with. It was *you* whose raw talent we saw on the court. And while we may have been the hands to help mold you, *you* had everything you needed to succeed baked right in. Because that's who you are, Del. This deal is no different. They wanted you because you're *you*."

"It is, though. It is different. Everyone else got their sponsorships because they put in the work. I'll always know this bigger deal I thought I achieved through dedication was actually because someone pitied me."

"Do you think that all these people, Lilian and me included, didn't have help along the way? Lilian and I both had loving families who helped us get to where we are. Austin, of course, had us his whole life, both for financial and emotional support. Nicola is a fine tennis player— I have no doubt she will become something great, as you all will—but her mother played professionally for years and her father has enough money to pay for her to train at all of the best facilities. Anya, well, we know what her family provided her." I laugh. It's true. The Morozovs have tennis embedded in their every cell.

"And if you point me in the direction of anyone else on the tour, I can tell you how they had someone supporting them to get to where they are. Because that's the nature of this sport. It's expensive, and you need resources if you're going to get here. Regardless of what those resources are and where they come from."

Eli scratches the back of his neck. "Look, Del. I may not be your father, but you are my daughter. I know you as well as I know Austin. I spend my year in your box because you are the daughter I have always wanted, not because I feel bad for you. I do it because I'm proud to call you mine, even if only in my head.

"I've seen you grow from the most mature eight-year-old I have ever met into the most hard-working woman. Your work ethic is something nearly unmatched by most on the tour. Sure, they all have what it takes to be professional athletes, but the work you put into tennis extends beyond that. It stretches back to the moment you were born into a life that most would struggle to come out of. At any point, you could have given up, but you didn't. So no. You have lots of things going for you, but I would never chalk up anything that's yours to something as fickle and indeterminate as *luck*."

My head rests on his shoulder, his head on top of mine. I marvel at his words because he's right. He's the father I always wished my father would be. He treated me like I was, and am, a Ward. Adopted or not. Blood or not.

And yes, I work hard, but that's for so many external reasons. For my siblings. For security. For the Wards, so they know their investment is paying off.

Except maybe I'm not an investment. Maybe no one expects me to do what I'm doing. Maybe the pressure I've always felt was external was actually my own.

I swallow. "If I quit tennis right now, would you be upset with me? Would you feel like I wasted…" What? His time? His money? His resources? All the above?

"I got to spend it all on you, and that could never be a waste. If you wanted to quit right now, I'd support you in finding whatever you want for your future. Lilian would too. Austin too, eventually, though he'd have a ton of questions and would probably beg you to reconsider so you could keep playing mixed once he's better." We share a laugh. "Though that ship has probably sailed."

I raise my head and meet his eyes. "What do you mean?"

"I've heard lots of great things about you and Matteo. Even Austin is sure you'll end up playing with him at every tournament you can until you retire."

"Oh. I don't know."

"Because you're planning on quitting?"

"No, no. That was just…I just wanted to know that it's okay. That when this stops being fun, the only thing preventing me from quitting is myself."

"Then what don't you know? Because if it's how that man feels, I'll tell you right now that, as someone who was so sure nobody would be good enough for you, he might be the one. Austin said he's never seen him so distraught. And I promised Lilian I would keep it quiet, but we both noticed the way he hung on your every word at tournaments. That man's been sure about you almost from the moment he met you, I think."

"He lied, though. He knew how I felt about accepting help, and he didn't think to tell me he pulled the strings of my sponsorship."

Eli sighs. "What did Stratosphere say was their reasoning for increasing your deal again?"

I think back to what Shay mentioned when she first told me. "I've been moving up the ranks." He holds one finger up, nodding for me to continue. "My social media has been growing. And they're looking for someone with my 'sunshine energy.'" Eli holds up three fingers.

"Three whole reasons why they wanted you. You passed every test, proved at every turn that you were worth their investment. Matteo just gave them the lead."

I pointed them in your direction, and you shined the way you always do.

He didn't push them. He dropped my name. And even so, I guess they could have done their research and decided against moving forward.

"Why is it so hard to accept help?" I ask quietly.

"Because you went so long without it. You became an island, self-sufficient and strong. You're proud of everything you've built for yourself and your siblings, as you should be." Eli looks at me pointedly. "But it might be time for you to realize that not all help comes from a place of pity. And it might not be a terrible idea to accept it here and there."

My chest aches.

I'm an idiot, too proud for my own good. I've pushed away the one person I've ever encountered who I can see a future with, who I can see standing beside me every day for the rest of my life.

"Eli, thank you. For everything. Now I'm so sorry, but I have to go."

twenty-five

K nowing he's likely asleep, I knock loudly, ignoring the odd glances from people walking down the hall or poking their heads out of their rooms. For once, I couldn't care less what they think of me.

After my second round of knocking, the door swings open to reveal a bleary-eyed Matteo, his hair standing up on one side, torso bare, and gray sweatpants haphazardly thrown on.

"Delilah?" Sleep clings to my name, his voice deep. His eyes flood with confusion, then happiness, then concern, his breath catching. "Are you alright?"

The air around me tightens, my stomach raging. Insistent. Heat blooms in my chest and creeps up my throat, just shy of burning me. My muscles feel taut as I point down the hall. "Do you want to go on a walk?"

Thick eyebrows furrow, but he nods, disappearing into his room and reemerging in a Stratosphere T-shirt and hat. "Where do you want to go?"

"The river isn't far."

Matteo gently grabs a strand of hair that's fallen out of my messy bun, as if to make sure I'm not an apparition or figment of his imagination. He drops it quickly, clearing his throat. "Sorry. Lead the way."

He follows me to the elevators. "How did you know what room I was in?" he asks, pressing the button. The elevator opens immediately, and we step inside.

"I asked Austin, but he was no help. He gave me four different possibilities. The front desk wouldn't give it out, which, in hindsight, is a good thing. Then I got to Francesca's room and begged her to ask Alessio." Sheepishly, I look away. "She wouldn't tell me anything until I explained what was going on, so she knows. Everything."

To my surprise, when I gaze back at him, his lips twitch subtly. "I think she's known for quite some time," he murmurs.

I don't get a chance to answer. The elevator doors open, and though it's after midnight, it's no surprise to see the lobby bustling with coaches and players; this hotel is where most choose to stay during the Australian Open. We make our way through the crowd, and when we step out of the main doors, a breeze darts around us, the sounds of the city magnified by how close we are to the main street and train station.

Putting a pin in our prior conversation, I say, "Sorry for waking you. I didn't...I had a small revelation and didn't want us to go another hour without talking."

"I thought I ruined any chance of you talking to me again," Matteo breathes quietly. He sounds so small, so hurt. I take his hand, watching the wonder on his face as he tightens his fingers around mine.

"I'm sorry," I reply, doleful. "I'm sorry I got upset. I'm sorry that I'm not good at accepting help from others, even when it's small. I'm sorry I left you like that, and that I let you believe we were done. I'm especially not proud of the way I handled the match today." I glance down at our hands, feel him anchoring me. "I…I just had things I needed to work through."

We pass a loud group of tourists leaving a restaurant, then turn to walk toward St. Paul's Cathedral. I can see the gears turning in Matteo's head while he digests my words.

"So you're…not mad at me about Strato?"

"I wish you would've told me. It was a long time to keep something from me, particularly when we got as close as we did. But at the end of the day, with that and everything else you've done to help keep my family together, I could never stay upset." We cross the main street and walk toward the Yarra River. When we're safely in the quaint park area, I finish, "It was overwhelming, hard to register and comprehend in the moment, but I will forever be indebted to you."

Matteo pulls me to a stop. Cupping my face with calloused fingers, he makes sure my eyes are on his when he says, "You are *not* indebted to me. You don't owe me a thing. Okay?"

"Okay."

His features soften. "And it's like I said. There are only so many strings I could pull. If they didn't want you, they wouldn't have pushed your endorsement through. You did all the work."

I can't help myself, even as another group of tourists

walks past us. I lean forward, pressing a chaste peck to his lips. "Thank you for giving them that push."

He's spent so long being terrified of the people in his life leaving in one way or another, there's still a hesitation in the tilt of his brow. Like he's not positive he's not dreaming. Like he fears waking up to an empty bed, this memory we're making becoming nothing more than his subconscious playing a cruel trick.

"I'm here," I whisper. "It's me. I'm not going anywhere. We're going to play doubles until we're old and wrinkled."

His eyes widen. "Does that mean…um, do you…" Matteo scratches the back of his neck, pink coloring his cheekbones. It's adorable from a man who seems so self-assured most of the time.

I step in and help before he loses his resolve entirely. "I would very much like it if you would be my partner on and off the court."

Matteo flashes me the most beautiful smile I've ever seen, all pretty eyes and straight teeth. He tugs me toward him and kisses me hard, a hand slipping into my hair. When someone whistles, we pull apart reluctantly and I slip my hand back into his, dragging him down the dirt walkway beside the river. Little ferry boats rock gently, the city of Melbourne lit up and casting a warm amber glow against the river water. The smell of food from the restaurants down the riverwalk waft toward us as we take a seat on a bench.

"Back to what you said about Francesca. What do you mean she's known about us?"

Matteo chuckles, wrapping an arm around my shoulders and pulling me into his body. "That woman sniffed me out like a wolf. Knew practically the moment I stepped foot in the facility that I wanted you."

"What? You're kidding."

"Nope. Half of what I said to her in Italian over the last few weeks had nothing to do with tennis and everything to do with asking her to be less obvious. When your back was turned, she made kissy faces at me and pointed in your direction."

I laugh, still shocked. "I had no idea. Does Alessio know?"

Matteo nods. "Yeah. The number of times he whacked me upside the head during my singles strategy sessions because I was thinking about you probably gave me a mild concussion. I got yelled at a lot when we were on separate courts too. He's very worried about my focus."

"As he should be, apparently." I rest my head on his shoulder. "I can't believe I was so oblivious."

"Very. I was sure you knew many, many times, but Francesca reassured me that you were clueless. Which is good. It gave me time to work my very limited charm."

I slap his chest. "You're very charming."

Matteo pulls my hand to his lips, kissing it softly before setting it in his lap. We observe Melbourne in all its glory, people drunkenly walking down the path in front of us or singing from restaurants behind us.

After a particularly rowdy group passes us by, I say, "There's one thing that doesn't make sense to me."

"What's that?"

"If you wanted to play mixed with me, why would you

offer me up for the endorsement? I could have gotten the deal and decided I didn't need to play doubles."

Matteo traces circles on my arm, putting his cheek on top of my head. "Because I cared more about you being okay than I did about getting to play with you."

I feel cleaved open. Raw. The warmth of his words, the depth of his love wraps around my heart to fill every void. Sticks to it tightly to protect it from any more hurt.

Over the course of the last couple of months, it has become increasingly clear that the press and other athletes on the tour don't know him very well. Now more than ever, it hurts me to recognize how utterly wrong they are.

"I love you," I say suddenly, almost desperately. I don't know when it happened, but the words have never felt more right. Pushing away to look into his eyes, I say it again. "I love you."

From his smile, he knows it means more than that. That I'll protect him from the words of people who know nothing about him. From their incorrect assumptions ever becoming something he believes himself. That I'll stand beside him at every tournament, win or lose, whether I'm physically there or in another country. That I'll spend every night I can beside him, holding him when he's reminded of the storms in his life.

That I'll love him until I'm laid to rest.

And when he whispers it back against my lips before kissing me, I know he means all of that too.

SHOTS FIRED

AUSTIN

More edits of the newlyweds now that they're official on socials

SAHAR

Austin, remind me to teach you what newlywed means

HARPER

Aw, stoppppp. These are all so cute.

NOAH

This is kind of obsessive

AUSTIN

Me? Or the people making the edits

NOAH

If you have to ask...

NIC REMOVED THEMSELF FROM THE CHAT.

AUSTIN ADDED NIC TO THE CHAT.

MATTEO LIKED "MORE EDITS OF THE NEWLYWEDS NOW THAT THEY'RE OFFICIAL ON SOCIALS"

MATTEO

Delilah is so pretty, I didn't even notice I was in those.

HARPER

AWWW.

AUSTIN

Barf

SAHAR

Shut up Austin

Two weeks later, I win my first Grand Slam quarterfinal match in a third-set tiebreak and immediately rush off to prepare for our mixed doubles semifinal match. Francesca gives me a giant bear hug when I reach her outside of the locker rooms, her smile almost as wide as when I told her Matteo and I were together.

The Wards are next, each hugging and congratulating me. Eli pulls away with tears in his eyes. "I knew you could do this. You were phenomenal, Del."

And though I promised myself I wouldn't cry until after my second match, I can't help it. I hug Eli again before hurrying to the area where Matteo is warming up, Francesca hot on my heels.

He was doing cone work on the grass, but the moment he sees me, he tugs me into a tight embrace. "Look at you. My semifinalist," he whispers against my temple. Past him, Nic shoots me a small congratulatory smile. Harper and Sahar, who are preparing for their doubles match, send me a thumbs up and kissy face respectively, and I giggle against Matteo's shoulder.

He steps back, searching my face, then my body. "How do you feel? Will you be okay to play? If you need to focus on singles, we can pull out."

I tap my chin and hum. "I've never known you to be so enthusiastic about pulling out."

His eyes widen, flicking around to make sure no one heard me. "Delilah," he groans quietly.

Chuckling, I add, "We will *not* be pulling out. I'm a little tired, but I have another match in me. Plus, I have a couple of days to recover before singles semis."

He scans me one more time, head to toe. "At least we know you're warmed up," he jokes.

"Exactly, so hop to it." I poke his chest, and he goes back to the cones.

Half an hour later, after lots of water, bananas, electrolyte drinks, and stretching, Matteo and I are called onto the court, the sun beating down on us. We barely win the first set, helped along by Matteo's aces and winners. I'm able to keep the ball in play, consistent until the end, when Matteo steps in and puts them away.

The second set is not as easy. The momentum shifts during the second game when Jeremiah Winter hits an angled winner, and no matter what we do, we can't seem to catch them on their heels. They've been playing mixed doubles together for a few years, and it shows. We knew this one would be harder than the last six we've played over the past two weeks, but as we head into the third-set tiebreak, I feel my energy nearing empty, and I'm not sure we're going to win this.

During the break, Matteo pours cold water on one of our towels and sets it across the back of my neck. "Do you want another banana? I have three of those protein shakes you like." He's been fretting at nearly every break, but he seems to know this time is worse.

I smile at him, resting my head against his shoulder. "I'll be fine. We're so close."

"Are you sure you don't want to pull out? I don't want you cramping or getting sick."

Taking the cool towel, I pat my face a few times, then his. "You know how I'm going to answer that."

Matteo sighs. "Fight?"

"To the death," I joke. "We're scrappy. I have faith in us."

We listen to Francesca and Alessio's pointers for the final few points before the chair umpire calls time. When I ask for a couple of balls for my serve, Matteo joins me at the baseline.

"Win or lose, I still love you." He's started saying this during every match, and though neither of us needs the reassurance, it's a reminder to both of us not to take things too seriously.

"Win or lose, I still love *you*," I answer.

Though we lose the match, and two days later, I lose my first Grand Slam semifinal, I don't regret a moment of the last two and a half months. I may have lost two semifinals, but I feel like a damn winner.

2 YEARS LATER

MATTEO

I slam a shot as hard as I can down the line, but Maria Kachura gets it back, volleying right at Delilah. She moves forward, takes it early, and perfectly places it so it passes behind Maria and is too far from Andrei Lepik.

"Game, set, and match, Anderson and Corsi. Six three, seven–five." I can hardly hear the chair umpire's words over the cheering.

I don't care. All I care about is the woman on this side of the net with me, whose smile is more radiant than the sun. It's fixated on me now, and when she does her favorite thing—drop her racket—I know what comes next. I take a step forward, and she comes barreling into my arms, laughing and crying.

"Matteo, we did it. Oh my god. I can't believe we did it." A giggle, her cerulean eyes bright, freckles dancing across her cheeks. Her Stratosphere visor has been knocked off her head, her blonde braid swinging. I grin as she places kisses on my forehead, cheeks, nose, chin. "You barely broke a sweat while winning a Grand Slam final," she says, laughing again. I see our opponents waiting at the net and know we should join them.

Screw it. I drop my racket to make her more comfortable, tightening my arms around her and spinning. We need to shake their hands in a timely fashion, but Delilah just won her first slam, and if she wants to laugh and cry in my arms, I won't let anyone stop her.

I kiss her on the lips quickly, and she pats my shoulder, her way of telling me to set her down. I do, and when we finally shake our opponents' hands, then the umpire's, Delilah jumps up and down, waving at a crowd that adores her almost as much as I do.

They go wild again.

Time moves at light speed. We sign and hit balls into the crowd. A stage is built, and a bunch of people come on the court. Thanks is offered to a couple of Australian tennis legends before our opponents give their speeches. Alessio and Francesca accept the coach's trophy.

The emcee turns to us with a smile. Delilah slips her hand into mine, and I squeeze. "And now, our Australian Open mixed doubles champions, Delilah Anderson and Matteo Corsi!"

More cheers as we step forward, hoisting the bowl-like trophy over our heads. I reluctantly give the camera the smile Delilah insists I use for photos, teeth and all. It's gotten slightly less fake over the years, though I'm sure she's the only one who can tell.

We set it back down, and Delilah takes the microphone. "Hi everyone! Thank you so much for being here.

I want to say a huge thank you to Maria and Andrei for a great match today. They played their hearts out all week and deserve a big round of applause for that." The crowd listens, cheering for our opponents.

"Thank you to everyone here in Melbourne for making this such a special couple of weeks for us. To my best friends, Austin, Nic, Harper, Sahar, and Maya. To my coach Francesca, my siblings, and Eli and Lilian for being here with us today and for supporting me to this point." Everyone in her box looks so proud of her, and even from here, I can see Lilian's and Eli's eyes brimming with tears as they hold onto each other, watching her like they're her parents. Which, as far as I'm concerned, they are. "Thank you to Alessio and Matteo's team for everything you guys have taught me over the years."

Delilah turns so she's facing me, that dazzling grin still holding strong. "And finally, thank you to the love of my life, Matteo, for letting me ride his coattails into this win." A few laughs. I join them, rolling my eyes because we all know damn well she's an integral part of this team. "Two years ago, we hopped on a plane to Melbourne together, and I was just hoping we would make it through the qualifying round. Now, I get to hold the trophy with you, and it's the sweetest win of my career so far. I love you"—she's choked up but shakes her head and pushes on—"*so* much, and I can't wait to spend the rest of our lives together, potentially winning a couple more of these."

Squeezing her hand again, I exchange a knowing look with Francesca because while I can't control whether we win any more, I can control us spending the rest of our lives together. The ring—which I purchased with the help

of almost everyone in her box, but especially Francesca—
in the pocket of my dress pants laid out for tonight's festiv-
ities is a step in that direction.

I was going to propose whether we won today or not,
but it'll be so much more meaningful with our first mixed
title in our pocket.

It's my turn to talk. Delilah gives me a peck before
pushing me forward. I rub a hand on the back of my
neck. There's so much I could thank everyone for, her
more so than anyone. For taking a chance on me over two
years ago despite what everyone said about me. For
showing up for me over and over again. For making me
smile and laugh every single day. For her beautiful heart
and kindness, even when people don't deserve it.

I settle on, "It won't come as much of a surprise that
Delilah executed that perfectly. So ditto." A collective
chuckle. "Thank you to the tournament staff, to our
teams. To Alessio specifically for putting up with me every
day. To you all for being here. And thank you to Delilah,
who has taught me more life lessons in two years than I
learned throughout the rest of my life before her."

The crowd cheers louder. Someone screams "We love
you, Delilah!" and she turns to the sound of the voice,
pointing in their direction and yelling "I love you too!"

Part of the reason my team and I thought it would be
a good idea to play mixed with her was exactly this; everywhere we go, every tournament she plays, every single
person in the crowd can't help but love her.

I'm like everyone else, no less obsessed with her than I
was the day I stepped onto the facility grounds and
remembered how incandescent she is.

The picture taking continues, and after the ceremony, cool down, and a press conference, we go back to our hotel room to rest. We have a big night ahead of us, plus Delilah has an assignment due for her online class, and I have a singles final to prepare for.

We settle onto the bed, my spine against the one million pillows, her between my legs, and my arms wrapped around her. "I have to finish my paper," she mumbles sleepily, her head turning so her cheek presses against my sternum.

She began online classes last year, though with the tour, it's slow moving. Without financial stressors, she's having more fun playing, so right now, the classes are for finding something she'll be passionate about down the road.

"Soon, tesoro. For now, revel in your triumph."

Delilah snorts. "You sound like a Stratosphere billboard."

"God, I do. I hate that."

"I'm glad Chase and the twins could make it. I feel bad I lost in the semis again."

I frown. "Why do you feel bad? They've gotten to see so much they wouldn't have otherwise. Plus, we just won a Grand Slam. That's reason enough for them to enjoy their time here."

She hums.

"Did Chase say something?" I ask carefully. Their relationship is miles better than it was a couple of years ago. He works as a mechanic now to pay for his community college courses and seems to be happy. They haven't had many issues over the years, but I'm forever on the lookout for trouble.

I never want her to feel the way she did that day we rushed to Tampa from the airport.

"No, no. They all seem happy. Excited for dinner tonight and to watch your finals match." Her lips curl into a sleepy smile, eyes closing. "A couple of years ago, I never would have pictured this, but I'm realizing it's all I could have ever asked for."

I kiss her temple. The twins both got their scholarships; Hazel is working toward a biochemistry degree, and Finn is a leading scorer at his dream school. I know Delilah wishes her parents were around to witness it all, but after everything they put her through, including her father disappearing from her life for good after trying out a treatment facility, I can't say I'm sorry they're not.

Delilah is the only parent her siblings ever had, and she is a better one than either of her parents were to her.

And after watching how hard she worked for her biological parents to care about her just to be disappointed time and time again, I stopped taking my father's attempts for granted. We're by no means in the best of places, but we talk for a few minutes once a month, and a lot of the anger I felt around our situation has dissolved.

Just one more thing I can attribute to Delilah—and therapy.

"I think there's something else that could make this moment better," I whisper.

One of her eyes opens, assessing me. "Matteo, if you propose to me while I'm half asleep and still grimy from our match despite my shower, I'll say no."

I bite back a laugh. "*Actually*, I'm going to find you

some disgusting ice cream while you take a nap. I need you on a nice sugar high so you're awake at dinner tonight."

Her eye closes, and she nods, though there's a hint of disappointment on her face when she says, "Good."

She's already asleep when I get out from underneath her, kissing her again and grabbing my wallet, phone, and hotel key. I have to meet with Alessio for an hour or so to go over strategy before picking up ice cream and getting ready for dinner.

When I step out of our room, a newspaper beside our door catches my eye.

The darling couple of the tennis world has finally taken home their first mixed doubles title. This comes two years after their first tournament together and their unprecedented semi-finals run...Has "Matteo the Malignant Narcissist" officially proved he's changed?...

What a crock of shit. I roll my eyes, resisting the urge to toss it into the trash. Delilah will want it plus five more to bring back to our house, so I add it to the list of things I need to grab for her before dinner.

Tucking it under an arm, I find the elevators, knowing nothing can bring me down today. Not because we won a Grand Slam or because I'm in the finals with a shot at another, but because tonight, I think, the love of my life will agree to be my wife.

Non vedo l'ora.

This one was hard for me, from drafting through edits. Addiction is something that has sunk its claws deep in the flesh of my family's lives. Many of my family members have endured it, and only a couple have had the wherewithal to wrench those claws from themselves to be better. I myself have not experienced it, nor have I had to witness it the way that Delilah did, since the members of my family were able to find their better paths before I was born or when I was very young. That said, it is still something that is woven in the fabric of my life and something I dearly hope I handled with the care it deserves.

Additionally, despite playing competitive tennis for much of my life and researching extensively about the ins and outs of the pro tennis tours, I took some poetic license to further the story—particularly as related to sponsorships and some aspects of offseason training. Also, while I know "Grand Slam" generally refers to winning all four majors in a year, both the WTA and ATP websites use the term to describe each of the majors, so I did the same. I hope that if you recognized any of these things, you were still able to enjoy!

acknowledgments

Huge thank you to my sensitivity readers Cassandra Diviak and Jenna Mae. Your dedication to ensuring I handled these important topics with care is so appreciated. Any mistakes made are my own. Thank you to my alphas —Marja Graham, Miah Onsha, H. T. Darrow, Giuliana Victoria, Cassandra Diviak, and Taylor E. Weston—for helping me find the big picture pieces that weren't working in my early draft. Thank you to my betas—Hannah Witherel, Kie Clark, Janelle The, and Jenna Mae—for helping me fine tune this story. Janelle, I am so thankful for your tennis eyes and that I finally found someone in the community to talk pro tennis with.

Thank you to Rachel for being one of my favorite people, alongside being the best editor and champion of my work. I am convinced you are my guardian angel.

Thank you to Miah and Laura for finding the little things, as always! Your attention to detail is forever incredibly appreciated.

Thank you to my and E's families for getting excited about all my bookish wins and for believing in me. I will never be able to thank you for all that you've given me over the last year and a half to help me achieve my dreams.

To my bestie gals Marja and Miah—I say it every

time. I would be lost without you. It's been less than two years yet I can't imagine how I functioned before meeting you. I love you forever.

To E—thank you for being my number one fan through every single thing. I can't wait to write more love stories inspired by the ways you love and take care of me (for the rest of our lives! you're locked in now!).

And last but certainly not least, thank you, dear reader, for picking up this book and taking a chance on me. Your support means the world to me. I hope you enjoyed reading Delilah and Matteo's story as much as I enjoyed writing it.

Vai Denton is an American author, romance enthusiast—especially if sports are involved—and book lover. She has spent much of her life struggling to find her identity between her two cultures, using books as a sanctuary. Her hope is that her stories provide readers with the escape she once sought. In each of her books, you can expect swoony, healthy relationships that will have you kicking your feet.

If she's not reading or writing about love, you'll find her playing tennis, watching football, Pride and Prejudice (2005), or any number of her favorite romcoms with her two cats and fiancé.

If you'd like to contact Vai, find her on instagram @vaidentonauthor or via email at vaidentonauthor@gmail.com